...And Hell Followed With Him

...AND HELL FOLLOWED WITH HIM

Paul Christopher

iUniverse, Inc.

New York Lincoln Shanghai

...And Hell Followed With Him

iUniverse, Inc.

For information address:
iUniverse, Inc.
2021 Pine Lake Road, Suite 100
Lincoln, NE 68512
www.iuniverse.com

ISBN: 0-595-32993-4

Printed in the United States of America

To Peg Christopher, who started all this mess years ago by giving me a dictionary of mythology to read. Thanks Grandma, I miss you.

CHAPTER 1

▼

Rain was coming down in sheets cold as ice when the man calling himself John Randall knocked on the front door to the Harlowe mansion, his big fist rapping against the dark brown mahogany. A wide-brimmed slouch hat rested on his head; its edge dripped a continuous flurry of water while he waited, more or less protected from the water by the dark blue coat that wrapped around his body, the frayed edge hanging down to his calves. Thunder boomed in the distance, echoing back at him through the night air, the occasional flash of lightning illuminating the area and giving him a glimpse of the ivy-covered walls of the mansion and the bent and twisted trees that loomed over the entrance. Randall glanced up at one particularly misshapen tree, noting that its branches almost seemed to be reaching for the front door as if seeking entry. The wind and rain only accented this effect, causing the boughs to bob and shift as if capable of conscious movement.

The door to the mansion opened, a ray of light spitting out of the inside, causing Randall to look away from the tree, squinting while his eyes adjusted. Eventually he saw that there was a small, straight-backed man in a butler's uniform looking at him, a polite smile on his face. If the butler was at all intimidated by Randall's massive frame he didn't show it. The butler just took a step back and bowed slightly as he gestured for Randall to enter. As he complied, his booted feet rapping softly against the tiled entryway, Randall felt a wave of cold wash over him, more intense than just the chill from the rain.

"Good evening, sir," said the butler. "You must be Mr. Randall. My name is John. Mister Harlowe is expecting you. May I take your coat and hat? They're awfully wet, I see."

Without a word Randall complied, setting down the heavy blue satchel bag that he carried his left hand onto the floor before he shrugged his coat off into the butler's waiting arms. He checked over the simple clothing he wore beneath, taking a moment to adjust the black suspenders that held up his matching trousers and smoothing the sleeves of his white dress shirt, all while John fumbled with the heavy, dripping mass. Eventually he had it folded neatly over his left forearm, and once he finished that Randall pulled off his hat and slapped it down onto the coat. The butler put a hand on the hat to keep it steady and took the opportunity to get a good look at Randall. Randall knew what he saw—not a handsome man. Beneath a pair of angled fair brows he had glaring, wicked eyes, clear blue in color but with a stare so piercing it made it difficult to look at them directly. His scalp was shorn clean, only a hint of stubble marking where his hair would be, and his ears protruded somewhat. His lips were of regular size, but pulled into an almost perpetual sneer. In coloring he was especially strange; several faint reddish lines marked his skin, reminiscent of scars that had healed long before. If anything, Randall gave an impression of great physical power and presence.

Once he was inside the house, Randall took a moment to appraise his surroundings. The house was immaculate, and every inch the home of a millionaire like Adrian Harlowe. The floor was black and white checkerboard tile, gleaming in the soft yellow light that came from the lamps set in bronze sconces along the walls. A pale green in color, the walls had a soft pattern painted onto them, too soft for Randall to clearly make it out. Huge windows with rigid steel frames gave him a view of the dark outside, high hedges dancing in the wind just beyond. A staircase beckoned nearby, as did a pair of huge brown doors on both sides of the huge entry hall. The crisp, clean scent of rain had penetrated into the entryway, but Randall thought he detected the lingering scent of cooked meat in the background somewhere. Perhaps the kitchen was nearby, he decided. In Randall's final estimation the house was beautiful, not to mention a damn sight more than most could afford.

As for Harlowe, Randall knew little about him; only that he had made his fortune in the steel industry and was considered one of the luckiest survivors of Black Thursday, only five years past.

John secured the visitor's wet coverings and reached out a hand. Randall just looked at it for a moment before he realized that the little man was waiting for his satchel bag. Quickly, Randall reached down with one heavy-fingered hand and snatched it up, feeling strangely defensive.

"I'll take this," he said gruffly, his voice deep. The butler straightened, a look on his face that could have said he was insulted. "It's fragile."

All offense faded quickly from the butler's face. "Very well," he said, walking briskly past and leading Randall to a specially prepared room. "Mister Harlowe will meet you in his study," he said, pointing towards the doorway on Randall's right. "The room has been prepared, up the stairs, down that hall, first on the left."

"Thanks," replied Randall, taking a last look around before swaggering easily through up to the second floor. He was immediately presented with a wide hall with walls the same patterned green as the entryway. Randall walked up to the first door on the left and opened it before poking his head inside. After checking that the room was in fact a study, he entered, looking from left to right.

There was no one else in the room, so Randall put his bag down by a large leather-covered chair and examined his surroundings. There were two chairs facing a large wooden desk and a fireplace to one side, inside which burned a small but warming fire. Several framed paintings depicting pastoral scenes decorated the walls and were for the most part unremarkable. Randall walked over to the fire and held his hands out before it, letting the chill seep from his fingers as he stared into the heart of the red-orange blaze. It was an inviting sight and his eyes lost focus, the fire seemed to expand and fill his area of vision. For a moment he let himself be mesmerized by it, but eventually he shook his head and looked away. The fire was soothing, yes, but he had things he had to do before he could think about relaxing. To that end, Randall walked quickly over to his bag and opened it, peering inside. He reached in and pulled out a jagged, roughly triangular piece of stone and looked at it. It was brown in color and covered in strange markings that looked somewhat like Egyptian hieroglyphs. For a long while he stared at the strange stone.

The door to the study opened and Randall looked up from his stone, facing the person who entered. He was tall, though a bit shorter than Randall and not as broadly built. He had thick black hair combed back from a low hairline, and a pencil thin moustache that crowned his top lip. Dressed in simple slacks and a smoking jacket, he carried a snifter of brandy in one hand while the other was thrust deeply into his pants pocket.

"Good evening, Mr. Randall," said Adrian Harlowe. "It's a pleasure to finally meet you."

"Thanks," grunted Randall. "Been looking forward to it."

Smiling, Harlowe took a sip of his drink. "I'm sure," he said, walking across the room and dropping into the chair behind his desk. He eyed the stone in Randall's hand for a moment, and then looked back at the bald man's face, apparently uninterested. "Can I offer you a drink?"

"No, thanks," said Randall. With an indifferent shrug, Harlowe gestured towards one of the chairs facing the desk and Randall dropped into it, his weight causing the cushion to let out a loud wheeze in protest.

"Did you have a long drive?" Harlowe asked, still ignoring the stone in Randall's hand. Randall looked at him, uncertain.

"About twelve hours," he said. He had come all of that way in order to bring the stone to Harlowe, and the man was ignoring it?

"I guess that's a long drive," replied Harlowe, taking another sip of his brandy. "Are you sure you don't want a drink? I have some excellent cognac."

Randall shook his head and his top lip rose a bit. "I'd rather get on to business," he said, a bit gruff. "I came a long way and we have an arrangement to finish."

For a moment Harlowe just fingered the rim of his glass, a thoughtful smile on his face. There was a trace of faint amusement in his eye, as if he thought the man before him a fool. "Fine," he said, putting the snifter on the desk. He reached out a hand, finally looking at the stone. "I assume that's the item in question?"

"Yeah," said Randall, putting the strange stone on the desk. Harlowe leaned forward and picked it up, his fingertips grasping it lightly. He looked almost afraid of what he held as he pulled it back, eyeing its carved surface with reverence and awe.

"It's perfect," he said quietly, allowing emotion to creep into his voice. With his free hand he gently touched the surface of the stone, running his fingertips along the glyphs and feeling every nuance of their depth and curves. After a moment he seemed to realize that he was letting himself slip, and he looked back at Randall, his veneer of indifference wrapping around him again. "What was our agreement?"

"Six million," replied Randall quickly. Harlowe smiled, putting the stone back onto the desk.

"That seems a bit excessive," he said, sliding the stone towards Randall. "Perhaps two would be more appropriate."

Randall's eyes narrowed as he leaned forward in his chair. "The deal was for six," he said. "You can't go changing things now."

Smiling, Harlowe waved a hand nonchalantly in Randall's direction. "Please," he said. "How much trouble did you go through to get this? Two would be a deal."

"But it wasn't *our* deal," said Randall, his voice rising. "You'll have what? Billions after this is through? You can afford six million."

Harlowe sighed as he sat back in his chair. "Fine," he said. "You're right, I can afford it. First, however, I must verify the stone's authenticity."

"It's real, all right," said Randall, sounding a bit insulted.

"Indulge me," Harlowe replied politely while he got to his feet. He crossed over to the wall to his right, opposite the fireplace, and lifted a painting off its hook. Randall raised an eyebrow when he saw the door to a safe behind the painting, which Harlowe lowered gently to the floor. He dialed the safe's combination and the door snapped open.

Inside were two stones that were quite similar to the one that Randall had brought—brownish gray in color, triangular, and covered in strange glyphs. Harlowe collected these and carried them over to the desk, placing them alongside the third stone provided by Randall. With slow, deliberate movements he aligned the stones together, taking a moment to figure out how the markings joined. Taking in a deep breath, Harlowe slid the stones towards each other, forming a larger triangle. The edges of the three stones met, and upon touching there was an audible snapping sound as the stones joined. The edges disappeared instantly, leaving no evidence that they had ever been three distinct objects; they had become one triangular whole, the markings joining to form a continuous network of symbols and shapes.

"Perfect," whispered Harlowe, his apathy gone again. "The stones are one, the way is clear." He laughed for a moment. "This is excellent, Mr. Randall. I must apologize for my earlier attempt at short-changing you. Six million souls will be just fine, once I have taken the billions that cover this planet. You have earned them, Mr. Randall. Trust me."

Harlowe looked up at Randall, and it was then that he noticed that Randall was pointing a pistol at him. He had been so absorbed by the stone that he hadn't noticed Randall taking the time to slip it from the satchel bag.

"What is this?" Harlowe asked, stepping back. The .45 Schofield revolver in Randall's hand was aimed at Harlowe's face, and Randall himself had gotten to his feet and was standing behind his chair. His sneer had grown into a full-fledged snarl, full of hate and loathing. "What are you doing?"

"My job," answered Randall, squeezing the trigger. The revolver belched a gout of smoke and a red-orange flash, and the thunderous report exploded through the room as Harlowe's head burst. Harlowe's body shuddered horribly, the contents of his skull splattering onto the wall behind him, and then dropped to the floor. Randall looked at it for a moment, still holding the weapon out in front of him, uncertain. Was that it? He took a step towards the body and nudged one leg roughly with his toe. The body wasn't moving—Harlowe seemed to be dead. Frowning, Randall crossed to the shoulders, keeping his weapon carefully trained on his victim. He knelt down cautiously, looking closely at the viscous matter that was oozing from Harlowe's shattered cranium. It was dark, thick stuff, but none of it seemed to be brains or any other recognizable human organ. Randall put his fingers into the steadily growing puddle and then looked at them—they were dark blue in color. Hesitantly he sniffed at the liquid, noting the slight scent of ammonia. Slowly and deliberately, he stuck out his tongue and tasted the heavy matter. It was sweet at first, but a harshly acrid aftertaste followed. Grimacing, Randall spat onto the floor and then straightened, satisfied. He backed away from the body, anger written on his face.

This thing was not, nor had it ever been, alive. It hadn't even been sentient. This was a construct, an android created for the purpose of drawing attention away from the real menace. This was a puppet, and what Randall was after was the one pulling the strings.

He had been duped, and now he knew it.

CHAPTER 2

▼

In the back yard of his house at 1128 Halfpenny Lane Philip Farwell knelt, a grave look on his face as he meditated silently. A comfortable black robe was draped around his body, a large gold medallion suspended around his neck and shining on his chest. In the flickering light of the torch-topped stakes arranged in an awkward semi-circle around him a bronze dagger glinted, its blade stuck in the ground, the handle jutting upwards. Alongside this and directly in front of Philip was a bundle of black cloth secured with dark brown twine, which he stared at with glassy eyes.

For nearly half an hour Philip had sat there, quiet, focusing his mind on the task at hand. Thoughts and images turned in his mind, strange geometric shapes and colored patterns that it took years of practice to hold stable for more than a few seconds. Philip kept dozens of them simultaneously floating in his head for the entire length of his solemn contemplations.

Before him the house stood like a giant withered and misshapen skull yawning in the blackness of night. Two brown-bordered attic windows watched him from the brown walls like great empty eye sockets, a single door to the kitchen set at ground level. Philip ignored the house as the cold night wind blew over him. There would be time enough to concentrate on it later. For now he had to prepare.

If the people in nearby Providence, just a mile or so away, knew even half of Philip's history they would have gathered up a lynch mob, complete with torches and pitchforks, and hung him from a tree. If he were lucky they would have tied the rope around his neck.

To the normal, everyday world he was just a harmless eccentric, a likeable enough fellow, if a little distant with those he didn't know, with an easy-going attitude that made him seem inoffensive enough. It was all a sham though, and the truth was that he would have slaughtered every last man, woman, and child in Rhode Island if he thought it would get him anything. He'd considered it on more than one occasion.

His teacher, Uncle Abram, had told him when he was a child of the weakness of small minds. What had he said? Philip thought back, tried to remember. "They're full of shit." That was it. "Not a single one of them has anything but mud and piss where their brains should be. Never forget that, Philip, and you'll do well."

He never had forgotten it and Uncle Abram had been right. He was doing very well for himself. The poverty that had stricken so many of the small-minded people hadn't touched him. Money was something that he never even thought about. Of course that was just something else he had to thank Uncle Abram for, the old man's fortune passing to Philip after Abram's untimely death...

Philip opened his mouth, began to whisper words in a language that was forgotten by history but not by people like him, people who still cared about the past and who weren't afraid to keep ancient traditions alive. Modern notions of morality or decency didn't influence people like that. They looked to the teachings of their forefathers and ignored the soft sentiments of the 20th century.

Philip stopped his faint muttering and pulled the dagger out, exposed its bronze blade to the cold and rain.

With slow, careful movements, Philip cut the twine around the bundle and slipped off the black cloth. He smiled when he saw that nothing had been damaged.

The child moved slightly as Philip looked her over, her eyes stared vacantly into the sky while her pink dress covered her pale skin. She couldn't have been any older than seven or eight, but Philip had never actually asked so he didn't really know. Her long brown hair still had the pink bows in it that had originally caught Philip's eye and her black patent leather shoes shined on her feet, white socks poking out. If she was frightened she didn't show it, her face tranquil and her eyes unblinking.

It would be some time before she came back to consciousness, thought Philip; his techniques of persuasion were quite potent. This child was his for the night. For a moment he wondered what her name was. He hadn't thought to ask. He'd just seen her at the park, playing by herself, and made his move. Old Uncle Abram's tricks still worked—the kid had gone stiff the second Philip put his hand to her forehead. There wasn't so much as a kick or a scream. Philip had learned more powerful methods, to be sure, but the classics were sometimes all he needed.

Philip concentrated on what he was doing. With surprising tenderness he reached out and put a hand on the girl's forehead, brushed away a strand of hair over her eye, and started to think about the shapes and colors that had been in his mind before. He could feel them charging his body with energy, warping the space around him. His thoughts seemed to be pouring out of his head, floating in the air over him and the girl, shaped from the very ether that permeated the universe. Philip tilted his head back as a warm feeling of ecstasy welled up in him.

The girl mumbled quietly. Philip ignored her and continued to look up at the black sky. It was time to begin.

"Come to me!" He cried out, suddenly, as he raised his bronze dagger high. "By my name and by my strength, come!"

A stroke of lightning split the night, and Philip laughed as thunder boomed all around him. Without hesitation he jabbed his own palm with the point of the dagger, drew it across the skin and a line of red trailed behind it. "By my blood I conjure thee," Philip continued, his voice loud. "Let my spirit be as a flame in the night, let my voice be the siren-call to guide you through the cold dark to this rocky shore."

There was a half-formed sensation of pressure on Philip's forehead and he let out an involuntary laugh. That was what he had hoped for. Something was trying to make contact with him.

For over a year Philip and his wife Helena had lived in that house, and they had purchased it for a very specific reason. It wasn't just because it was situated on a lonely country road, far from prying eyes, but that had certainly appealed to them. No, it was because Philip had sensed that something very old and very powerful infested the ground beneath that house. Since moving in he had labored night and day to contact the entity, to conjure its potency up from the earth and set it free.

The Christians and the Jews could go on until the sun burned out about their so-called God, but Philip knew he had something more deserving of the title beneath him. This was something older than man, older than the continents. This was a feaster from the stars, an unknowable and unstoppable force that just waited for someone with the skill to release it. Others had tried while still others had fallen victim to the entity's latent power, their minds and bodies twisted and corrupted, but none of them had managed to coax the presence from the ground.

Philip would prove that he was their better. He would turn the creature loose and follow its wake as it ran rampant over the unsuspecting world.

To that end Philip smeared a thumbprint of blood onto the little girl's forehead, left a dark crescent-shaped stain. "Be thou drawn to this," he said, calling again to the presence. "Come to this offered jewel and fill thyself. Reveal unto me the power and the glory of thy majesty!"

The presence reacted. Philip could feel it rise up from the ground and could almost smell it as grew stronger. It crackled in the air, fluttered like invisible butterflies against his cheeks.

"Yes," Philip whispered, exultant. There had been doubts before he started but he had known in his heart that the ritual would work. Everything he had studied, everything he had read about the house and its invisible inhabitant said that the thing was attracted to imaginative minds, especially those belonging to children. That's why many of the families that lived here before him roused the creature from its rest, much to their dismay.

On the ground the little girl stared, her mouth open, her eyes rolled back in her head. Philip had no idea what the presence was doing to her and he didn't care. All he was concerned with was giving the presence what it wanted. If he did that maybe it would give him what he wanted.

What did Philip want? Why, the power to dominate all things, of course. Was there any other purpose to sorcery? Uncle Abram taught Philip to set his sights high, and he did.

More thunder rolled in from the distance. Philip got to his feet, his hands held high, and called out again, his thick dark hair whipping in the wind.

"From the void I beckon thee!" He shouted. "From the abyss I summon thee! Come into this world! Break down the walls! Throw open the nine gates! Take your place as master of this pitiful planet and let thy hunger strip it clean!"

Another bolt of lightning forked over him. The pressure on his forehead grew stronger, and he could feel the boundaries between the material and immaterial begin to bulge. He knew he was close. He just needed to push it harder. The presence had slept for thousands of years; it needed help to shake off its lethargy. It sensed the child he offered and wanted to taste her mind but couldn't do it without his assistance.

The little girl whimpered. Philip looked down at her and, just like that, the presence was gone. "No!" He shouted. He looked around quickly, searching for the unseen spirit that had been there only a moment before, unable to accept that it had left him.

"No!"

He almost shrieked the word the second time as he dropped back onto his knees, his body trembling terribly. It was all gone, the power he had felt flitted away like it had never been.

"Damn!" He spat. He had been so close!

Philip looked at the child, still seething with rage. The little girl had her eyes closed and looked almost asleep. Her peaceful face only made him angrier. He'd give the girl to his wife if the presence didn't want her. That would teach the little bitch a lesson.

But there was still the issue of his failure. This was not the first time he had come this close only to lose everything at the last second. He'd tried almost everything—Lemurian chants, the *Codex Infernum,* readings from the Black Book of Heinrich Hull, even a particularly humiliating ceremony from the terrifying Bone Grimoire—but all of it came to nothing. Why wasn't it working? There was no mistaking the fact that the entity had pulled back. It had chosen to abandon him. Why? He knew that the creature was attracted to minds, imaginations, and memories, but what did it want? Was it tired of children?

With a thud Philip flopped onto his back, his arms and legs spread wide. He sighed, stared up at the sky. Maybe that was it, he mused. Maybe the ancient entity was weary of the cacophony of a child's mind. His sources had indicated that it liked young minds, not that it was exclusively drawn to them. Certainly he had evidence that all sorts of people could rouse it. If anything it liked people who had some power over the spirit world, people like Philip.

There was no way he was going to put himself on the chopping block, though. That was far too risky. He had refused to let it influence his mind, kept it at arm's length while he worked on using different bait. He knew plenty of folks that would have made good sacrifices but that was the very reason he dare not go after them. Simply put the power they had made them attractive but that same power prevented him from taking them. Children were just easiest to get his hands on.

Unfortunately children clearly weren't working. Fine, he decided. If the entity wanted to be fussy then he would get someone better, someone it had never sampled before.

This, of course, begged the obvious question: where was he going to find someone like that?

CHAPTER 3

▼

"Damn it."

Randall whispered the oath as he went back to his satchel. He reached inside and drew forth a ball-peen hammer, which he quickly struck against the tablet on the table. The stone shattered at the first strike, and Randall swung two more times, reducing the tablet to a multitude of broken fragments. Without hesitation he swept these pieces into his satchel, then pulled out another revolver. As he checked that the second Schofield was loaded, Randall was glad that John had not searched him for weapons at the door. He pulled out a pair of worn and cracked black leather gun belts and strapped them on quickly, crisscrossing them across his waist before stuffing the revolvers into the empty holsters, and then went back to the satchel for one final item. The large Bowie knife and sheath clipped easily onto the left hip of his gun belt. Ready, he turned towards the door.

John was out there, and he was the real enemy.

Randall crept to the door and slowly pulled it open. With a quick glance out the doorway, he went back downstairs, his pistols ready. His boots made only the slightest sound on the tiles as he made his way down the hall. He moved deeper into the house, waiting for the butler to make his move. The android had been well made; its smell and mannerisms had all been too convincing and Randall hadn't recognized it for what it was until he had tasted its insides. John knew his business—this would be no easy hit. Finding out about the transaction had been simple, so had the business of killing the real Mr. Randall and assuming his identity. Randall had been a coward and an idiot, so getting his fragment of the stone tablet had been an easy task. John, however, looked to be a different matter entirely. The man who had taken Randall's name would have to be very, very careful.

So, when he was wandering down the central hall on the first floor of that magnificent house, he was being careful. This, however, did him no good at all. The sound of a muffled cough told him that he was not alone, nor was he going unseen. Randall spun around quickly, bringing his weapons to bear, and saw John standing at the foot of the stairs. The butler's face was devoid of expression, and Randall noticed that the smell of cooked meat was much stronger now.

"So," said John, his voice calm, "you've decided to break the deal, eh?"

"Never had a deal," said Randall. "Randall died three nights ago. You're going to join him."

Smiling, John just shrugged. "Doubtful," he said. He glanced at the muzzles of the big six-shooters and then at the false Randall's sneering face. "You might kill me, I don't doubt that, but I really don't think I'll be joining Randall, wherever he might be."

"Makes no difference to me," said Randall, starting to get tense. This was taking too long, he knew he should just pull the triggers and be done with it, but something was holding him back. Was it fear? Maybe. More likely it was curiosity. He wanted to see what John had up his sleeve.

John's eyes narrowed. "Who are you?" He asked.

"Name's Sebastian Cobb."

John's eyes widened, and he chuckled softly to himself for a moment. "I should have known," he said. "This is going to be a very interesting experience, Mr. Cobb."

John attacked, moving too fast for Cobb to fully react. A long, red-black tentacle came lashing out from over John's left shoulder, whipping at Cobb's face like lightning. Cobb managed to shift his bulk slightly, not enough to completely avoid the deadly missile, but enough to cause it to miss its mark. The tentacle slashed across Cobb's shoulder, the wicked barb on its tip gouging through the fabric of his shirt and tearing a rent in the meat beneath. Cobb winced, the pain only registering slightly in the back of his brain as the tentacle retracted. It hung in the air over John like a serpent, ready to strike again, and was soon joined by a multitude of other similar serpentine limbs radiating out from behind John's back. For a moment neither of them did anything, then the tentacle that had struck Cobb lowered itself, bringing the bloody tip down to hang alongside John's mouth. He extended his tongue, which was longer and thinner than any human's, and tasted the blood and small chunk of meat that hung from the hook.

"Delicious," said John, the tentacle raising. "Let's try for the whole carcass, shall we?"

Cobb leapt back just in time to avoid the combined onslaught of all of John's cruel tentacles, which drove forward with the intent of impaling him. Cobb threw himself to one side, the hooks barely missing him. Some struck the tiles of the floor, cracking them into fragments; some found nothing but empty air. Cobb righted himself quickly, drew a bead on his opponent, and fired his revolvers. The dual blasts echoed through the enclosed hallway, and John was propelled back by the force of the bullets striking him in the chest. He staggered, his tentacles flailing madly; his normal limbs following suit as blood splattered from his torso. Cobb pressed the advantage, his thumbs pulling back the hammers of his guns and firing a second pair of shots into John's abdomen. Firing a third time, Cobb grunted as a wild tentacle caught him over the right eye, the barb slashing a shallow wound above his eyebrow. Blood spilled into his field of vision, getting into his eye and causing him to lose balance for a moment. It was all that John needed, even wounded as he was. A pair of tentacles flashed out and wrapped tightly around the bald man's neck while a third swatted the weapons out of his hands.

Feeling the crushing pressure around his neck, Cobb reached up and grabbed the tentacles with his huge hands, but he couldn't exert enough force to pull them away. Still on his feet, with blood streaming from his body, John smiled and began to lift Cobb into the air. Cobb's legs kicked wildly as John pulled him closer, slowly tightening his grip around his opponent's neck.

"You should have stayed away," John hissed as he pulled Cobb closer. Cobb's eyes had rolled back in his skull, indicating he was close to going under. John's eyes filled with glee and two more of his tentacles slapped around Cobb's ankles, supporting his opponent's weight, easing the pressure on his neck. "You would have been safe for a while."

Cobb's vision cleared and he turned his eyes back to John's evil face. "For a while," he said, his voice guttural, spittle popping onto his lower lip. "But then what? Everyone on earth a slave?"

"Don't tell me you care about that," John replied with disdain. His face began to shift and change, the flesh starting to expand. "I know too much about you to think that the humans on this planet mean anything to you."

"You think I want you and that loser Kilroy running everything?"

John suddenly giggled like a maniac schoolboy, an act made more disturbing by the fact that his face was bulging and starting to turn pink. "Kilroy is only a tool," he said. "He thinks that in a few days he'll have more power than he needs. He's a small man with small desires. Humans are all the same."

Snorting, Cobb pulled harder at the tentacles around his neck. John responded by anchoring their barbed tips into his shoulders. Cobb grunted from the pain. "You're a hunter, Cobb," said John, his face still bloating. His eyes were turning yellow, and when he talked, his long tongue slavered from his open mouth like an angered lamprey. "You kill demons like me out of spite. You have no love for humanity."

Taking one hand away from the tentacles that bound him Cobb fumbled at the Bowie knife on his belt. John paid no attention, his eyes still focused on Cobb's. "With the tablet you brought me, I can finish them, Cobb. I can rid this planet of humanity once and for all. Change it into what it was always meant to be. I can open the gates of hell and let my kind run free on the surface. Wouldn't that be wonderful? Think of the unbridled carnage and slaughter, all throughout eternity. The earth would be a boiling, shattered mass, and then the rest of Creation would follow. World by world we would eat away at everything that lives, never ceasing until we had mastered all. You made that possible, Cobb, you brought me the stone that would ensure total victory for me and my kind."

"Big deal," whispered Cobb, finally yanking his knife free. With a mighty swing of his arm he slashed a deep wound across one tentacle. John growled, pain registering on his face, and Cobb struck again, this time hacking clean through. It split open and a spray of black-green ichor shot all over Cobb's head and shoulders. Cobb ignored it and severed the other tentacle with a single stroke. The limbs restraining his ankles weren't enough to keep him balanced, and the Cobb fell forward with his arms outstretched, right into John.

A roar spat from John's mouth just as his face split down the middle. Cobb flew towards him while the wet halves of John's human head flopped to his shoulders and revealed the unearthly thing beneath. A great central eye burned within the mass of bubbling, supernatural flesh that quivered beneath John's human visage, ringed by several smaller, staring eyes. A small, fang-filled maw opened beneath the eyes just as Cobb landed knife-first on the creature. Its point sank into John's great eye with a spurt of green fluid and John screamed, his true mouth letting out a terrible wail and his tentacles straightening in neural agony. The limbs binding Cobb's ankles released before joining the rest of their brethren in involuntary exultation of their body's defilement, and all of Cobb's weight came down onto the floor, his knife still buried in John's eye. Wrenching his weapon free, Cobb stabbed again, this time driving his blade deep into John's narrow neck. A savage smile on his face, he gave the knife a twist, pulling the wound open and bringing another spurt of black-green ichor. John's mouth narrowed, a sharp hiss issuing from his inhuman lips.

Suddenly, John's tentacles shot into the ceiling, their barbs grabbing the tiles and holding, and then flexed mightily. Lifting his legs, John brought his knees up between himself and Cobb and then thrust them down again, pulverizing the bones like they were made of glass. The tentacles in the ceiling gave a great heave, and John cast off his human body like it had gone out of style, leaving it behind on the floor, the weight of the ruined legs holding it down while something wet and huge slid out through the back and shot into the air. The stench of rotting flesh blasted Cobb's nostrils instantly and he nearly gagged, his stomach wrenching in his gut.

Once he put off the foul stink, Cobb looked up and saw John's true form hanging from the ceiling, giggling at him. The thing was a red-black color, a bit more red than the tentacles, vaguely cone-shaped with a bumpy, glistening skin. The central mass ended in a large tongue-like slug foot, which contracted and expanded strangely while Cobb watched.

"Hello, Sebastian," a voice inside of Cobb's mind whispered, "at last we truly meet."

John didn't seem to be in any hurry to come down, so Cobb took his time in retrieving his pistols. John's dripping face turned slowly on its wounded neck, watching him as he moved.

"I'm glad you killed Randall," he said, using the sibilant, hissing voice that Cobb heard in his mind. The creature's mouth didn't move when the words came, and Cobb guessed that it had no organs that would approximate the sounds of human speech. Those were left behind in the inert bag of meat crumpled on the floor. "Did he beg for his life?"

"Yes," said Cobb as he sheathed his knife and lifted his pistols. "I thought I had gotten everything he knew. It looks like I was wrong. He didn't say anything about you."

An eerie titter escaped John's mouth—a physical sound, not a mental one. For a moment, Cobb wondered why a demon would be able to make that sound and not speak.

"You're a dangerous opponent," John complimented. "And I'm certain that if we started fighting again you would kill me. I know this, Sebastian, and I have no desire to die. More than that, I have no desire to be killed by you. I know what that means, Sebastian, I really do. If you kill me I will be more than just dead—I will cease to be. I have heard this about you."

Cobb smiled. John was right—if Cobb killed him, the demon would be more than dead; he would be gone forever. Cobb wasn't human, and hadn't been for almost two hundred years. He was immortal, he had power that separated him from his race and he could kill a demon in a way that made sure it would never come back. Demons like John, as Cobb had come to understand it, were hurled from this world and back to their own if their body was destroyed, an event that caused the creature a great deal of pain and made it unable to reform for quite some time. It would be reduced a mindless essence, roaming the nether-hells until it was able to coalesce again. The process might take centuries.

This was, apparently, a humiliating experience, though Cobb had little first-hand experience with that. Demons, though, especially the stronger ones, seemed quite reluctant to experience it, but Cobb had the ability to make sure they could never come back. He had done it before and John knew about it, and John was clearly scared. He was right to be.

"I know what you want," said John, still undulating near the ceiling. Cobb listened, his smile slowly transforming back into his normal sneer. "I know what you're after."

"What's that?" Cobb asked, dubious. The demon chortled.

"Revenge," he said. "And I can see that you find it."

Cobb took a heavy step forward, his brow tightening with anger. "Liar," he spat. "You couldn't."

Intimidated, John pulled back and made a wet, bubbling sound. "Listen to me," he implored. "Demons talk, they gossip like human women, maybe worse. I heard a story once about a demon that was killed by someone who wore the shape of mortal man. This was different than anything that had happened before, though. This demon was gone, its essence purged. Nothing like that had ever happened in the history of your world. Years later when the name 'Sebastian Cobb' began going around, some wondered where he came from. It didn't take long for a few of us to figure things out, asking the right questions to the right agencies."

Growling, Cobb took another step forward. "Don't lie to me, demon," he threatened. "I know your kind and I don't trust you."

"Just let me go," offered John. "Kill my body if you want, send me into the abyss for a few centuries and let the others laugh. They won't laugh once they know I escaped total destruction. Please, Sebastian, don't obliterate me. Go on and kill Kilroy. I look forward to seeing him in the Pit, anyway."

"And what will you give me?" Asked Cobb. The offer sounded genuine—he'd seen such fear of destruction in other demons. Being immortal creatures of spirit, demons had no real conception of death. Not true, everlasting death. They never had to accept the reality of it like humans and other mortals did. They never had to deal with the uncertainty of what was beyond. The idea of that certainty made someone like Cobb terrifying to them—he brought a whole new possibility to their existence, that of utter annihilation.

"I'll show you how to use the tablet you brought me," said John, lowering. "I'll teach you its power—you could master the human race with that, not to mention many others. You could summon and kill all the demons you want, including the ones who could tell you what you're after. Think of that Sebastian, think of everything you could have."

"I don't want it," said Cobb, quietly. "I don't want any of it."

"I know what you want," said John seductively, daring to come back down to the floor. He slithered closer on his slug foot, his tentacles disengaging from the ceiling and coming down to within an inch of the floor in a gesture of submission. "I know you'll need power to accomplish what you want. Listen to my offer, Sebastian," he said. "There are things happening in hell that you could never understand, and if you want to take your revenge you'll need the power I can offer you."

"No," said Cobb, looking down at the floor as he thought about what John was telling him. The offer of power was tempting, of course, for anyone. The Muir Tablet was a powerful talisman, capable of great many things. Cobb had his desires, too, and here John was offering the chance to make them become reality.

"Why do you think I came to this pathetic world?" John asked, drawing within a few feet of Cobb. "Why do you think I went about collecting the fragments of the Muir Tablet? I wanted power, Sebastian. With that tablet I could have the power I need. Think of it, Sebastian, you could help me. Together, we could make sure no demons ever invaded this world ever again. Get the tablet and bring it to me. You'd have your revenge and I could be safe."

Cobb's eyes narrowed and he looked at the demon, suddenly becoming aware of how dangerously close he was. It was too late, though. Cobb's pistols were yanked out of his hands a second time and John's tentacles snapped into the air, coming around Cobb from behind. They sank their points into the meat of his shoulders, back, and thighs and Cobb roared as hot pokers of agony lanced through his body.

"Of course," John said, lifting Cobb into the air like he had before, "I could just give you to Kilroy as a plaything. Or, even better, I could take you back to hell with me."

Cobb clenched his teeth, ignoring the inhuman laughter that gurgled from the demon's jaws. Using the only weapons he had, he threw out his arm and stuck the fingers of his right hand into John's eye, reaching into the gash that his knife had made before. John screamed and thrust his barbs into Cobb's shoulder and forearm. He pulled desperately at his opponent's limb, but he couldn't force the hand out of his eye. Cobb bared his teeth like a wounded animal, pushing his fingers deeper into John's wound, splitting it completely open. Heavy black goo spilled out, and this time John's scream was both physical and mental, his small mouth letting out a high-pitched shriek that mixed with the mental wail that exploded in Cobb's mind. The barbs in Cobb's body twisted, sending new waves of pain through him and he let out an involuntary groan, but he kept his hand where it was.

"You're dead, demon," spat Cobb as he pulled his hand to one side and tore the eye in half. John's howl grew louder, and he released Cobb before slithering away. Cobb fell heavily to the floor, a large chunk of John's eye still clutched in his thick hand. Discarding this quickly, Cobb leapt at the retreating demon, not willing to let it get away from him. He hurled himself at the misshapen thing, just as its body began to tremble violently. The smell of ozone filled the hall, and a pale nimbus of blue light started to envelope John just as Cobb fell onto him.

"Oh no you don't," Cobb whispered, recognizing the signs. John was trying to discard his physical form, trying to run back to his own realm and save his existence. Cobb would have none of it. His big hands slapped onto the sides of John's central mass and held on tight, the muscles of his shoulders and arms bulging. "You're not going anywhere."

"Please," John implored weakly, as a quantity of greenish-black filth vomited from his ruined eye. "Let me go. I'll never bother you again, just let me go."

Cobb could feel the eerie flesh under his fingers begin to soften and fade—the demon would vanish soon. He had no other option. Exerting his will, Cobb snarled, and he began to *feed*. John howled, his essence being ripped from him, the glow fading. Cobb closed his eyes, drawing the energy from the demon's mass, sucking the life out of him. The pale blue light disappeared altogether, and John's body began to darken, the flailing of his limbs growing steadily weaker.

In a moment it was over. John's body went limp, his tentacles dropping to the floor as he blackened. His hideous head swayed from side to side with his narrow mouth hanging open, and a weird hissing sound came from within before it tilted backwards, all unearthly life gone. Cobb released the empty husk, letting it fall to the chamber floor with a sickening squishing sound. Opening his eyes he looked down at it with an expression of disgust. John's body lay still for a moment, and then it began to twitch slightly. As Cobb watched, the corpse began dissolving in the open air, no longer maintained by the demon's life force.

Unmoved by something he had seen many times before, Cobb turned away from the melting corpse. He was tired, and the sickly feeling of John's polluted essence was still swirling around in his gut—he knew it would fade, but for the moment he had to deal with it. It was always the same; he would take the essence of a demon, sometimes it would make him stronger, sometimes it didn't, but it always disgusted him. Unfortunately it was the only way to make sure they were finished for good.

Cobb shook his head, hunted down his revolvers, and replaced them in their holsters. John's body was almost completely gone now; Cobb glanced at it only for a moment before leaving the main hall, heading back to the study.

Once inside, Cobb was glad to see that Harlowe's corpse was still where he had left it. The last thing he needed now was for the android to get up and attack him. Satisfied that Harlowe wasn't going to offer him any trouble, he went looking through the rooms until he found a master bathroom. Inside, there was a huge white tub, and Cobb glanced quickly at its carven images of cherubs before turning on the water. He pulled down his suspenders and took off his shirt, letting out a quiet grunt. His muscles were stiff and his joints popped as he moved; the fight against John had been taxing.

With casual disdain Cobb dropped his filthy shirt onto the floor, turned away from the tub, and looked into the long wall of mirrors on the opposite wall. He saw himself reflected there, half-naked, covered in blood and ichor, his pants crusty. He froze, regarding his reflection with wide, blank eyes.

"Who are you?" He asked himself in his mind. "Why are you here?"

CHAPTER 4

▼

The answers came too quickly, and he didn't like them. He was Sebastian Cobb, born 1752, a servant of the British government in the Americas.

Putting a hand to the side of his face, he leaned forward, peering closer at his reflection, looking at the shaven scalp streaked with black. He ran his fingers under his chin, then up to the eyebrow that had been wounded early in his fight with John. The cut was almost completely gone, only a narrow line was left behind. It was just another to mark each day, another wound that would heal and disappear in a miraculously short period of time. The soothing sound of the bath filling brought a strange calm to Cobb as he looked at himself, thinking back to his past.

He remembered that night in 1783 when the war ended. He remembered hearing that England had recognized the colonies as free, he remembered the exultation of knowing that he was living in the midst of history. He had been 31, a man with a family. His wife, his daughter, they had both been the source of his strength during the nightmare. They had loved him as much as he had loved them, and he had loved them with a depth that few could ever understand. If not for them he would have lost hope many times during the war, but the hope of giving them a country that they could call their own kept him going as it did the countless others that fought. It had been enough and in the end it had paid off. The war ended and America was victorious. He went home a hero in the eyes of his family, and he couldn't remember a time when he had been happier.

If only it had lasted.

He remembered the night of 1787, the night that they had come. He remembered pain and he remembered loss. His heart lurched when he saw the blood in his mind, saw the wet crimson on his hands and felt the hot fetid breath of something horrible on his face. The sights and smells in his mind were broken by screams and inhuman laughter, taunting Cobb from the past and daring him to lose himself in the endless drift of memory.

Cobb shook his head, coming back to the present. Turning away from the mirror, he saw that the bath was full almost to the edge. He turned off the water quickly, stripped off the rest of his soiled garments and then got in. The warmth soothed him, the feeling of the dried filth coming away from his skin even more relaxing. He submerged himself, staying under for a few seconds before bringing his head back up, taking in a huge breath of air and letting out an almost involuntary bark of satisfaction. He smiled, wiping his face and scalp, cleaning off the blood and filth. It felt good to be warm; it felt good to be clean. Leaning back against one side of the bath, Cobb gently lowered his head to the rim and closed his eyes.

More memories came back to him. He remembered running through the cold night, remembered the feeling of his musket in his hand; remembered the fear that had crept up his spine like an icy spider. He entered the forest, not hesitating for a moment in the face of the natural fears he had about being in such a secluded place. The Indians held no terror for him now; the threat of wild animals could do nothing to sway him from his purpose. His family needed him; he would do anything to save them.

He remembered shuffling through the brush, following the trail that had so obviously been left. His feet struck the dry earth with deadly urgency as he noted every broken branch and every misplaced twig by the light of his lantern, holding his musket out protectively. How long did he pursue his quarries? He couldn't remember. He did remember finding them, though. He remembered that very well.

Opening his eyes, Cobb sat up in the bath, taking a bar of soap from a holder on the nearby wall and began cleaning himself in earnest, working up a lather and spreading it onto his arms and shoulders. The water around him was cloudy with sweat and grime, not to mention the blood and ichor that was coming off his skin in wet flakes. He rinsed himself off, oily dark water swirling around him, remnants of the soap lather floating on the surface. He dunked himself twice more, wiping off his bald scalp and face, then stood, water splashing off his body noisily. A large white towel was on a nearby rack; he took it off and padded himself dry before leaving the tub. Standing before the mirror, he finished his drying, then wrapped the towel around his waist and looked at himself, satisfied. He was clean again, looking and feeling more like his extremely old self.

"Help us!"

The scream was loud, and it took a moment for Cobb to realize that it was coming from his mind, from the depths of his memory. He tensed, looking around, and saw that he was standing at the edge of a clearing in a forest, watching the people in black hoods as they chanted around a Godless altar. He couldn't remember how many there were, maybe five or six. Where was his wife? Where was his daughter? He cried out to them, all but one of the heathens turning to him while the last kept up the chant. There was a chill breeze moving through the surrounding trees, causing them to sway and dance almost in mockery of his fear.

There was fighting; Cobb remembered fighting. He remembered the sound of a gunshot and the stench of burnt gunpowder. There were screams and pain, all of these senses and sensations combined in his mind to form a gray, clouded mass that was impossible to see clearly. Why couldn't he remember everything? Even the next day he had been unable to do that. What caused him to quickly forget the details of what could have easily been the most significant night of his life?

One image wasn't gone, though; no matter how much Cobb wished it would go. When all was said and done, the chanting had stopped, the men in black were all dead, and Cobb held the bodies of his wife and daughter in his arms, their blood spilling onto him. He could feel the warmth leaving them, his mind racing as he contemplated the fact that he would never hear them laugh or cry, never speak to them, and never feel their love touch his heart again. He held them while they died, everything that had made his life perfect dying with them.

Cobb screamed, both in his memories and in Harlowe's house, the sight of their dead bodies wrenching his heart almost from his chest. He fell onto the floor of the bathroom, his mind hurtling back from the past into the present. Mercifully, he passed out shortly afterward.

Cobb woke slowly, the tile cold against the side of his face. He lifted himself up, his big hands on the floor, and looked around. There was no sunlight coming in through the windows—it was still nighttime. He walked out of the bathroom and into the hallway beyond; there was a clock on the wall, it read 3:52. If there were any human servants that worked in the house they would be along soon to get things ready for the day. That raised a question in Cobb's mind: Had there ever been a human named Adrian Harlowe? Or had he always been a construct, an artificial person made by a demon to draw attention away from the real threat. Harlowe had built his empire only a few years before. Perhaps he had simply never existed as anything other than a decoy. Manipulating a financial empire would have been child's play to a demon, especially in the wake of the chaos of the stock market crash. There were many possibilities, too many to consider.

Taking his time, Cobb searched the master bedroom, located after a few minutes of wandering the halls. He stripped off his damp towel and went through the huge closet, looking for something to wear. Adrian's clothes were a bit small, but he eventually found a pair of trousers that were only slightly snug. The shirt was a different matter, however. Anything with buttons and a collar was right out; he decided on an undershirt. It hugged tightly against his thick torso, but at least it covered him. He looked around the bedroom some more, just on the off chance that there was something interesting lying about, but came up with nothing. So, he decided to check out the rest of the house.

An hour later, Cobb was finished. His search had turned up little apart from some fine silverware and a few bottles of bourbon, which he placed in a large black travel bag found in a hall closet. Finally he returned to the study. A quick search of the desk turned up a .38 revolver that had been placed in the middle drawer, a small box of bullets nearby. Cobb pocketed this almost as an afterthought, nothing else of importance in the drawer. A second drawer, however, turned up something very interesting.

It was a small envelope, clearly an invitation of some sort, still sealed. Tearing it open, Cobb saw that the invitation consisted of a small card, bordered in red, which read:

"You are cordially invited to a celebration of His Infernal Majesty, to be held at the home of Benjamin Kilroy, August 1st, 1934, please arrive before midnight."

Kilroy was the next target on Cobb's list before he would be finished with his current affair. From what Cobb knew Kilroy operated some kind of brothel in New York State, one that catered to more than just the usual kind of people that frequented brothels. Randall had told him that it was Kilroy who had located all of the fragments of the Muir tablet, sending Randall to collect them while John held the secret to unlocking their power. They were, Randall said, planning to unleash the Tablet when the astronomical conditions were right, but that wasn't for another six months. It seemed Kilroy had plans for the intervening time. Summoning demons was always a good way to avoid boredom for people without regard for things like sanity or morality. Slipping the card into his pocket, Cobb turned his attention to the nearby wall and its safe. He'd deal with Kilroy in good time, but for the moment he had more immediate concerns.

Cobb didn't know the combination to the safe, but there were other ways to open things. A quick rummage through the satchel bag turned up a bundle of dynamite and a roll of tape. Cobb looked at the bundle of thick sticks; he had brought it as a "just in case" tool. He was glad he did. He removed a single stick from the bundle and taped it to the safe door. It took a moment for him to stow his belongings down on the first floor, and then he went back to the study and lit the fuse. A second later he was running down the stairs. At the bottom Cobb knelt down and covered his ears, his eyes closed tightly.

The explosion was very, very loud.

Cobb opened his eyes, a slight smirk on his face. There was something thrilling about explosions—they were something he had learned to enjoy. Picking up his satchel bag, he made his way back to the study, his feet crunching on the flakes of paint and other debris that the shockwave had shaken loose from the walls. He almost laughed when he saw that he blast had torn the study door from its hinges and thrown it across the hall. Looking through the open doorway, Cobb let out a satisfied grunt when he saw that the safe door had buckled; it was lying on the floor.

Cobb entered quickly, realizing that he was taking too long in the house. It was just after 5 in the morning; it was very possible that someone could come to the house at any second and catch him rooting around and blowing things up. He looked into the safe, glancing momentarily at the black, circular blast mark that surrounded the opening. There was a small metal box, which proved to be unlocked. Inside was a pile of hundred dollar bills and a few pieces of jewelry. Cobb threw all of this into his satchel and a few minutes later he was making his way out of the house, bags in hand. His big Studebaker was parked out front, and it didn't take long for Cobb to load up his belongings and drive off, bidding Adrian Harlowe and his demonic butler farewell.

The road back to town was short, and it wasn't long before Cobb found himself driving past the sign along the side of the road that read "Coopersville, Population: 1,350." It wasn't one of the biggest towns in New York State, but it wasn't bad. Cobb had only spent a night before going off to the Harlowe mansion, but he seemed to like it as much as any other town. The hotel he had booked himself in was average, which suited Cobb just fine because no one asked questions of strangers passing through. He would have preferred spending the rest of the day in bed in his hotel room, but circumstances wouldn't allow it. Sooner or later someone was going to notice the local millionaire being dead and start asking questions, especially of strangers passing through. Cobb didn't want to deal with that.

So he drove through Coopersville without stopping, sparing less than a glance at the small town and its earthy charm. The chugging of his engine was the only sound he paid attention to, ignoring the curious glances from the people on the street. The stock market crash had been hard on small towns like Coopersville and it showed. There were men sitting idly in front of the general store, staring blankly with hollow eyes as Cobb passed by, something very real missing from deep inside. Cobb had seen it before, in many towns since that day a mere five years in the past when the bottom fell out of the American economy and hope disappeared. He was learning to expect it.

He drove out of Coopersville, leaving its inhabitants and all thoughts of their suffering behind. There would be other towns, other places with the exact same problems and the exact same people sitting in the exact same places. To dwell too long on the specifics of one place would invite madness.

CHAPTER 5

▼

There air was unusually cold the night that Benjamin Kilroy had his gathering to honor the Prince of Darkness, but it was somehow appropriate and in no way unwelcome, considering how hot August normally was. The guests chafed a bit at the black robes, but the basement was cool and once the wine started flowing people stopped complaining.

Kilroy had gone all out for the occasion, stocking some very good chardonnay for the guests and making sure there were plenty of hors d'oeuvres to go around. There were at least twenty people assembled, some hardened occultists, others curious novices, but all were willing to participate in the ritual that Kilroy had gathered them for. It was surprising how many people were willing to traffic with the dark powers of the underworld as a means to escape the mundane and the increasing tedium of modern life.

Benjamin Kilroy himself was a complicated man, a scholar and a poet, the heir to a long line of wealthy businessmen whose family dated back to Plymouth Rock. At 38 years old he had established a reputation for himself as a purveyor of a great many dark pleasures, a man who made it possible for people to indulge whatever wicked whims they could come up with. Bestiality, necrophilia, voyeurism, pederasty, just about anything was possible if you asked Kilroy, just as long as you were willing to pay the price; the severity of which was based on exactly what you wanted. No one cheated Kilroy; he had plenty of loyal customers who were willing to make sure that no one jeopardized their own pleasures by annoying him.

The last of the guests had arrived by 11 p.m. Kilroy greeted them warmly, dressed in a black and gray suit, his thin black hair pushed back from a high forehead, a snifter of brandy in one hand. He ran a finger along the length of his thin black moustache, smiling amicably at the arrivals, a husband and wife named Jennings, a pair of decadent old perverts that had been patrons of Kilroy's for years.

"Welcome, Loretta and Terrance," said Kilroy, gesturing towards the main hall of his rather quaint home, where the others stood conversing while servants circulated food and wine. There was a faint scent of incense in the air, mixed with the odor of the expensive floral arrangements that Kilroy had procured for the evening. Kilroy always like yellow roses, and he had masses of them set against the walls of the hall, so that no matter which way he faced he could see them. "I'm so glad you could make it."

As the Jennings couple mingled, Kilroy looked around at the others. Most of the people he had invited were present, all except for Adrian Harlowe's butler, John. An interesting fellow, this John, clearly Harlowe was not the brains of that operation. Truth be told, Kilroy knew little about John, only that he was in control of the entire Harlowe fortune and was a man of bizarre tastes. That and the fact that he was promising him power over the entire world if the fragments of the Muir Tablet could be acquired. While the plan seemed far-fetched, even for someone like Kilroy, he had decided to put his faith in John and had committed his associate to the task. He wasn't worried, though, Randall usually came through. Kilroy had hoped that John would have shown if only to tell him the state of the plan. He hoped nothing had gone wrong.

If John even had a last name Kilroy didn't know it. There were things he did know, though. Teenage girls were the butler's favorite; virgins especially, and they were procured at a high cost. Sometimes he would go through three or four in a night, satisfying his cruel lusts on their young bodies, leaving them bruised and terrified wrecks by morning. Kilroy was never so uncouth as to spy on a guest, but the way the girls reacted to their nights with him had always made him undeniably curious, especially since in Kilroy's dealings John was a quiet, friendly man, always prompt with a payment and more than willing to stay an hour or two for brandy and cigars afterward. The girls would certainly never speak of it, and Kilroy could see that pressing the point would have been fruitless.

The only time that Kilroy had even entertained the notion of turning John away was after one of the girls, a 14 year old named Ginger, had slashed her own throat with a razor blade after one night with John. But the girl had always been a little off-center; Kilroy used that as an excuse to give up on turning away someone with as much financial clout as John.

But John had not shown, nor had he phoned or otherwise contacted Kilroy to let him know that he was coming.

Still, Kilroy had hoped that the mysterious manservant would have made an appearance. The others were there, though—the Jennings', the MacReadys, the Brighton twins, Anton Smythe, Nicholas Rasmussen from California, six members of the Unquiet Dark, the Farwells, a strange little man named Gunnam, the hauntingly beautiful Victoria Mundy, and finally a pompous but capable industrialist called Gregory. All members of a very secretive group, all united by their common interest in the powers that mankind was right to fear.

None of them knew what was really in store for them. They might have had an idea, but Kilroy knew that there was no way they could foresee his plans. There would be no end of surprises in the following hours.

Taking a sip of brandy, Kilroy stood before the assembled throng and raised a hand, calling for their attention. Eventually they quieted themselves, forgetting their inane banter and looking to their host. Smiling, Kilroy addressed them.

"Good evening to you all," he said, his baritone voice loud and practiced. "Welcome to my home. Some of you know each other, but all of you know me. You know that I have called you here tonight to witness a miracle, something that I think you will all enjoy."

The throng applauded this, using that same quiet and reserved clapping that one usually heard at a golf tournament. Kilroy gestured for quiet and continued. "Some of you will be familiar with what you will witness, the practices and principles well-known to you, while for others this will be an entirely new experience. I expect that those who are knowledgeable of such things will guide the others, so that everything goes off without a hitch. There can be no beauty without risk, and though the risks of what we are about to do can be great, the rewards are worth it. Trust me when I say that I have taken every possible precaution."

With that, Kilroy led his mumbling and muttering guests into the basement, where everything had been prepared. There were armed servants on the main floor, more than capable of dealing with unwanted visitors, should they arrive. It was unlikely, but Kilroy didn't like leaving things to chance.

The basement was huge, specially built to be expansive, since Kilroy never knew what he would need to put down there. The walls were flat gray stone, unremarkable but good at keeping the moisture out when it rained. Even so there was a musty damp smell to the place, the kind that all such places had. There were two ways up to the first floor, two sets of stairs opposite each other leading from the main chamber. A storeroom was connected to it, and this had been packed with everything that normally rested in the basement, the main chamber cleared out to make room for the ceremony. To that end, a large red pentagram had been painted on the smooth stone floor, seals and sigils of mystical significance drawn on the edges. The circle measured twenty-five feet across easily; when one summoned the Devil one liked him to be comfortable. Several of the guests walked around the perimeter of this circle, nodding silently as they examined the markings, their own expertise evaluating their host's work. The uninitiated just watched, marveling at what they were seeing.

In the corner was set a pile of candles, braziers, and other accoutrements. Taking a long white candle from this mess, Kilroy lit it quickly, smiling at the group.

"Now it begins," he said, ushering the throng towards one corner, in order to give him room to work. The candle flame flickered strangely before him, casting eerie shadows on his face. He turned to the circle and placed the candle on the floor.

"To the reaches of the dark I call thee," he began, his voice clear and calm. "By the spirits of the night I call thee. By the blood of my kin I call thee. In the name of all unholy things, summon I thee to this prepared place."

His arms were raised above his head and his hands were open to the ceiling. "Come to us, glorious and powerful lord of Hell, come to us in the form that pleaseth thee. Give to us, your faithful servants, the pleasure of your countenance. Come! We beg you!"

And then Kilroy slipped into some strange language that few in the world understood, including one or two of his guests. He chanted in the guttural, low tongue, his voice growing louder and louder, his eyes wide with exultation. The guests watched, silently, while Kilroy started to shout, caught up in bizarre, otherworldly exultation.

Finally, he stopped, apparently exhausted, his hands slapping down to his hips, his head low. Nothing had happened; no fire, no smoke, no roaring hell-spawned thing—nothing had appeared. Some of the crowd began to murmur softly, Kilroy ignored them. The ones who stayed quiet were the ones who understood what was going on.

The candle flame flickered once, and then the circle burst into flame.

"Yes!" Kilroy shouted as he raised a triumphant fist. The flames rose higher, restricting themselves to the perimeter of the circle, impossibly refusing to spread like a normal flame should. They grew almost to five feet high, lashing back and forth, yellow-orange tongues that should have seared Kilroy from the heat but did not. Nothing about the flames was natural.

The uninitiated in the crowd were taken back by the sudden conflagration and the rancid odor of sulphur and ash that filled the basement, but they did not cry out. Instead they stood fascinated by what they saw, what burned before Kilroy's silhouetted form. Kilroy himself was euphoric, watching the flames with fascination. Eventually they calmed, lowering down to a burning ring only a few inches high, revealing what had answered the call and now stood in the center of the circle.

The thing was man-shaped, with two arms, two legs, a torso and a head, but that was where the resemblance stopped. Standing almost ten feet tall, the demon was covered in matted blue-black fur, its hands and feet ending in great, clawed appendages, its head surmounted by a pair of huge, curved black horns that projected from its forehead. The face below the horns was more a wolf's face than anything else, with a pair of staring yellow eyes and a fanged muzzle. Saliva dripped from the jaws while it looked at the group of humans, mockery in its eyes. In its left hand it gripped a long, gnarled staff of bone, topped with a huge human skull.

"Who summons Bifrons?" The demon demanded, its voice a horrible roar. Several of the assembled group shuddered and Kilroy dropped to one knee, a supplicant in the face of eternal damnation.

"I do, my lord," he said. "We have asked for the blessing of your company for this night."

"You have the wonderful stink of sin upon you, mortal," said Bifrons, taking a step towards him. Glancing at the crowd, the demon waved a claw. "All of you do. What blessing could Bifrons give you?"

"We seek pleasure and wealth, my lord," replied Kilroy, bowing his head. "Power and glory such as only the lords of hell understand."

The demon laughed, its guttural, barking chuckle echoing off the walls of the chamber. "Such things are beyond your comprehension," it said. "For what price would you buy them?"

The crowd mumbled for a moment, and Kilroy moved over to stand between them and the exit. It was time for him to get to business as he had planned. "These," he said, pointing at the crowd. "Take them, my lord, they are for you!"

Again the demon laughed, the guests quickly realizing that they had been betrayed. Kilroy had brought them together to feed to this beast in exchange for its patronage. Anton Smythe, tall and strong, stalked forward, an angry look on his face, but Kilroy shot him through the knee with a pistol that he plucked quickly from a pocket. The crowd gasped, fear in their eyes, while Smythe clutched at his wound, whimpering. "Take them, lord, they are yours!" Kilroy repeated while he waved his gun at the rest of the group to keep them back.

"Even souls such as these are pleasing, mortal," said Bifrons. Then, it sniffed at the air, like a dog scenting something on the breeze. After a moment it looked at Kilroy, its eyes narrow. "But you can not buy my pleasures now."

Kilroy was stunned. "But, lord—"

"Death has come for you all."

No sooner had Bifrons pronounced the sentence than the body of one of Kilroy's servants came crashing down the steps, his face drenched in blood. Everyone turned to look upon the body, which lay still on the floor, a pool of dark red forming underneath the head.

"What the—" Kilroy began, his question cut off by the sound of heavy footsteps on the stairs. The demon behind him forgotten, Kilroy felt the comforting weight of the gun in his hand while everyone waited for the intruder to show himself. The first thing that they saw were his boots, black and cracked, covered to the heel with a pair of black canvas pants. A long blue coat flapped around the ankles, whipping back and forth with every step. Eventually the intruder was fully visible, his hands gripping a sawed-off double-barreled Stoeger coach gun. His face was a twisted mask of rage, his large nose bleeding slightly, his pale eyes slits as he stared at the crowd. Beads of sweat showed on his bare scalp and there was a tear in the left breast of his coat, bloody fabric visible beneath.

"Who are you?" Kilroy demanded, his gun wavering while the colossus stared him down. Cobb answered by pointing his shotgun and firing, sending a blast into Kilroy's stomach. The man of pleasure spun completely around with the force of it, and to his horror staggered across the ring of quietly burning fire before he could recover his balance. As soon as he did he almost forget the massive wound he had suffered, for he realized that something far worse had just happened.

He had fallen into the circle.

Bifrons roared when the mortal entered his reach, the magical power of the circle no longer protecting him. With eyes wide in horror, Kilroy cried out as the demon slapped its claws onto his body, grabbing him by one shoulder and one leg and then lifting him into the air, his joints popping as Bifrons rent his limbs.

The guests screamed and mumbled, turning away from Cobb and the demon and making for the opposite staircase. Cobb dropped his shotgun to the floor and reached under his coat, yanking his Schofields out of their holsters. No one was escaping while he could do something about it. His lips pulled back and he opened fire, sent bullets into the fleeing people. Several of them dropped right away, others managed to avoid the slaughter and ran up the steps.

After the last of the guests had fled, Cobb turned his attention back to the demon. It seemed unconcerned with him or what he was doing, focused as it was on mutilating Kilroy's screaming body. The human bled from a dozen wounds, each of them enough to kill anyone, but still he did not die. Quite simply, Cobb knew that Bifrons was not going to let him.

Eventually Bifrons dropped the wet body to the floor, looking intently at Cobb, who was reloading his revolvers patiently and ignoring Kilroy as he whimpered in the circle. Nearby Anton Smythe still sat against the wall, clutching his bleeding knee, clearly oblivious to what was going on. Cobb holstered his pistols, picked up his shotgun and, without ceremony or the slightest hint of human emotion, emptied the second barrel into Smythe's chest. Smythe was dead in moments, gasping out his last breath while Cobb replaced the cartridges.

"Well done, warrior," said Bifrons, pleased. "Slaughter suits you."

"Shut up," muttered Cobb, slapping shut his shotgun. He knew that the demon was confined to its circle. He had no need to hurry. "You and I have business."

Crossing to the other side of the chamber, careful to avoid touching the burning circle, Cobb turned over the bodies on the floor, making sure they were dead. He had managed to shoot seven of them before they escaped and only one of them was still breathing. Pulling the Bowie knife from the sheath on his belt, Cobb finished Mrs. Jennings with a thrust to the abdomen, up under the ribcage and into the heart.

"They were mine, you know," said the demon, casually watching Cobb. "This one," he nudged the still living body at his feet, "promised them to me."

Cobb wiped his blade clean on Mrs. Jennings' dress and sheathed it. "I don't care," he said.

"No, I expect you don't," replied Bifrons before kneeling down and stroking Kilroy's quivering body in a strangely gentle manner. "This one will provide me with much sport. I like the way he screams."

"You've got other things to worry about," said Cobb while he walked over to the edge of the circle. He could sense the power of it, could feel the energy it radiated churning in the air even if no one else could. The demon loped over to stand before Cobb, leaning down so that its eyes were even with his.

"You wish to kill me?" It asked, amused. Cobb didn't flinch. He merely stared while the hot breath of the demon washed over him. The thing smelled like it existed on a diet of raw meat and feces, and Cobb could almost hear the massive heart beating within its breast.

"I wish to question you," Cobb replied, resting his shotgun on his shoulder. He'd planned on killing Kilroy anyway, but the fact that the pimp had taken the time to summon this demon had given Cobb an idea. "Look at me."

Bifrons complied, and its eyes bored into Cobb, their hateful glare withering to all but the staunchest target. "What do you see?"

Head tilting a fraction of an inch, Bifrons grinned. "Power," it said. "And rage. Plenty of rage."

"What am I?"

The demon almost seemed surprised by that question and it pulled back a bit, eyes narrow. "You don't know?"

"I was born a man, demon," Cobb replied. "I know that, but I want you to tell me what happened to change what I was."

"That's an expensive question, little one," said Bifrons, its mocking tone returning. "Do you wish to pay such a price?"

"You tell me or I'll kill you," growled Cobb, his temper flaring as he inched towards the edge of the circle. "I'll suck the life right out of you and fucking eat it."

Bifrons laughed. "Truly I think you are capable," it sighed.

"You know I am."

The great demon leaned closer and examined Cobb with narrow eyes. "You are more than you think," he said, "but less than you could be. It almost saddens me to see you diminished so."

"No riddles, demon," said Cobb. "Tell me what I am."

"You are familiar," said Bifrons. "Very familiar, though I cannot place the taste of your spirit. Part of it is human, part is...something else."

Cobb grew angry. "Tell me!" He shouted. "Tell me or I'll jump in there with you and we'll see who comes out!"

The demon's slavering lips pulled back into a hideous smile. "I am not in the mood for combat," it said as it reached down and lifted Kilroy's pathetic body in one claw. "I have my prize. Some other time, perhaps."

Again the fiery circle flared. Cobb took a step back and lifted a hand to ward off the flames, and then they were gone. The flames, Bifrons, Kilroy; all of them had disappeared. Only a blackened circle on the floor remained.

Ignoring the fact that Bifrons had told him nothing, Cobb wondered what kind of torture Kilroy was already enduring, but he pushed that thought from his mind quickly. Whatever it was, Kilroy deserved it.

Cobb took the time to go through the corpses, and he snatched up all the jewelry and cash he could find. He had expenses, after all, and without any sort of regular income he had to make do with what he could get from people like Harlowe or Kilroy. He had no desire to grow wealthy, and would have given anything for the chance to live a normal life, but that wasn't going to happen anytime soon. He would make his way as best he could, and if that required he steal from dead servants of evil then so be it. They didn't need it anyway.

Cobb lingered only a moment once the bodies were looted, pausing to take in the quiet of the chamber that had once been host to a denizen of the pit. Some of the guests got away, but Cobb didn't really care. The ringleader, Kilroy, had been dealt with, and it was unlikely that the survivors would try anything like this again anytime soon. He would have liked to have it out with the demon, but sometimes they just left like that. Besides, Bifrons hadn't been up to anything nefarious, he had been summoned by humans and was contained. John had been running loose in the world with the clear intention of conquering it; it was a completely different situation. When Bifrons was finished he had left, that meant that Cobb wasn't going to waste any anger over his escape.

Having had his fill of the chamber, Cobb bounced up the steps, his coat flapping around him. The wound on his chest had already closed, and in a day or two any trace of it would be gone. One of the servants had been a better guard than Cobb had expected; the shot had been a good one and if Cobb were mortal he would have died. But, if there was one thing Cobb knew about himself, it was that he wasn't mortal. At a hundred and eighty-two years old he could safely say that. Of course, he had a lot more evidence than just his age; there was also the fact that in those years he had been shot, stabbed, disemboweled, hung, drowned, and once even decapitated. Through it all he had stayed among the living, coming back to consciousness after enough time had passed for his body to repair itself. If there was a way for him to die he didn't know what it was.

And he wanted to know. He wanted to die, he was tired after so many years of facing horrors that no man was meant to face. That is to say, he wanted to die a clean death, a mortal death. He didn't want to have his essence drained, his mind destroyed, or his soul consumed. These were all common hazards in his line of work. No, Cobb wanted to die like a man, wanted the rest that he deserved. So far nothing had been capable of killing him, but that didn't mean he wasn't willing to try.

Until then, though, there were things that needed stopping. People like Kilroy, things like Yulgo Kharan. By driving them away or ruining their plans Cobb got a little bit of revenge, acquired a modicum of satisfaction that the thought that they were stopped. Something very like them had made him into this thing that he was, this unknown quantity that seemed capable only of killing, and if he couldn't have his revenge on it he would take it on its ilk. And, of course, there was always the hope that that one day one of the things he fought would be capable of killing him. That was something best left to the subconscious, however.

On the main floor of the house Cobb went to the pantry, looking for something to drink. That was just about one of the only escapes he had left—alcohol. After a night like this, Cobb liked nothing more than to drain a few bottles of whiskey or vodka, drinking himself into a stupor and then passing out into black oblivion. When he was drunk and unconscious he didn't dream, and that was just fine with him. His dreams were worse than the reality he faced.

Locating a bottle of what smelled like cognac, Cobb took a swig and closed the bottle, savoring the taste on his tongue. It was woody, but good.

A scraping noise came from the hallway, and immediately Cobb had one of his revolvers out, the cognac bottle clapping against a countertop. He forgot about it and walked quietly to the doorway, his gun out before him, eyes narrow. Were all of the guards dead or had he missed one?

Cobb had come to within inches of the doorway when the woman appeared, tall and beautiful, if terrible. The fact that she had been one of the party guests barely registered before she slapped away his gun, her blow far stronger than her size would suggest, her crimson eyes burning and her fangs glittering. Before Cobb could recover she was on him, leaping onto his massive body, wrapping her legs around his waist and sinking her fangs into his neck. Groaning, Cobb staggered back, her thighs like a vice around him, and crashed into a set of cupboards. He felt her suck the blood from him.

Vampire.

The word resounded through his mind like someone was shouting it at him across a crowded room. He'd met such creatures before, of course, and knew they were real. In fact once he had had an interesting conversation with one; some little weasel-faced man named Matthias. He had explained a great many things about vampires, like for example they could only be killed by decapitation or exposure to sunlight, or by bleeding them dry. There was also some sort of war going between the most powerful vampires, apparently they were engaged in a very clandestine campaign against each other, but all of this was academic. Cobb forced himself to focus on the fact that at that particular moment there was a vampire drinking his blood and he needed to do something about it. With a mighty heave he threw the woman off him, her mouth disengaging from his jugular with protest.

She crashed to the floor, her reddish-blonde hair whipping around her head. In an instant she was on her feet, smiling at Cobb while he tried to recover his strength. The vampire had drained a good deal of blood from him; he could sense it. His vision was out of focus and his feet felt like they were made of wood.

"Wonderful," said the vampire, her tongue and lips dark red. Her face was flushed, and she seemed charged with energy. "I knew you weren't mortal."

"Leave it," muttered Cobb, clenching a fist in an attempt to loosen the muscles. "You're going to pay for that." The revolver was still in his hand, he pointed it at the woman and fired, the report like thunder in the small kitchen. The bullet crashed into the wall, however, completely missing its mark; the woman had stepped to the side fast enough to avoid the shot. It was something else that Cobb should have remembered about vampires—when they wanted to they could move very, very fast.

"That was stupid, lover," said the vampire, laughing. "You can't kill me with those toys."

Pointing the gun again, Cobb cocked the hammer back and was about to fire a second shot when the woman appeared only inches away from him, her hands on his neck. She wasn't hurting him, however, her touch was gentle. She leaned in close, her face next to his, and took in a sharp inhale through her nose, smelling him.

"Wonderful," she whispered, her flesh cold. Cobb felt a pressure on the side of his temple, even though nothing was touching him. It was strange, almost like something getting into his head. "You are perfect. We've got such plans for you."

Cobb's strength was returning, and he reached up with his empty hand and thrust his fingers into her hair, his lips pulling back. "Go to hell," he barked, yanking her head roughly and smashing her in the nose with his revolver. The vampire gasped, blood shooting from the wound, and staggered back, her expression a mixture of rage and confusion. Clearly she had not expected Cobb to recover that quickly, and in fact she looked more insulted than hurt by the attack. With a grunt she kicked him in the stomach, the force of her blow throwing him against the wall. He slid down onto the floor, the gun still in his hand, and in a flash she was gone.

For several moments Cobb sat on the floor, trying to get his head together. Having one's blood drained did a number on their cognitive faculties. He was content to sit there, feeling the tingle in his feet, until he recovered.

Until then, however, he was free to wonder about things. Who the hell was that woman? He asked himself that question while he sat on the floor of Kilroy's kitchen, the cold weight of his revolver resting alongside him in one hand. He remembered vaguely as one of Kilroy's guests, but apart from that he didn't have a clue. Being a vampire would have made it easy for her to get out of the basement safely—as she said she couldn't be killed with Cobb's "toys." She wasn't as invulnerable as she pretended, though, and if he ever saw her again he'd show her that.

Cobb felt strong enough to stand so he got to his feet with a weary groan. It was time for him to be on his way. He allowed himself a bit of satisfaction, however—Kilroy and John were taken care of, Randall dead before all of them, and there was nothing more to fear from the Muir Tablet or anyone who would abuse its considerable power. He'd spread the remains of the shattered stone at the bottom of a river before coming to Kilroy's, it would be some time before anyone gathered up all the fragments again.

That didn't mean that Cobb was done with everything, though. There was one more matter to deal with while he was in the area, and this was something a little more personal. He had a score to settle with something very old and very unpleasant, something that a small blurb in a newspaper had alerted him to only a month before. He hadn't seen it since 1849, and the last time they had fought Cobb had underestimated its strength and it had bashed his head in, leaving him for dead. He'd had a lot of time since then to learn more about the thing, and he had come across the tools to make sure it didn't hurt anyone else ever again.

Once that was finished he would consider tracking down the vampire woman. She had said "we have such plans for you," and that was something he couldn't ignore. He'd find out who she was and he'd kill her. Then he'd kill her accomplices, whoever they were. It was what he did.

CHAPTER 6

▼

Ed Roberts took a long, deep breath, the faint stink of his last cigarette still in the air. He shuddered in the cold night air, the coming New York autumn making its presence known by the chill wind that had picked up just after nightfall.

What was he doing waiting on the docks at night? He didn't really know. The story, of course, was that some cargo was coming into town that night and that it needed to be secured on board his ship, the *Beatrice*, but Captain Pierce had been strangely vague on the matter. The client was offering a huge amount of money, more than would be offered for any legitimate cargo, and that was the problem.

Ed could smell a dirty deal a mile away and even though the *Beatrice* had moved contraband before there was just something strange about this whole situation. A man named Davis had contacted Captain Pierce, and the pair of them had spent a long period of time conversing privately. Eventually they had come out of the captain's cabin, and Pierce had announced that they were going to ship a crate from New York to Hong Kong. That alone was enough to give Ed pause. In 1930 the *Beatrice* had been in Hong Kong and Pierce had run afoul of some port authorities. They hadn't been back since.

What had Davis said to him to convince him to go back? It couldn't have been the money; it may have been a lot but it wasn't enough to risk incarceration in a Pacific jail. Something else was going on. Maybe they had blackmailed him. Whatever the case, they had insisted that they be allowed to put the cargo aboard ship as soon as they arrived, which happened to be at night. Apparently they didn't want to leave the crate locked down on the docks overnight, attesting to the fact that it probably wasn't legal.

A faint engine sound crossed Pier 42, causing Ed to look up. The headlights shone in the distance, growing slowly closer, and he looked up at the side of the *Beatrice* looming beside him. One other crewmember, a stout fellow by the name of Gilbert, was on the main deck, waiting to operate the cargo crane that would lift the crate onto the ship. He could see Gilbert standing on the deck, wrapped in a heavy black coat, and waved to him as the truck approached. Gilbert responded in kind, and Ed turned to greet the coming truck. It pulled up nearby, the engine rumbling loudly. It was a big truck, the kind with a covered cargo area.

"Hi," Ed called over the engine noise as the truck parked and a man popped out of the passenger side door. The man was in his late twenties, dressed in heavy clothing and wearing spectacles. He walked over and shook Ed's hand, a grin on his face.

"I'm John Norris," he said as the wind picked up. "I'm here for Mr. Davis."

"Ed Roberts, First Mate of the *Beatrice*. You've got your cargo?"

"In the truck," John replied. "I'll need your help getting it out, is that okay?"

"Sure," said Ed, glancing up at Gilbert, who nodded and went off to take his place in the crane. The driver of the truck climbed out—a tall, gangly man with curly black hair—and together they went to the back of the vehicle. The driver hopped up into the rear and a moment later Ed heard a scraping noise before one side of a large packing crate appeared.

"We'll use the ramp," said John, getting the steel slope in place, his arms flexing as he pulled it out from its housing under the truck. The edge of the ramp slapped against the wooden pier with a dull thud and the driver started to push the crate down. John and Ed assisted by pulling on the thick iron chains that wrapped around the crate's midsection. Ed was tempted to ask what the crate contained, but he knew better than to make such a mistake. If the captain said they were taking it then they were taking it and he didn't need to know anything else. Besides, if it was illegal (like he knew it probably was) then the pair loading it might not appreciate any questions. "Now remember," added John, "this is to be picked up by a man named Fletcher. No one else gets it. Clear?"

"It's all arranged."

The crate slid down onto the pier, leaving the ramp slowly. John and Ed were able to slide it a few more feet, into a better position for the crane, and then they stepped away. John went over to talk to the driver while Ed waved at Gilbert to begin. It took a moment for Gilbert to start up the crane, and as John and the driver replaced the ramp under the truck, John's eyes caught a strange sight. He wasn't certain, but in the half-light of the docks, John could swear that there was a huge, dark streak marking the path that the crate had taken from the back of the truck. The ramp was gone too quickly for him to be sure, but when he looked at the pier, where the crate had crossed it, there was about two feet of uneven dark streaking. Ed knelt down, curious, and touched the surface of the pier; it was wet. He held his fingertips up to the failing light and saw that they were red. It didn't take him long to recognize what shade of red, either.

A hand grabbed Ed's lifted wrist and he let out an involuntary cry. Straightening, Ed saw that John's hand was wrapped tightly around his forearm. "That was stupid," said John, his eyes hard. The crane was starting to lower, Gilbert unaware of what was going on. "You didn't have to do that."

"I didn't," muttered Ed, terrified. "I mean, I don't know anything—"

"Too late," interrupted John. The driver was watching them, a sneer on his face. John waved a hand towards the deck, towards Gilbert, and the driver went off, presumably to deal with him, clambering up the ramp onto the ship with practiced grace. An evil grin on his face, John produced a long, narrow-bladed knife from under his coat.

"It's no big deal," he said. "It's been a while since he's fed anyway, and he needs something for the trip."

His fear paralyzing him, Ed could barely breathe. His face was ashen, and a cold sweat had broken out on his forehead. Someone screamed on the ship; a few seconds later something heavy dropped off the deck and landed on the pier nearby. Ed's eyes went to it; it was Gilbert, a dark hole in his neck. That was as much as Ed could handle. He let out a rattling, choking cry.

What happened next was more unexpected than everything that preceded it. The driver was stalking down the ramp, back to the pier, a bloody ice pick in his hand, when the sound of gunfire rattled through the night. The driver was the first to go, cut down on the ramp by a hail of bullets; his body wriggled on the planks for a moment before dropping into the water. John reacted quickly, spinning Ed around and wrapping an arm around his neck while he looked up at the shooter. Standing on a pile of packing crates on the far side of the pier, Cobb was just a black silhouette, his long blue coat flapping in the darkness as he glared from beneath the brim of his slouch hat. The Thompson smoking in his hands was pointed at John, who held Ed like a shield, his knife at his throat.

"Go on and fire," said John, madness in his voice. "Shoot us both!"

As if in answer Cobb's gun popped once and a bullet whizzed over Ed's shoulder to tear off John's ear. John cried out, spun, and fell, a hand going to the side of his head. Ed fell forward and scrambled away like a frightened rodent once he realized that he was free. John ignored him and leapt over to the crate.

"Save me, lord," he implored as he grabbed desperately at the chains. "Save your loyal servant!"

Cobb raised the barrel of his weapon, curious, and suddenly the box that John supplicated to burst at the sides. Quickly a pair of huge, dark hands reached out and grabbed John's head. He let out a terrifying wail, his skull pulverized in the grip of the malformed thing he called master. In an instant he was dead, and the crate exploded in a shower of wooden fragments, the chain securing it dropping to the pier. Cobb watched with casual interest as Yulgo Kharan revealed himself; a huge, hunched and bloated monstrosity from the distant past.

Standing nearly twelve feet when fully erect, Kharan usually crouched. The huge hands on the ends of his long arms dragged, his claws of black glass scraped the ground quietly. Everything about him was huge; his arms and legs were like stumps, his massive belly hung low, creating the illusion of lethargy and indolence, but his strength was said to be limitless. His stone-like hide was a repulsive grayish pink color, mottled with spots of black and patches of coarse black hair. Most terrible of all, however, was his face. He was known as the Great Pig for a reason, for there was a distinctly porcine aspect to it, with a great snout and a pair of wicked tusks set beneath the beast's small, deep-set eyes. Wiry bristles surrounded the snout, dripped blood and putrid matter. With a pig-like snort, Kharan fell upon the body of its worshipper, rending it horribly with its claws while hungrily slurping down the flesh, his jaws crushing the bones before also sucking them down. In seconds John's corpse had vanished, only a pool of blood and traces of viscera remained.

Cobb sneered. He remembered that the monster's hunger knew no bounds, and its worshippers were often taken when other fare wasn't available. The last time they had met Kharan had ended up in a cave near Wales, venturing out from time to time to suck out the internal organs of anyone it could find. It had an insatiable appetite and purely alien drives; the beast needed killing.

Having fed, the Pig turned its eyes on Cobb, the defiler who had interrupted its journey. Cobb was still atop the pile of crates, his Thompson pointed, a faint hint of amusement in his expression. He had watched Kharan feed with only mild interest, thinking it a fitting end to the beast's thrall, ignoring Ed as the sailor ran for his life.

"Remember me, Pig?" Cobb asked, his voice gruff. "It's been a while, but I think you do."

Kharan snorted and wheezed, its beady eyes burning, and suddenly let out a vicious snarl. Cobb chuckled.

"I thought so," he said. "Glad to hear it."

With that, Cobb opened fire, his Thompson barking at his side. The bullets smashed against Kharan's hide but did not penetrate and even though the beast held up an arm before its face in a protective gesture it was clear that the weapon was useless against the Pig. After a long moment of steady fire Cobb let up, the failure of his efforts not causing him the slightest worry. It had been a token effort, anyway. The Pig lurched forward, its giant feet smashing against the pier, and Cobb dropped the gun, letting it clatter to the pier as he lifted the weapon that had been his true choice to use against the eons-old monster coming at him. Resting by his feet, the iron pry-bar was about four feet long, terminating in a wicked chisel-tip at one end. Cobb scooped it up in his black-gloved hands, the weight reassuring, then leapt down to meet the Pig's charge. Swinging the bar in a vicious arc he caught Kharan in the side of the head, bashing the Great Pig's tough skull with tremendous force. Kharan squealed and lashed out with a claw. The blow sent Cobb flying across the pier and he crashed against a crate, the wooden planks cracking with the impact and his hat flopping off. Blood poured from his ears and nostrils while he got back up, the bar held out before him, a huge grin on his face.

"Come on, Pig!"

Cobb shouted the challenge and rushed the monster with the bar pointed like a spear. The chisel point struck Kharan in the neck with a shower of sparks, and Cobb followed by striking him again with the other end. Kharan growled, the blows causing him real pain, and swatted at Cobb. The big man dodged, however, and continued smashing at the monster. Cobb had a plan, but it required him to not only immobilize Kharan but also penetrate the thick hide that protected it. What soft lead couldn't pierce hopefully blunt iron could smash through.

The Great Pig's flesh cracked under the strength of Cobb's blows, bringing forth a trickle of glowing orange liquid. Smoke ran from the wound—Kharan's blood was like molten metal, boiling under the surface through organs impossible to describe. A barbaric yawp issued from the Pig's maw, a signal of its unfamiliar agony. In the millions of years since it crossed the vast gulfs of space and descended to our world it had never known such a feeling as pain, never fought a creature like the one that was beating it mercilessly, madness gleaming in his eyes, seemingly unafraid in the face of the Pig's wrath.

"That's right," howled Cobb, continuing to lay into the monster with the iron bar, which had bent slightly from the strain. "Come on! Come on you fucking thing!"

Kharan lashed out, grabbing Cobb's arms while he was raising them in preparation for another stroke, and with a brutal grunt it twisted the limbs back with a ghastly popping sound from the joints. Cobb winced and the iron bar dropped from his hands to clang uselessly against the pier. Desperate, he kicked Kharan in the groin, his booted foot smashing into the beast.

Unfortunately, Kharan was not designed like earthly life, and he had no vulnerable external genitals to crush. Cobb's boot merely struck a bare expanse of impenetrable skin. The beast paid little attention and lifted its opponent into the air in order to whip him back down into the pier. Striking the planks hard, Cobb heard a crunch from his shoulder and he realized at once that his right arm had gone numb. The Pig kicked him in the stomach, the sheer force of the impact sending him flying across the pier to land on the blacktop beyond. He rolled a few more yards, leaving a wet, sticky mark with each rotation.

The Pig bellowed, the sound splitting the night. Drops of its orange blood fell onto the concrete and created blackened, deformed pits as the thing loped towards Cobb, saliva pouring from its jaws. Cobb pushed himself up into a sitting position, his right arm hugging protectively to his side, and reached into his coat pocket with his left hand. After a moment of hurried fumbling, Kharan growing closer by the second, he produced a bundle of three sticks of dynamite. He wasn't in love with the idea of using explosives on Kharan, such devices produced uncertain results, but he had little choice. Given the chance the Pig was going to consume him like it had John, and even as much as Cobb desired death he didn't want to be joined forever with the Pig, which is what being eaten by the thing entailed. Consumed victims were drawn into the monster's unfathomable consciousness for all time, a tiny mote washed away in the sea of the god's mind to spend eternity in the maddening grip of Yulgo Kharan.

Cobb wasn't about to let that happen. He lit the fuse that dangled from the dynamite, took a moment to make sure it caught, and then threw the bomb at the lumbering creature, one arm raised over his face. The dynamite struck the pavement and rolled, sparks falling from the fuse, and ended up by Kharan's feet. The Pig ignored it and just as it was about to take another step the bomb went off, exploding into a huge flash of fire and smoke. Cobb felt a blast of hot air wash over him, along with assorted debris, and when he looked back Kharan was laying on its huge belly, silent and immobile, only a few feet away.

Knowing that Kharan wasn't dead—there was no way that a few sticks of dynamite could kill something like the Pig—Cobb got quickly to his feet, a bit of feeling coming back in his right arm, and recovered his pry-bar. He limped back to Kharan's inert body and levered it onto its back, no easy task considering the monster's weight. It lay with its eyes closed, the maw hung open and its hideous green tongue lolled to one side. Cobb had to work fast; time was of the essence for the Pig could wake at any moment and there was still much to do.

He knew as much as any one man could about Yulgo Kharan, and he knew that no earthly force could truly kill it, for it would not die as a man died. That didn't mean that it couldn't be trapped, though.

The granite-hard hide of Kharan's torso was cracked and split from Cobb's attacks and the explosion. Its viscous, luminescent blood flowed from its wounds. Cobb squinted in the face of the waves of heat that surrounded the body, and after taking in a deep breath he drove the chisel point of the pry-bar into a large crack in Kharan's chest. The monster groaned but remained stunned, and Cobb struck again. It took four more blows, but eventually Cobb managed to bury the point about an inch.

It would have to do, he decided. It was clear that Kharan was about to regain consciousness. With a mighty heave, Cobb pulled the pry-bar back, wrenching open the Pig's wound and exposing a large gash of glowing orange. A blast of heat, greater than before, struck his face, and his skin tightened and grew dry. Ignoring his discomfort, Cobb reached under his shirt and drew forth a small piece of metal on a chain around his neck, making sure to keep the opening wide.

The amulet was very, very old. Cobb had tracked it down at the turn of the century during an errand that had taken a great amount of effort on its own. He had first heard of its existence while searching for a way to settle his score with Kharan, and even if he couldn't kill the Pig he would take the next best thing. About the size of a quarter, star-shaped and covered in strange sigils, Cobb ripped the chain from around his neck and leaned down to drop it into the burning wound. Instantly the amulet began to glow, the furnace beneath Kharan's skin turning it white-hot. Cobb knew that it wouldn't melt, though, protected as it was by the enchantments that made it the only weapon that could end the menace of the Great Pig.

Satisfied and knowing that his time was almost gone, Cobb yanked the pry-bar free, its tip blazing like a hot poker. The wound snapped shut, trapping the amulet within. Almost immediately Kharan reacted, ancient forces working under its skin. With a howl the beast sat up, suddenly aware of what had been done, and slapped Cobb away with a powerful backhand. Gibbering, Kharan lurched in frantic movements, knowing that something that it actually feared was going on. The amulet was crafted by sorcerers in ages past for the express purpose of subduing creatures such as it, and it had no defense against its powers once they were released.

But they had yet to be released, and the Pig knew it, which is what made it so dangerous. Cobb had begun the ritual but he had not finished it and the Pig would fight to prevent him from doing so. He staggered; still groggy from the blow, and wiped blood from his chin while trying to clear his head. The amulet was in place but there was more that had to be done. The words still needed to be spoken, but they weren't clear in his mind anymore. How did the ritual begin?

Kharan snorted and came at him, bashing him in the side with one great fist. Cobb rolled onto the ground, his coat draped around him, his face streaked with blood and dirt. He was weakening; the Pig was doing too much damage. Desperate, Cobb got to his feet as the Pig came back, only barely managing to dodge another massive blow that would have crushed his skull. His boots striking the ground sharply, Cobb ran from the Pig, trying to get some distance in order to complete the ritual. Unfortunately Kharan wasn't to be thwarted so easily, and it gave chase, its thick legs driving it forward as Cobb made for the ship that would have taken the Pig across the Atlantic. Scrambling up the ramp onto the deck, Cobb turned and saw Yulgo Kharan leap from the pier and clamber onto the ship after him.

Seeing that there was nowhere else to go, Cobb faced the beast as Kharan rushed him, opening his mouth to begin the chant that would activate the power of the amulet buried in the Pig's flesh. Kharan moved too fast, however, even for its massive size, and it struck him at full-bore. The Pig lifted him into the air, its treelike limbs wrapped around Cobb's waist, pinning his arms down. He felt the Pig's tusks pierce his abdomen and let out a choked cry, the taste of blood and bile in his throat. He had to say the words and he had to say them loud or it was over.

Kharan squeezed, ignoring Cobb's kicks to its chest and belly as he struggled in its grip. Joints popped and bones cracked and Cobb ground his teeth together, trying to work through the pain. He squirmed like a worm dangling on a hook and managed to actually slip an arm out of the Pig's grasp. Out of reflex he struck his fist in a hammer-like motion against the monster's skull, but even though Cobb could have dropped a buffalo with such blows he could do nothing against the Pig. Kharan tightened its grip, and Cobb spat up a mouthful of blood onto his chin. Desperation took control and he slapped his hand onto the Pig's shoulder and started draining its energy. He was reluctant to use this weapon, but he was starting to black out and he needed to do something.

Kharan paused, as if uncertain. Its grip relaxed only a fraction, and as Cobb felt his mind expanding in the way it did when he fed, he realized that something was wrong. Yulgo Kharan's mind and essence were too powerful, there was too much there for him to absorb. It was like a bottomless well, a roiling sea of alien energy that went on forever. And it hurt. It stung Cobb like lightning. He tried to stop, tried to reverse the flow of energy and for a moment he was afraid he wouldn't be able to. His hand seemed stuck to Kharan's body, as if he and the Pig were truly joined. Kharan must have known what Cobb had attempted, for it let out an exultant bellow as Cobb's hand came unstuck and trembled in the air over the Pig's shoulder. Eyes wide with the closest thing to fear that he had felt in decades, Cobb tried remembering the words that would activate the amulet while the Pig squeezed him tighter.

"*Azgh...*" he muttered, the words coming back to him. His voice was weak; the ritual would be stillborn if he couldn't get more volume. "*Azgh,*" he tried again, managing to suck in a big enough breath. Kharan heard the word and must have recognized it if the rage-filled roar that issued from its throat was any clue.

"*Azgh harrl marbarb,*" Cobb cried, desperate, feeling something rip deep inside his torso. "*Ka-rin eises schaur...*"

The Great Pig released Cobb and he fell sprawling to the deck, sucking in great breaths and trying to get his body to calm itself. Yulgo Kharan turned and looked as if it intended on escaping, but it moved slowly, like it was drunk, swaying from side to side. Knowing that the ritual was working, Cobb continued the chant, shouting the words so loud that his voice cracked more than once. He repeated the mantra again and again, each time causing Kharan to grow more lethargic in its movements. Finally it turned to face him again, a strangely passive look on its inhuman face, and then it dropped to the deck, curling its legs beneath one another as if meditating. Resignation and even sadness appeared in its expression as it regarded the being that had defeated it. Cobb repeated the chant one final time and the beast closed its eyes, becoming as inanimate as the stone it appeared to be.

Cobb did nothing for a long while, merely laying on his back, propped up on his elbows, staring at the giant, peaceful statue that had once been a bloodthirsty pig-man from the stars. His whole body ached; he knew he was bleeding internally, and though he'd be fine by morning there was a real risk of passing out. That wouldn't do at all, since there was no telling how long he'd be unconscious. The explosion was sure to bring the authorities—it was a miracle that they hadn't come already—and he didn't want to be around when they arrived.

With a low groan, Cobb got to his feet and went back to the pier, searching for his pry bar. Finding it, Cobb returned to the ship and jammed the end under Kharan's body, leaning forward and shifting the statue towards the water. It was strange being that close to Kharan without fear, knowing that it could do nothing to hurt anyone in the state it was in. It would be millions of years before the stars aligned themselves in the proper way to allow Kharan freedom again.

Eventually Cobb pushed the statue off the edge of the deck, the massive form tumbling into the dark water below. It would sink to the bottom, which wasn't very far from land, but it was far enough. Anyone looking for Kharan would think that it was still alive and roaming the countryside, the possibility that someone had actually beaten the monster inconceivable to its worshippers. No, they would search for a living monster, never considering the possibility that it was just sitting near the pier, silent.

Watching the water, Cobb thought about Yulgo Kharan, and he realized that he had just closed an important chapter in his long life. For eighty years he had planned this, searching for a way to stop the Great Pig, and now it was done. Kharan's minions would eventually be free of its corrupting influence; it would take time, but soon enough the servitude would seem like some horrible nightmare, hazy and indistinct. They would go back to their lives as free men.

As the sound of engines came up from the distance, Cobb realized that he had never really hated Kharan. He never even hated what it represented. It was no demon, no abstract manifestation of human unconsciousness. Rather it was a creature from another part of the universe, a monster that hailed from stars where physical laws differed from those on earth, alien and unknown. It had come to ravage and to consume, but that didn't make it evil. It only did what it did out of need, not malice. Humans were like cattle before it, and just as low in its eyes.

With a weary sigh, Cobb recovered his lost hat and put it on. He picked up his Thompson, still laying on the dock, and rushed away, into the darkness, away from the coming crowds. He might not have hated Kharan, but that never meant that he was going to let it go. It did what it did, but so did he, and once their paths crossed only one could walk away. For a moment Cobb wondered if Kharan had once been a creature like him, a being trapped by its own sense of alienation and regret over what it once was. Did it represent what Cobb would become if he weren't careful, if he didn't find the answers he was looking for?

CHAPTER 7

▼

It was around 2:30 in the afternoon when Philip got out of bed. He rubbed his eyes while Helena lay alongside him, her pale body still in the inky blackness of the bedroom. The tall man slid from the silk sheets and walked naked to the adjoining bathroom to relieve himself, a contented smile on his face. He washed his hands and splashed his face with water, driving away the vestiges of sleep, before he looked at himself in the mirror. His dark blond hair was a bit messy and he needed to shave, but it was the dark red line on his chest that caught his eye. With care he touched the fresh cut with hesitant fingers, and a faint burning pain spread out from it. Helena could be careless sometimes during their love-making and her fingers sometimes ended in more than just long nails. The positive side to this was the fact that the smell of fresh blood would drive her into a frenzy, and during sex this could be an amazing experience, so Philip usually shrugged it off and bought lots of iodine. The pain meant nothing to him anyway. A long time ago he had learned to endure pain.

A few minutes later he stood in the shower, and as the warm water ran over him, streaks of red from the wound on his chest mingled with the water in swirling patterns as he soaped himself. Helena would be comatose until nightfall. Her kind didn't really sleep in the human sense of the word; they went dormant and appeared to be nothing more than corpses until the sun went down. Then they rose to their version of living. Philip intended to use the intervening time to attend to some matters that had been lurking in the back of his mind lately.

After showering, he dressed himself in a pair of black trousers and a white shirt, careful first to attend his injury with iodine and cotton. Feeling more himself and truly awake, Philip paused to kiss Helena gently on the forehead before he left the bedroom.

Philip walked to the kitchen and made some breakfast. It was more like lunch, but since it was his first meal of the day he thought of it as breakfast. He downed a ham sandwich and glass of milk quickly while thoughts churned inside his head. For days he had contemplated the existence of Sebastian Cobb, talking to his various contacts and gathering what information he could. Helena's explanation of what she had seen in Cobb's mind painted a picture of an unstoppable killer, an occult-powered madman who hunted the dark powers of the universe, destroying anything in his path but fundamentally confused about the details of his own existence. He knew no more about his own nature than Philip or anyone else. Cobb didn't know where his immortality stemmed from, and didn't even appear to want it. Well, if death was what Cobb wanted, Philip would be more than happy to help him on his way.

His meal finished, Philip headed down into the basement, into the darkness below the house where years ago, a man named Edward Buford had found his brother's hideous legacy. Down there was where unearthly presence of whatever it was that infested the house was strongest, and Philip thought about that story as he walked down the creaking wooden steps.

Terrance Buford, a local banker, had bought the house in 1898, after it had been abandoned for several years, and immediately set about rebuilding it. During that time, young Matilda Jenkins, the 11-year old daughter of a local baker, went missing. The last person to see her was a playmate named Henrietta Philby, who said that she had seen Matilda skipping happily down a road holding the hand of a tall man dressed in black. Since she looked happy, Henrietta had thought nothing strange of it until she heard that Matilda never came home that night. Unfortunately, she could offer no further description of the man other than he was tall and that he looked like a gentleman. For three weeks people searched the town and the areas around Providence, trying desperately to find the missing girl, but to no avail. The community banded together to offer their support to the Jenkins family, and eventually everyone moved on. Matilda's family, however, never lost hope.

Three months later, a second child, Natalie Vickers, disappeared. A month later another girl, Alice Renfield, followed suit. In both cases there was a single witness, a child, who claimed to have seen the missing girls with a gentleman in black. The community nearly went mad with fear and the local law enforcement resolved to find this mysterious man in black, as well as the missing children. Initial searches for Natalie and Alice came up with nothing, however, and a pall of fear descended on the Providence folk. No one allowed his or her children to be alone for any amount of time. The streets became empty, the doors barred at night and the windows were shuttered in an effort to keep the stalking beast at bay. Anyone even remotely suspicious risked being beaten in the streets, and the sight of a man dressed in black clothing became more than just remotely suspicious.

Eventually, though, Terrance Buford had an accident. An oil barrel was being loaded into a storehouse near the bank when the pulley came loose, causing it to crash down onto the street. The noise of the barrel bursting spooked some horses pulling a carriage nearby, and they thundered down the street, trampling Terrance as he exited his bank. Terrance was dead before the bystanders got to him, and he was buried two days later in the family plot at the nearby graveyard. Several upstanding members of the community attended the ceremony. In the days that followed, however, his family made a horrifying discovery.

Having no wife or children, Terrance's home and possessions reverted to his brother, a local alderman named Edward. While Edward was going through the house, he came across a large wooden chest in the basement, secured by a heavy iron lock. The key was nowhere to be found, so Edward broke it open with a sledge. Inside the chest were the three missing girls, their corpses piled on each other, their throats slit and their eyes cleanly removed.

The authorities thoroughly investigated the house before they declared that the mysterious man in black was found. The bodies bore surprisingly little damage, apart from the obvious. Their dresses were still intact and free of blood, and those that saw them said that there was something eerie about the almost peaceful looks on the girls' faces. If it hadn't been for the vacant pits where their eyes should have been, it was said, you would have thought they were sleeping.

After all of that Edward sold as many of his brother's possessions as he could, then packed up and left Providence for Boston, hoping to escape the scandal that his brother's actions had caused. No reason for Terrance's homicidal activities was ever determined, and since he was dead, no further inquiry was deemed necessary. Some took solace in the fact that the families of the girls were given a sense of closure.

As he entered the basement, Philip wondered exactly how much solace there had been. Could a parent really be satisfied knowing the name of their child's murderer? Was satisfaction even possible? Philip had killed many children. He wondered if the parents of his victims would feel better knowing who he was.

The basement was lit with a pair of bulbs that hung from wires while the walls were roughly hewn and lined with brick. The floor was packed earth, which gave the room a musty scent. The air was always cold, a mixture of the heat-sucking effect of the floor and the supernatural particulars of the house. Here Philip had set up as his workshop and study, with bookshelves against two walls while a long wooden table for his tools and other odds and ends was set opposite the entrance. The items on the table included a large object in the center, about a foot and a half high, covered in a draping black cloth. Near this was set an old, yellow-paged book, sitting open to reveal the haphazard, chicken-scratch handwriting inside.

Philip eased himself into the chair sitting in front of the table. Alongside him on the table was a thick roll of parchment, which he picked up and opened. The seals and symbols on it were dawn in a circular pattern, only making sense if read from the outward edges towards the center. This was something that he had stolen from a British nobleman named Edward Glenbury, an ancient spell for waking a creature called the Million Staring Eyes. He had hoped to adapt the spell to his own needs and rouse the spirit of the house, but meeting Cobb had distracted him from that.

With a shake of his head, Philip tossed the parchment casually onto the table and stared at the black-wrapped thing in the dim, pale light. For a long moment he looked at the object, his face unreadable, and then he reached out and pulled off the black cloth, revealed what lay underneath.

It was a head.

Any antiquarian would have given his eyeteeth for a look at the thing that Philip had in his basement. The workmanship and quality of its construction were obvious, even to a layman. Made of riveted brass, the head sat on a vague stump of a neck, its eyes and mouth closed in an expression that spoke of quiet repose, as if it were sleeping. Often Philip admired the simple elegance of its design, the subtle beauty of its curving, smooth surface and the glint of the metal in the soft light.

Getting the brazen head had been a difficult task and he appreciated it, even if there were times when he didn't always admit it.

Philip reached out a hand and touched the head, ran his fingertips over the formed eyebrow ridges, scraped against the rivets there. He smiled at the feeling of the metal against his skin.

And then the eyes opened.

Philip made no motions of surprise, didn't jump out of his chair, and otherwise gave no indication that the head's wet, glistening eyeballs were a shock to him. In fact they weren't, for he had long known that the head was alive. Roger Bacon had constructed the head in 1257, and it was he that had given it life, a story that was well known but rarely discussed. No, he didn't scream, he simply looked at the eyes, his mouth a straight line.

"Good afternoon, Philip," said the head, the mouth moving like that of a ventriloquist's dummy. The brass jaw slid straight up and down and revealed a very human-looking set of white teeth and tongue. The voice was very deep and had a slight echo, while the words were well enunciated as if spoken by a trained actor or public speaker. "It's been a while."

"Hello, Head," replied Philip, slowly. "I have questions for you."

"Of course you do," replied Head, rolling its eyes. "You only talk to me when you have questions."

"Why else should I talk to you?"

Head looked at him. "Roger used to talk to me all the time," it said. "We talked about philosophy and whether or not flowers could dream."

"I don't care if flowers dream," said Philip, slightly annoyed. Head could be very, very frustrating sometimes.

"I'm aware of that," sighed Head. "You want to know if I've made contact with the spirit of this dwelling, don't you?"

"Have you?" Philip perked up a bit.

"No," said Head, flatly. "It's a most unfriendly entity you've got living underneath you, Philip. Downright antisocial, if you don't mind me saying it."

Philip waved a hand. "Fine, fine," he said, impatient. "Do what you have to, but that's not what I want to know about right now. I need to know about a man named Cobb, Sebastian Cobb."

"Ah, yes," said Head, incapable of smiling, but the tone of its voice betrayed faint amusement. "I've heard of him. What's your interest with Cobb?"

"That's none of your business," Philip replied. "What can you tell me about him?"

"What I can tell you is only a little of what I know," answered Head, narrowing one eye, "but what I do know is only a fraction of what there is to know. Cobb is a fury, a predator and a killer. Unaware of his own nature, he preys on the spirits of the dark and their followers, sending demons and gods to their graves while their followers are ground into the dirt."

"I already know that," said Philip. "Tell me something else."

"He's the treader of the dust," Head continued, ignoring Phillip's command. "He reflects the Maw of Hell. Something noble was cut from him a long time ago, and in its place he feels the pulse of damnation. You would do well to avoid him, Phil."

"I know he's tough," said Philip. His irritation was beginning to show. "But there's got to be a way to get at him. Some way to take his power."

"There's always a way," whispered Head. It closed its eyes and its voice became distant. "Your wife has already tasted his essence. Use that. She can get to him."

Philip thought about this. "I don't want her getting hurt," he said, finally.

Head's eyes snapped open. "You're awfully protective of your vampire bride," it said, haughtily. "That doesn't make much sense. You know she could snap you in half with a flick of her wrist, saucy trollop that she is."

"Watch your mouth," spat Philip. Head could be vulgar at times, especially when it talked about women.

"Or what?" Head challenged. "You'll hit me with a stick? I'm a brass head, Philip, there's very little you can threaten me with."

"I'm sure there's some demon who wouldn't mind having you for himself, down in hell," said Philip. "How would that suit you?"

Somehow, without shoulders, Head managed to give the impression of a shrug. "I think it would be fine," it answered. "Just think of the conversations I could have with a demon. I don't have a soul, Phil, I'm just magically animated and as such I have no fear of death or destruction."

"Fine then," said Philip, "I'll bury you under the ground, someplace where no one will ever find you. Think about that. You wouldn't have any conversations with anyone, ever."

"Someone always finds me, Phil," said the mischievous Head. "You did, after all. Enough of the threats, though, you're boring me. We can just agree that you can't do anything to hurt me, but you don't need to anyway. I just want to help, that's what I was built for."

"So help. Quit wasting my time with riddles."

Head laughed. It had a quiet, manipulative laugh. "Now if I did that, I'd be breaking my own rules," it said. "And that's something I couldn't do for Roger. What makes you think I'd do it for you? The price of knowing things is knowing things, and that's something that needs to be done alone."

Tired of Head's rambling, Philip tossed the black cloth back over it with a grunt. He snatched up the handwritten book as he got to his feet and headed towards the door. As he put his foot on the first step, though, he heard Head call out to him, its voice muffled by the cloth.

"The wife," it said, "remember the wife. She's got his blood in her veins now. Remember that when you're fumbling between her thighs, Phil. And never forget: People who kill gods make a lot of enemies."

Disgusted, Philip switched off the lights and submerged Head in darkness while he went back upstairs. He sat in the living room, Head's words in his brain. What did it mean, "use that against him?" He knew one or two tricks, invasive techniques that could exploit the fact that Helena had drank Cobb's blood, but they would be messy and could damage Helena if not done with extreme care. Those were risks more suited to people that you didn't care about, rather than someone you loved with every fiber of your being.

No, there would have to be some other way, some other method that could ferret out Cobb's weaknesses and bring him to an end. He knew people. There were favors he could call in. There were even other survivors of the Kilroy attack who would be happy to help him exact a little revenge, just as long as Philip kept his specific intentions to himself. If they knew he was trying to take Cobb's power they might want to get their hands on a share, and that would be problematic. No, he would keep that a secret and just ask around. No one could be untouchable. Someone had to know something.

Philip looked at the clock in the living room and saw that it was almost 4 p.m. The sun wouldn't be going down for four more hours or so, meaning Helena would be out until then. Tonight was their special night together, when they went hunting down by the taverns, when the drunks came wandering out. Philip loved watching his wife work, luring men and women into dark alleyways with her mysterious beauty and then ripping their throats out like a wild beast, sucking two or three of them dead before they would return home to their bed.

But that was for later. For now he had things to do. Philip went into his study on the second floor, the book still in his hands. An important piece of history, that book. It was because of that book that he had most of his knowledge about the house. He dropped into his chair and flipped through its dry, wrinkled pages. In his hands he held the journal of Lucius Cromwell, the man who owned the house before Terrance Buford. Discovered about a year before, the journal of was an interesting read for anyone willing to take the time to decipher its rambling, bizarrely phrased paragraphs. In fact, it was because of the journal that Philip knew what he did about the presence in the house.

It seemed that shortly after moving into the house Cromwell began sleepwalking, his nightly excursions taking him into the basement. He would wake up there in the mornings, lying on the dirt floor, dressed in his nightclothes, terribly confused and only remembering bits and pieces of strange, nightmarish visions. A student of the occult already, Cromwell began conducting rituals in the basement, intent on making contact with whatever it was that called him downstairs every night.

Eventually something had answered. From what Philip could ascertain from Cromwell's ranting, the thing beneath the house was extremely powerful, older than humanity, and restless. It hungered after dreams, lusted after the multitude of experiences and thoughts found with the human mind, and that's why it touched the minds of sensitives who spent long periods of time in the house. That's why children were affected—children had sensitive, creative minds. Most of these people had no conscious knowledge of what was happening to them. Cromwell only figured it out because he already sensed the presence in the house and knew how to talk to it. But he had been too stupid. As the journal entries went on, it seemed clear to Philip that the thing beneath the house had taken control of Cromwell. It dominated his personality and kept him inside the house at all times, just listening to his thoughts and feeding off his dreams. Cromwell became the house's pet, and he died in the house alone.

Philip had other plans, though—he wanted to communicate with the presence and have access to its power, not become a lapdog.

He knew there had to be a way. Head was usually good at figuring out such things, even when it was being difficult, and he knew that eventually it would find a way to interest the presence. That was one reason Philip wanted Cobb. Head had told him that some beings took an interest in immortal creatures, creatures with power like their own, and that the thing beneath the house was like that. It didn't care about Head because Head was an artificial thing, and Philip had tried a few rituals using his wife, but they had come to very little, mostly because Philip wasn't willing to endanger her. They'd thought about capturing other vampires, but that was risky business; Philip had no desire to attract their attention. Vampires always had friends.

So Cobb would make a good alternative. As Head had told him, someone like him was bound to have enemies. If he could find someone who had a grudge that he could exploit, maybe he could take Cobb as a prisoner. If it didn't work, there was always the possibility of stealing Cobb's power. After all, he seemed to have plenty of it, and power was something that Philip enjoyed a great deal.

Philip sighed and shut the book. There had to be some way to get to Cobb. Who was he? What was he? Someone had to know, someone always knew. Maybe what Head had told him about using the link between Helena and Cobb was his best chance—he knew some tricks, some ways to exploit the natural telepathic link that was formed when a vampire bit someone. It wouldn't be much, but maybe he could get inside of Cobb's head and root around for a while. There had to be something in there that a more detailed examination could dig up.

It was worth a try. At the very least it would amuse him.

CHAPTER 8

▼

It was three in the afternoon when Cobb woke up, the last of the alcohol having cycled through his system and sobriety back. As he sat up on the hotel room bed, dressed only in his boxer shorts, he ran his fingers over his bare scalp and looked out the window. The sun was streaming in through the thin muslin curtains, leaving yellow patches on the brown carpet while his clothes and gun belts sat on a nearby chair. An empty bottle was on the sheets next to him. Cobb picked it up and examined the traces of brown liquid hugging to the bottom. Kilroy's bourbon had been better than some, but not as good as the stuff he had gotten from Harlowe. Now, though, it was all gone, and Cobb had thinking to do.

After he arranged himself on the edge of the bed, his feet on the floor, Cobb grabbed one of his Schofields and held it on both palms. The pair was from 1872—he'd bought them as a matched set from a dealer in Arkansas. The belts had come at the same time. Cobb wore two because it was easier to replace a single belt instead of getting a whole new two-gun rig. The leather was cracked with age but still serviceable and the creak of it as he walked had become a comforting sound over time.

With a sigh Cobb broke open the revolver and popped out a cartridge. In the diluted sunlight he saw that it was one of his wadcutter rounds, flat at the tip, designed to rip apart the insides of a fleshy target. That was very useful in his line of work. He'd wished he'd had a chance to see how well they had worked on the vampire.

The memory of the vampire was still strong in his mind, even though he didn't know her name or what her beef was with him. He could still see her face and her glaring red eyes, her pale skin and angled features, and could feel the touch of her cold skin against his. The smell of her hair and perfume clouded his memories and he paused a moment, trying to push her from his mind.

Cobb didn't often go up against women, but that didn't mean he wasn't a realist. Corruption had little regard for gender and women could be just as foul as men. The fact was, though, that he wasn't really used to fighting members of the fairer sex. Sometimes he just didn't think about it, sometimes he regretted it, but he never hesitated. A hundred and fifty years of wandering and hunting had honed his reflexes to the point where he almost went on automatic when the fighting started, his conscious mind submerging itself in a sea of instinct that drove his limbs forward, allowing him to do what needed to be done. When that happened it didn't matter who or what Cobb's enemies were, all that mattered was that they were enemies and that meant that he would fight until they were as dead as he could make them.

After emptying the rest of the bullets from the revolver, Cobb got to his feet and went to a large trunk set at the end of the bed—his luggage. The clasps along the seam were undone and Cobb nonchalantly kicked it open, exposing the contents to the light. Inside in a neat pile was the entirety of Cobb's wardrobe, only a few changes of clothing, and alongside that were his weapons. This was a far more diverse collection than what he wore. The Tommy gun was in pieces, disassembled to make it easier to store, while the pistols and knives were stacked on top of boxes of ammunition. Three bundles of dynamite were tucked away in a corner, nestled against a roll of fuses. Many of the weapons were decades old, all showed the marks of age and heavy use, but diligent cleaning and maintenance had kept them in working order. The cleaning kits were in wooden cases strapped to the underside of the lid. Cobb found the one for his revolvers, tossed it onto the bed, and sat next to it before he set about disassembling the Schofield.

Cobb's thoughts wandered while he cleaned the gun, examining the individual parts with a practiced eye, looking for signs of wear or damage. He thought back to that night in 1787 for a moment, but that line of imagery was pushed out almost instantly. Cobb hated to remember that night, hated to remember the sight of his murdered wife and daughter, hated the fact that the next few hours were completely gone. Rather he skipped forward, to the next day, when he woke unharmed in his bed and thought for a moment that what had transpired had only been a dream. That blessed bit of self-delusion had only lasted a few minutes, unfortunately—he eventually realized that his wife and daughter were gone. Riding out to the area where he had seen them die he found the bodies, still tied to a stake, limp and lifeless in the early morning light. Cobb had broken down at that point, jumping from his horse and falling to his knees, the horrible realization that this was something that couldn't be undone crashing down on him. He wept before their bodies, tears streaming from his face while he slumped forward onto the blackened patch of earth.

An aching pang appeared inside his chest while Cobb sighted down the barrel of the Schofield and rolled it gently between his hands to check for deformity. Finding none, Cobb brushed it out, images of cutting his wife and daughter's bodies down from the stake in his mind. He remembered putting them on the back of his horse and riding to town, taking them straight to the chapel so they could be prepared for burial. He still remembered the words of comfort that the minister had said to him just after he explained what had happened before the magistrate.

"Rest assured that they are with God now," the minister had said. "He has taken them into His graces. They are free from all earthly pains."

Cobb had taken little comfort from that.

He had led them both to the clearing where the murder had taken place, showed the bodies of the dead cultists as evidence. The minister prayed and the magistrate muttered oaths upon seeing the unholy place, the waxen corpses of robed men still motionless in their own dried blood. Maggots churned in their eye sockets even though they had only been dead a few hours.

The presence of the bodies and Cobb's reputation as a proper and honest businessman had saved him from suspicion, and no further inquiry was made apart from attempts to identify the cultists. No one in the town had seen them before, so it was conjectured that they had come from some other province. Probably drifters or thieves, was the eventual consensus. Why they had chosen Cobb's family, and why they had left him behind and chosen to take just his wife and daughter were questions that had never been answered.

That fact grated on Cobb when he thought about it, and he had thought about it every single day since.

Cobb wiped down the parts of the gun and then slowly reassembled it, checked the tiny screws and springs before he inserted each of them. Once the weapon was whole he slipped it back into the holster on the chair and got dressed, threw on a plain white shirt and pulled black socks and boots onto his feet. Someone had to know who had been invited to Kilroy's party, and Cobb wanted to find out whom that woman was. She had struck something in him, something told him that he needed to track her down, and not just because she was a vampire. That "we have plans for you" still unnerved him.

After he put his boots on Cobb slipped into his heavy blue coat. A fresh line of stitching marked the shoulder that had been torn open during the assault on Kilroy's. With slight indecision he dug around in his trunk for a moment before he pulled out a small .38 revolver. He stuffed this into one pocket. He didn't like to go into the regular world heavily armed, but it never hurt to have something along just in case he needed it. Once the gun belts and Schofields were safely hidden under the bed Cobb left the hotel room, the door locked, and exited the building through the lobby. Thoughts of his past disappeared and he focused on the emptiness he felt in his stomach. He hadn't eaten in almost two days, his only sustenance in that time being whiskey and bourbon. It tended to bring on a sense of starvation once it was out of the body.

Cobb's gray Studebaker was sitting out front on Broadway Street, waiting patiently for him. Nodding past the clerk at the hotel desk, Cobb walked out of the building, felt his stomach rumble. One thing he knew about himself was that he could go a long time without eating. Once he had gone three weeks without food or water, trapped in an underground cavern in Maine, and while there had been hunger pains at first they had eventually faded away. Cobb just forgot about them, no weakness or dehydration reminding him about basic human needs. As soon as he had dug himself out, though, he had feasted himself silly at a local restaurant, raising a few eyebrows on the other patrons while he consumed three whole chickens, a loaf of bread, and six bowls of soup. That had been good soup.

But the fact of the matter was that Cobb liked to eat, even if he didn't have to do it very often. It was one of those things that reminded him of his humanity, like sleeping, something else he only occasionally needed yet enjoyed. It was a normal thing that normal people did. There was also the fact that food usually tasted good, and Cobb's life was relatively short on pleasures. He took them where he could get them.

Out on the street there were a few people who glanced at Cobb as he walked towards his car, avoiding their gaze as best he could. He didn't feel comfortable facing other people, especially since so many of them seemed so dead inside. That didn't surprise him, though. What else could he expect in such a time? So many people had lost their souls, empty holes marking where they had once kept their purposes and identities. In other cities at other times he saw men on street corners selling apples or women selling more intimate wares, all trying to make ends meet in a time of financial famine. Eighteen million people were out of work, eighteen million people couldn't afford to feed their children or keep themselves warm at night. How could anyone be surprised by the never-ending supply of misery in the world?

Cobb turned his thoughts back to food as he reached his car and shifted his bulk into the driver's seat. He was trying to decide what to eat. There was a nice little diner about three blocks from the hotel. He'd gone there a few times and liked the owner, a greasy-haired little man called Pops who made great coffee. They had good roast beef sandwiches; Cobb was in the mood for three or four of them, dripping with gravy. His mind made up, Cobb slipped the key into the ignition gave it a turn.

And then the car exploded, a giant ball of flame blossoming like a huge red and orange flower on the street.

CHAPTER 9

▼

Doctor Henry Halloway looked up from his clipboard at the sound of someone entering the First Avenue city morgue, a small smile on his narrow face as he puffed on a cigarette. Detective Charles LeGrasse of the New York City Police Department adjusted the lapel of his brown suit coat, scratched at his collar a bit, and generally looked about as uncomfortable as he possibly could as he walked in. That wasn't an unusual sight to Halloway, who understood that the morgue wasn't a place that many wanted to be in. It was cold, after all, and filled with corpses. The cloying smell of formaldehyde and alcohol filled the main examination area, and the lights bothered the eyes, especially after one came in from the sunlight.

The doctor crushed out his cigarette. He was leaning against a counter near a sink, taking a break from one of his more unpleasant job duties. "Good afternoon, detective," he said, his face pale in the stark white light of the morgue. "And how are you today?"

"Lousy," said LeGrasse. The detective was older, a portly man with a big moustache and thinning black hair who always smelled of cheap aftershave. "I need to see the Casey body."

A thoughtful frown appeared on Halloway's face and he put down his clipboard. "All right," he said, and he led the policeman over to the bank of drawers set into the nearby wall and opened Casey's. He suppressed the urge to be dramatic as he pulled out the body on a long track and removed the sheet, exposing it to the light. "There he is," was all he said, still smiling.

"Great," the policeman said. Casey's body was black and shriveled while his mouth was open in a silent scream of agony. It wasn't much to look at.

"Is there something wrong, detective?"

LeGrasse shrugged. "Probably," he said. "You heard about Casey's hotel room?"

The doctor shook his head. "No," he said. "Should I have?"

"It was filled with weapons," replied LeGrasse absently while he put a hand to his neck and massaged it. "The man had a damn arsenal in there. I need to find out why."

"Well, he's not going to tell you much," said Halloway. He turned his head slightly and looked at the body. "He was tall."

LeGrasse looked at Halloway for a moment, and then back at the man he knew as Jack Casey. "A little over six feet, according to the hotel staff," he said. "Big, scary lummox. Shaved his head."

"There's a lot of muscle left on the bones," Halloway said, his voice that of a practiced pathologist. "I think he cooked slowly. Probably wasn't killed right away. The force of the explosion would have stunned him. Pulverized his organs, if he was lucky. You said the bomb was under the gas tank?"

"Yup," said LeGrasse. "Ignited the fuel supply, blew the whole car to hell."

"Poor bastard."

LeGrasse grunted. "Don't be so sympathetic," he said. "This guy was probably some kind of torpedo."

Halloway's head snapped up. "For who?"

"No idea, but you remember the Castellammarese War two years ago?"

"Yeah," said Halloway. The Castellammarese War occurred when mob bosses Messeria and Maranzano had gone after each other, a conflict that had ultimately left Lucky Luciano in charge of the New York underworld. "You think Luciano's calling in favors from out-of-towners now?"

"Maybe." LeGrasse bent down and looked at the corpse's face, the large head pulled back in its silent throes of agony. "If he is, what would this man be expected to do? Or, and this is more likely, is someone gunning for Luciano? They would need people like this, heavily armed and, by all descriptions, tough."

"You're sure he's not a local?"

"I don't think so. I've been checking the SID files but there's only so much that can be done in a few hours. I can't find any mention of Casey's name, though."

"So you've no idea who he is?"

LeGrasse shook his head. "Don't even know if 'Casey' is his real name. Who-ever he *was*, he was in town for some major business. Was anything else on him?"

The doctor shrugged. "He had a piece of metal fused to his hip," he said. "Looked like a gun, probably a .38."

LeGrasse nodded and looked back at the body. Suddenly he reached up and stroked his chin, a frown on his face. "Does this corpse look different to you?" He asked.

Halloway's brow crumpled. "What do you mean?"

"I mean it looks different," the detective replied. "Almost bigger, thicker."

With a small chuckle Halloway shook his head. The body looked exactly the same to him as it had when brought in. "Must be the light in here, detective," he said. "Or you're just tired."

LeGrasse said nothing. For a long while he just looked at the body with that frown on his face. "I'm going back to the station," he said at last, his voice low. "If anything comes up let me know."

With that he turned on his heel and walked out of the morgue. Halloway stared after him for a moment, a confused look on his face, and finally he just shrugged and slid the drawer closed, a smirk on his face. What did LeGrasse think, that the body was somehow changing? Corpses didn't change, except to get even more decayed and desiccated. They didn't change. They rotted.

The detective gone, Halloway returned to his work, namely an autopsy in the other room that he had started just before LeGrasse had turned up. The body was of a young woman, laid out on a table, incisions made on the front of her chest. She had been fished out of a garbage heap the day before, no visible cause of death. Track marks on her arms, however, suggested morphine or heroine use, and judging by the blueness of her lips and slight bluish cast of her skin Halloway was fairly certain that he would find evidence of an overdose. One of the harness bulls had identified the woman as Red Sally, a prostitute from the lower side of Brooklyn, lately of Luciano's string of whorehouses.

Standing alongside the naked corpse, Halloway felt a twinge of sadness. The girl couldn't have been older than 25, and she looked to have been attractive. Halloway had a soft spot for pretty girls, and he didn't enjoy cutting them open on examination tables.

The autopsy went routinely, Halloway catalogued the girl's insides and found that she had died of oxygen starvation, probably the result of an overdose. Quite simply, she had stopped breathing. Halloway yawned as he made his notes. It was getting late and he was tired. He wondered while he wrote, thought about what the detectives would decide. Had Red Sally overdosed in a hotel room? Had some john got rid of the body in order to avoid complications with the police? Or had she threatened to blow the whistle on someone, who killed her by inducing an overdose? That kind of thing actually happened.

His job finished, Halloway loaded his blood-coated instruments onto a single metal tray and took them to a nearby shelf. He whistled softly to himself and tried not to think about how long of a day he'd had. His assistant, a lazy bastard named Gaines, had called in sick, leaving Halloway to do all the work on his own. Not that he minded. Most days Gaines just caused more problems than he solved. Halloway sighed and wiped his hands on his apron before turning back to Red Sally.

Then something behind him moved.

Halloway felt his heart leap. He hated it when people entered the morgue too quietly and snuck up on him. He spun around, but saw no one in the doorway to the adjoining room. Slowly he walked over to it and peered around the corner to the right, towards the entrance to the morgue.

No one was there. Halloway frowned and looked around at the main room, at the bank of drawers to his left, where most of the bodies were kept. He could have sworn he had heard something, but clearly no one was there. Maybe someone had come in and then changed their mind, he decided. Oh well, no skin off his nose. He turned back to his bloody tools and took a few steps, and then heard the noise again. This time it was plain that he had heard something. There could be no denying it. Again he went back into the first chamber, looked around. It had been a louder sound, almost like a scrape and a bump noise.

It came again.

Halloway jumped, the sound intrusive, a hard knock. It had come from the drawers he decided while a cold sweat popped onto his forehead. Something in the drawers made that sound, something moved. Halloway knew that he should get help, but instead he took a few slow steps towards the drawers, towards the area where the sound had come from. It was the drawers on the right, nearest the door. With a trembling hand he reached out and took hold of the lever of one of the drawers, the one that he was sure the noise originated in. The thought that someone was alive inside terrified him. How could that be possible? The bodies were examined. They were all pronounced dead before being brought to the morgue.

The lever was cold, but Halloway's skin was colder. He twisted it, released the lock on the drawer, and pulled it out, half expecting someone to leap up from the slab as soon as they hit the light. The body didn't move. It just lay on the slab, the pale skin waxen and the knife wound on the neck dark red. This was Harold "Longtooth" Carter, a petty thief and drug pusher. The doctor shook his head and relaxed a bit. He wondered if the noise had been some faulty piping in the ceiling, a trick of the acoustics making it seem like it had come from the drawers. Halloway slid the drawer shut and laughed softly at his own foolishness.

And then the knocking resumed.

This time there wasn't just one knock and then silence. This time it was a mad, frantic banging from the drawer above the one he had just opened, from Jack Casey's drawer. Terrified again, Halloway backed away from the drawers, a hand by his gaping mouth. The banging lasted a few seconds and then stopped, replaced by a methodical, heavy knocking on the door. The drawer shivered with every impact, and Halloway realized that whatever was in there was trying to pop the lock, trying to force the drawer open. His bladder loosened and Halloway backed himself into the corner, tears in his eyes as he slid down into a crouch, muttered like a frightened child. Whatever was in there it was pissed off, and Halloway was too paralyzed by terror to do anything about it.

With a bang and a crash, the lever on the drawer snapped off and the drawer slid open, banging as it reached its full length over the floor. The blackened body floundered and rolled off, slapped onto the linoleum, and that's when Halloway realized that it was moving of its own accord, a charred nightmare that reared up to stare at him with baleful eyes, the burned meat cracked and wet in places.

"Please," sputtered Halloway as the thing stared at him with bulging eyes, its teeth white in the blackness of its face, a rictus grin without lips or flesh. "Please, don't hurt me."

The black thing crawled towards him, pulled itself along on the floor by its hands, its legs dragged uselessly behind it. As it approached Halloway could hear it breathing, every breath labored and forced. It came within inches of him, the eyes glistened in the pale light and that horrid grin leered at him. Halloway shut his eyes, his mind on the verge of breaking.

As it pushed itself up the corpse that moved reached out and grabbed the doctor by the lapel, forced him to look. Halloway's eyes were wide and the touch of the thing's fingers nearly gave him a heart attack. Seeing it that close didn't help, either.

The thing drew close to Halloway's face and its nightmarish visage sent shivers down the man's spine. While he stared, he became aware that it was making sounds, something he only noticed when he forced himself to listen past the sound of his own heartbeat pounding like a piston in his chest. Once past that, though, he could hear the grunting noises that came from between the monster's clenched teeth. They sounded like tires against gravel, guttural and low, coming in rhythmic, definite patterns. Slowly Halloway realized what was going on.

The monster was trying to talk!

His lips parted into a broad, open frown, Halloway stared in disbelief as the thing grumbled. Somewhere in the back of his mind he realized that the monster's jaw muscles weren't capable of opening and closing the mouth enough to speak, and the lack of lips didn't make it any easier. In fact, Halloway was fairly certain that the vocal chords weren't all there. But the thing was still trying to talk to him, and it looked to be getting frustrated by the fact that it couldn't.

"I can't understand you," said Halloway, his voice wavering. His skin had somehow managed to get paler. "I don't know what you're saying."

The thing's grip on his coat tightened, its eyes showed its anger. An idea popped into his head and Halloway pulled a pen from his pocket. He held it up and the thing's eyes turned to it quickly.

"Can you write?" He asked. The thing's teeth clamped together. "You know, write?"

After a moment the thing reached up and snatched the pen from Halloway's hand and slithered away, left him alone in the corner. It scraped the pen against the tiles, but the ink couldn't find a purchase and soon the monster looked frustrated again. Fearful of the thing's wrath, Halloway jumped to his feet and grabbed his clipboard, the one he had written the details of Red Sally's autopsy on. He dropped this onto the floor next to the thing and it looked up at him, its shriveled head twisting up and then back to the clipboard. Almost resentfully the thing took the clipboard and wrote a single word on it, holding the pen like an ice pick. Halloway looked at it, his natural curiosity overriding the bone-chilling fear.

"Where?" Halloway said, reading the word out loud. He thought about it for a moment and then understood. "Where are you? You're in the morgue. Your car exploded, it was a bomb."

The thing grunted, then wrote on the clipboard again. Halloway looked at it, his forehead wrinkled.

"Who did it?" The thing had written.

"I don't know," answered Halloway, actually laughing. "I'm a pathologist, they don't tell me shit."

Apparently the thing didn't appreciate Halloway's humor and it reached out, grabbed the cuff of his pants with a growl. Immediately the doctor froze as his fear came back. With its other hand the thing scribbled again, wrote simply, "Get me out of here." Halloway stared at it, not certain how to answer.

"I don't know if I can," he said, eventually. "I mean, Detective LeGrasse thinks you're a mob hit man, he found the guns in your hotel room and he's worried there's some kind of gang war coming."

The thing thought about this. Again it wrote. "Guns, where?"

Halloway shrugged. "The evidence locker at the 32nd Precinct, I guess."

The thing pointed at the "Get me out of here" again, as if to repeat it.

"I can't, really I can't."

Resigned, the thing wrote again. "Bandages," it wrote.

"You want bandages?" The doctor asked, his fear of the thing's anger making him eager to please. Part of him dearly wished someone else would come down to the morgue and rescue him. "Of course."

Two minutes later the doctor was wrapping the thing's limbs with brown cloth, an uneasy look on his face while it sat on his examination table. The thing was staring at him, its eyes hard, as if it suspected him to try and run at any second. But for some reason Halloway was compelled to stay, to see where this situation led. So far the thing, despite its outward strangeness, had not really threatened him. As a doctor Halloway felt a compulsion to help the broken and damaged wretch before him and it was clear it needed it. Halloway was not a religious man, but his experiences with corpses had given him a sense of kinship to the dead, and the fact that this corpse was up and moving around was fascinating to him. Yes, the sane thing would have been to run screaming at the first opportunity, but morbid curiosity drove him on.

"There," said Halloway as he applied the last bandages to the thing's head. Its entire body was covered, the only gaps left, other than the eyes and mouth, were over the joints and under the armpits to allow movement. Bits of blackened flesh peeked out around the eyes and the neck, but that was it. "How's that?"

The thing nodded, looking like an Egyptian mummy that had come to life. Carefully and with some hesitation, it dropped down from the table, lowering its feet first as if testing to see if the legs could support its weight. After a moment it was clear that they could, and it stood before Halloway, tall and imposing, its eyes staring out at him.

"All right, then," said Halloway. He clapped his hands together, pleased. "Let's see what we can do for you."

CHAPTER 10

▼

Cobb was not in his right mind, to put it simply. The bomb had shattered his bones, burned off all of his flesh, cooked and pulverized his organs. That included his brain. It was probable that not everything had fixed itself yet. Waking up in the morgue drawer had been the easiest part, the shock of that nothing compared to the injury. He was in a real situation now, though—stuck in the morgue, his weapons, clothing, and cash confiscated, not to mention his complete lack of skin. None of this would do.

Nothing really hurt, his nerve endings weren't together enough to send impulses, and he still couldn't talk. He wondered how long complete regeneration would take. First thing was first, though. He needed to get out of the hospital and make it to the police station.

Halloway lit up a cigarette and puffed at it quickly. Silently Cobb walked over to the doctor, grabbed him by the shoulders, and punched him squarely across the jaw. The doctor flopped to his side, landing in a heap, unconscious. He had decided that it was better if Halloway had as little to do with him as possible. Cobb hadn't hit him too hard. He'd wake up in a little while and have nothing more to do with the madness of Cobb's life. He might have a headache, but that was a lot better than the alternative.

Without another thought Cobb rushed towards the exit, sliding his drawer shut as he passed. Luckily it was getting late and there weren't many employees around to notice him. As he neared the front door, he checked first to see that the coast was clear, and then made his way to the back parking lot.

He was out of the city morgue, but he still needed to get to the police station and reclaim his trunk. That would be the hard part.

Cobb pressed his back against the wall and looked out at the parking lot. Right away he saw a man in a hat and long coat unlocking a large Ford. Cobb moved fast, hunching down and using the other cars in the lot as cover, his cloth-wrapped feet scraping the pavement only slightly. The target was just about to get into his car when Cobb reached him and grabbed his shoulders from behind. The man let out a yelp as Cobb yanked him back and threw him into a tight sleeper hold. It took only a few seconds to choke the man unconscious.

The poor bystander subdued, Cobb laid him gently on the pavement. He ignored the fellow's quiet mumbling and looked around to make sure that no one had noticed. Cobb took his victim's keys, coat, and hat, with as much care as possible. He didn't want to hurt the man; he was just a bystander after all. Cobb got into the Ford and started the engine, his pearly white teeth clenched tightly as he pulled out of the parking lot.

He supposed he could have just let his belongings go, but that didn't sit well with him. He needed them, for one thing. The guns, knives, and explosives could probably be replaced, but there were other things in his trunk, things that he hoped would still be there when he found it. The money was important, that was certain. Without that he would have a very difficult time moving around.

Cobb drove straight to the 32nd Precinct. He didn't much like the idea of a frontal assault, but he knew the longer he waited the harder it would be for him to get his things back. The fact that he was gone from the morgue would be noticed quickly, even if Halloway didn't blabber his unbelievable story as soon as he woke up to anyone that would listen.

The street was nearly empty when he pulled up against the curb, just down the block from the station. Cobb stared at the front of the building through his borrowed windshield, unable to frown but desperately wishing he could. Walking through the front door was probably a bad idea since he couldn't count on being unobtrusive in his current condition. He thought about grabbing a cop and using his uniform, but the chances of finding one that fit were small. Cobb was, after all, a large man, even burnt as he was.

For a long time Cobb just sat in the car, in the dark, looking at the police station. It was close to 10 p.m. when Cobb decided to get out of the car, glad that the street was relatively empty in front of the station. The fact remained, though, that he wasn't wearing any clothes or shoes, he just had his stolen coat and hat. If anyone got a clear look at him they were sure to notice that he was wrapped completely in bandages.

There wasn't much else for him to do, though, so he got out and stood on the street for a moment in the safety of the shadows, glancing around. There were a few folks around, but it was otherwise silent. Quickly Cobb walked over to stand in a darkened corner near the station door, pulling his hat brim low and keeping his head down. In the black he waited, patiently, a hunter looking for his prey.

It came eventually. A uniformed policeman walked out of the station and past Cobb's corner, but Cobb didn't let him get much farther. He flowed out of the shadows with practiced grace and snatched the policeman's revolver out of his holster before he tucked it under his armpit. The cop barely noticed until the muzzle pushed up against him.

The policeman froze as Cobb put a hand on his shoulder in a gesture that could have been interpreted as friendly by anyone who happened to see it. The iron-like grip he exerted felt like something far different, however.

Cobb leaned in close and grunted softly in the cop's ear. The policeman, feeling the gun against his ribs, sucked in a quick breath. "Look," he said quietly, "this is really a bad idea. You don't want to do this."

Cobb ignored his words and shoved him gently towards the station. The cop looked at the looming building and frowned. "You want me to go back in there?" He asked.

Cobb grunted and prodded the officer again. Shrugging, the cop did as he was told and started walking towards the front door.

"They're going to burn you, you know that don't you?" The cop asked, annoyed. "I mean, walking into the station with a cop at gunpoint? How stupid can you get?"

Cobb just wanted to get this over with, so he shoved his revolver hard against the cop's ribs to shut him up. He couldn't speak, but he wasn't about to let his things get pawed through by the police and whatever experts they called in. They'd put their grubby fingers on weapons, relics, and sources of information that he had spent several lifetimes putting together and that couldn't be allowed to happen.

They entered the police station and Cobb did his best to appear like he was just standing alongside the policeman. He covered the gun in the cop's ribs while he kept his head low. There weren't many people around, just another cop behind the front desk, his face down as he scribbled on a few papers. There were a few other administrators walking around, but it didn't look like anyone had noticed Cobb or his unwilling companion. There was a single civilian in the waiting area; a short, fat man who looked almost like he was falling asleep in his chair.

"So where are we going?"

Cobb grunted softly, uncertain how to indicate what he was after. Finally he just gave up and shoved the officer towards the nearby restroom. The were alone inside, and the cop managed to get a look at Cobb in the mirror, clad in bandages, his hard eyes visible through the openings that Halloway had left.

"Jesus," he whispered. Cobb ignored the statement and pushed the policeman towards the sink, his revolver at the cop's head. The policeman watched, his hands coming up, while the nightmare in front of him shifted the gun to his left hand, took a pen from his coat pocket, and scribbled on the concrete wall, the ink just barely showing against the paint.

"Evidence," Cobb wrote, with some difficulty. The cop looked at it, Cobb drawing a question mark underneath it to clarify his desire.

"The evidence room?" He asked. "You want that?"

Cobb nodded.

"Okay," said the officer. He looked back at the end of his own service revolver. "Up the stairs, second floor. Take a left and go down the hall. But you'll never get in there. There's a guard on duty."

Cobb tossed away his pen and grabbed the cop by the shoulder, turned him around forcefully. The policeman yelped in protest but it didn't stop Cobb from hitting him. The revolver smacked the back of the cop's head and the cop dropped into an inert heap on the tiled floor. Ruefully Cobb looked down at him and silently measured the man—he was at least a foot shorter than Cobb, there was no way his uniform would fit. His teeth clicked together faintly and Cobb tucked the policeman into the stall, under the toilet, obscured him as best he could. At least he had a gun, he thought to himself. The policeman had been useful getting him into the station, no one had looked twice at the uniformed officer or his companion, but now he was just a liability.

Stepping out of the restroom, Cobb decided to keep it simple. His eyes going to a small red box on the wall on the other side of the hall, he walked quickly over to it. It was a firebox, complete with glass front and brass hammer on a chain. He snatched up the hammer and smashed the glass to start the bell ringing. In a moment people were coming out of the woodwork, running down the stairs from the upper floors and heading towards the front doors, mumbling and questioning each other. Cobb shrank back to the restroom, closing the door but leaving a slight partition so he could watch, satisfied. After a few seconds he realized that he had cleared the building as much as he was going to and he exited the restroom. He rushed towards the nearest steps, following the policeman's instructions.

Eventually he reached the door to the evidence locker, and the desk before it was empty, the guard nowhere to be seen. It was the best chance he was going to get. Cobb ran towards the door, grabbed the knob and gave it a hard turn. It resisted, and he growled angrily before he threw his weight against the metal. The locked door shook on its hinges, but it did not give. Frustrated, Cobb drove his shoulder into it again, to the same effect. Strong as he normally was his condition had him severely weakened.

"Hey," shouted someone from behind. Cobb turned to see another policeman walking towards him, a confused look on his face. "What the hell do you think you're doing?"

Cobb snarled and rushed the cop, the poor man's eyes widening when he realized that the thing he was talking to was not like him. The cop's gun was out quickly and he fired a single shot. The bullet went right through Cobb's shoulder but did nothing to stop his approach. Cobb hit him at full speed, hurled him painfully to the tiled floor. The cop groaned, and Cobb reached down and picked him back up, shoved him roughly to the door.

Cobb pushed his face against the evidence locker door in an act that couldn't be interpreted as anything but "open this." Fumbling at his belt, the policeman found his key, stuck into the lock and twisted it quickly. Cobb threw the cop back to the floor, the door to the locker open, and stepped inside eagerly.

In the corner his trunk sat, a paper tag fixed to the one of the handles. He tore this off quickly, popped the latches and threw open the trunk to see if everything was still in place. It looked to be, if a bit moved around.

Cobb loaded one of the Schofields and shut the trunk, lifted it in one hand while holding the gun in the other. Just as he was about to leave the locker, though, something caught his eye. He turning his head and saw his hat, quietly on top of a shelf, a manila tag hanging off the wide brim. He would have smiled if he could have, glad that he had not been wearing it when his car exploded, and plucked off the stolen hat and threw on his own after yanking off the tag.

The fire bell stopped, and Cobb knew that he only had a few seconds to get out of the building before it was swarming the police. Rushing past the evidence guard, who watched him go by with disbelief in his eyes, Cobb headed toward the front door, not interested in hunting for a side way out. Unfortunately this took him right to Detective LeGrasse, who had returned from the morgue and was walking back inside the building.

LeGrasse froze, his eyes locking onto Cobb, who was driving towards him, intent on bowling the old man over.

"Stop," LeGrasse ordered, a hand out. Cobb pointed his gun at the old man's face, not having the time to mess around. As soon as he saw the extended barrel, LeGrasse cleared his path, watched Cobb walk briskly by, the weapon trained on him. A crowd was just outside the door, and several people saw Cobb and some shouted while others cleared out of his way. Cobb shoved through them before enough of them noticed him to be a nuisance. He could hear LeGrasse behind him, the old man calling desperately for him to stop.

Once clear of the crowd Cobb broke into a dead run, into the dark, and disappeared between a pair of buildings that sat quietly across the street from the police station.

He heard police following, but he didn't care. He had to get away, had to get clear of their eyes. They were disoriented and confused, it took little effort to escape. A fire escape helped, and he crouched on a rooftop, safe for the moment.

Finally he had some time to think. Here he was, charred and fleshless, barely able to feel anything. He had been planning to leave town but now he had a reason to stay. That explosion had been no accident, it had been a bomb and that meant someone was responsible.

He was going to make that someone pay.

CHAPTER 11

▼

Detective Charles LeGrasse sat in his office, a pensive look on his face, holding in his hands a worn newspaper and staring intently at a photograph of a man who had called himself Jack Casey. The black and white photograph depicted a tall, bald, fierce-looking man, standing with one foot on a corpse, a pair of pistols on his belt. The headline above the photograph read "Arizona Bounty Hunter Casey Ends Career of 'Reckless' Bill Smalls."

The newspaper was dated June 18th, 1894.

With a heavy sigh LeGrasse dropped the newspaper onto his desk, shaking his head. His search for Jack Casey had turned up little more than the New York Gazette from forty years ago, and it was unlikely that the Jack Casey he was looking for was the same Jack Casey depicted. Although from what Halloway told him he might be likely to think that if he weren't a logical man.

Halloway had given him a story that, quite frankly, he was unwilling to believe. Stories about bodies coming to life and crawling around were more suited to the pulps, not real life. Still, there had been something about the way the doctor told the story that lent itself to credibility, but LeGrasse wasn't about to buy it. Not when a more likely explanation was that Halloway succumbed to the chemicals they used in the morgue or simply exhaustion. It was entirely possible that Halloway only dreamt the part about the charred corpse attacking him.

Of course that raised the question of what had happened to the corpse. Casey was the only one missing. If he didn't get up on his own then where did he go? Perhaps there was a more sinister cause of Halloway's delusions. Perhaps Casey's associates, whoever they were, had decided to reclaim his body and his possessions to throw the police off the trail, and perhaps they had knocked Halloway out. A blow to the head or something similar would have been just as likely to cause the doctor's hallucinations as anything else. The man that had threatened his way past LeGrasse after the bogus fire alarm certainly seemed like the type to do that sort of thing.

Turning his thoughts back to Casey, LeGrasse looked at the collection of information on his desk, ignored the old newspaper. None of it added up to much, Casey simply did not exist. The only real police record he had was of a mysterious explosion in Pittsburgh in 1931, where the top three floors of a Harlowe Inc. regional office were blown clean off. Investigating officers had arrested a man calling himself "Jack Casey" in the area, but questioning had come to little so he had been released, and later attempts to find him were unsuccessful. That was all there was, besides the old newspaper. But LeGrasse dismissed that particular scrap as coincidence. If he were looking for the same Jack Casey as the one in the article the man would be in his 60's and as such not a likely suspect.

Out of plain curiosity, however, and just in need of a break, LeGrasse had done some more digging on the 1890's Casey and found that no less than 27 men had been captured or killed by the bounty hunter between the years of 1892 and 1895. Then Casey simply disappeared, probably retiring. Disappearing in the 1890's wasn't a difficult thing, after all, especially for a loner type like a bounty hunter.

All of that was interesting, but had nothing to do with the Casey he was tracking. Details on his Casey were important in that through them he could find Casey's associates, maybe even the people who had stolen his body and beaten Halloway and the other officers, not to mention finding an explanation as to why Casey was in town. That, more than anything, was what LeGrasse was after.

Slowly LeGrasse pulled a worn pipe from his desk and popped it into his mouth. He lit it with a wooden match from a desk drawer and the sweet smell of tobacco filled his office while he sat back in his chair, deep in thought. He glanced at the clock on the wall, noted with some surprise that it was after five. He was late for dinner. Quickly he threw his information on Casey into a drawer and put on his coat and hat, his black pipe still perched between his lips.

Katharine, his wife, hated it when he was late, and he hated upsetting her.

There were a few people at the station. As he left LeGrasse nodded hello or waved a hand at people he passed, wondering silently what Katharine would have waiting for him. He hoped it was meatloaf. Katharine made great meatloaf.

Finally making it to his car, LeGrasse slid into the driver's seat, his face a bit red for having rushed. He wasn't as young as he used to be, and too much of

Katharine's cooking had had its way with his shape; LeGrasse was a considerably large man. He slammed the door shut and put his key into the ignition.

Just then something touched the right side of his head, just behind the ear. LeGrasse froze as he recognized the unmistakable shape of a gun barrel pressed against his skull. He glanced at the rear-view mirror and saw the long cylinder of a huge revolver held by a black-gloved hand. He couldn't see the face of the holder, the angle was wrong.

"Quiet now," said a low, deep voice quietly behind him. "Start the car."

His breath coming softly, LeGrasse reached out and turned the key in the ignition, brought the engine to life. The gun at his head shifted slightly and a hand snaked around his shoulder, reached under his coat and pulled his revolver from his shoulder holster. The gun disappeared to the back seat, leaving LeGrasse completely unarmed.

"Drive," the person in the back seat commanded and the detective complied. He wasn't afraid, more concerned, and he recognized the gun that he had seen in the mirror.

"Where am I going?" He asked, pulling out onto the street.

"The docks," said his passenger. Resisting the urge to shrug because he didn't want to make any sudden movements, LeGrasse thought of the fastest way to the docks, and then began navigating. The person behind him said nothing while the drove, he just held his weapon to LeGrasse's head, and the detective wondered if he was going to be dead soon. It didn't seem likely. If this were an assassination attempt he would already be dead. More likely this was a scare tactic, something to keep LeGrasse from poking his nose into something that others would rather he stayed away from. The gun was one of the old revolvers that had been in Casey's trunk, so LeGrasse reasoned that whoever took Casey's body was the man in the back seat.

They neared the waterfront and the man in the back directed LeGrasse to a lonely corner of the docks, near some huge cargo containers. "Pull up here," he said.

"Don't try anything funny," he warned, his face close to LeGrasse's ear.

"Wouldn't dream of it," said LeGrasse. The door behind him opened and his guest got out, commanded LeGrasse to do the same. They stood together on the street, LeGrasse turning to look at his kidnapper. Cobb, however, kept his face turned down, the brim of his hat confounding the detective's attempt to get a look at his face even though a bit of reddish-pink skin around the neck and jaw were still visible. LeGrasse could see that he was a big man, however, dressed in a blue shirt and black pants, covered by a long gray coat that hung down to his shins.

"Get into the back seat," said Cobb, grabbing LeGrasse's elbow and urging him forward. While the policeman complied he glanced around, saw that there wasn't anyone around to notice too much. It was a Monday night. The workers were gone for the day.

The detective was more than willing to go along with Cobb's demands, knowing that it was possible he would get some information if he played ball. He had no idea of the scope of Cobb's actions or even what he was all about. To him this man was an associate of Jack Casey's, a criminal and nothing more.

"So what can I do for you?" LeGrasse asked while he got comfortable, the casual tone of his words hiding the fact that his heart was pounding at a hundred beats a minute. As much as his intellectual mind could say that he probably wasn't going to get killed his fight or flight reflexes were kicking him in the groin.

"I need information," said Cobb as he got into the backseat alongside LeGrasse.

"You're one of Jack Casey's friends, aren't you?"

Cobb paused. "Uh, sure," he said, after a moment. "I'm one of Casey's friends."

LeGrasse smiled. "Here for some business, then? Looking for Luciano?"

"Not really," Cobb answered. "I want to know about the car bombing that…killed Casey."

"Revenge, huh? Typical."

"You're investigating Casey," replied Cobb, impatiently, "so I think you know something about who killed him. Who could set up something like that?"

Shrugging, LeGrasse dared to glance around the brim of Cobb's hat. The shadows hid his face well, however. "Probably about a dozen guys," he said. "It's too common a skill these days. The bomb that hit Casey though was a rush job, sloppy, really."

"So who works like that?"

Smiling, the detective shook his head. "You know I can't just tell you that," he said. "I'm a policeman, not a stoolpigeon. I don't help out people like you."

"You should," said Cobb, leaning in close. "Help me and I'll help you. Give me a name and I'll make sure he doesn't blow anything else up, ever again."

"Sorry, there's a process to law enforcement, and I work by it."

Suddenly Cobb grabbed LeGrasse's wide shoulder, his grip like a vice. LeGrasse winced, surprised by the roughness of it. "Give me a name or I'll kill you," Cobb whispered, deadly serious.

"Can't kill a cop," grunted LeGrasse. He wanted desperately to give in but knew that if he did it was likely that he'd be killed. "Have the whole New York police force on you if you did."

"I don't care," growled Cobb, "and you're an idiot to think I would. This isn't a mob thing, LeGrasse. This has nothing to do with Luciano. This is something you can't possibly imagine."

Cobb's grip tightened and LeGrasse felt tears sting his eyes. "Try me," he muttered, feeling like he was going to pass out any second. No sooner had he made the challenge than Cobb whipped off his hat and gave the policeman a good look at his deformed features. LeGrasse sucked in a breath, shocked by what he saw. Cobb was a nightmare, his half-formed flesh glistening, and muscle tissue visible through semi-transparent layers of fat while veins pulsed. His eyes stared large and terrible, his eyelids soft and translucent.

"Look at me," Cobb ordered as LeGrasse tried to turn away. "Take a good, long look. Do you think I work for anyone you've ever met? You think I'm just a friend of Jack Casey's? You think he even exists?"

"Jesus," whispered LeGrasse, staring at the nightmare that held him in an iron grip. "What the hell happened to you?"

"The bomb did this to me," replied Cobb, his teeth white behind his misshapen lips. "Blew me to hell and I haven't gotten better yet."

"It's not possible," said LeGrasse as Cobb released him. Slowly he put his hat back on while LeGrasse stared, his curiosity overriding his fear like Halloway's had. "You can't be Casey. He's dead."

"I don't care what you believe," said Cobb, pulling his slouch hat low. "It means nothing to me whether or not you believe I'm the same guy you pulled out of that wreck a week ago. I just want to know who did it."

LeGrasse was answering before he even knew it. "There's a guy named Baker," he said. "Wesley Baker. Used to work for Maranzano's crew before he went down. Now he's freelance. I heard he's laying out a lot of money right now, and explosives are his thing. We were going to bring him in but I needed more evidence if I was going to make a charge stick."

Cobb smiled at the detective, took in a deep breath. "There, that wasn't hard," he said. "Thanks."

"You really are him, aren't you?" LeGrasse asked. "You really are Jack Casey."

Cobb snorted through the yellowish cartilage of his nose. "That's not my name," he said. "Now, give me your handcuffs."

LeGrasse hesitated, but the look in Cobb's eye forced compliance. Cobb took the handcuffs and got out of the car. His revolver reappeared, the muzzle pointed at the policeman. By Cobb's instruction LeGrasse shifted his body closer to the door, allowed Cobb to handcuff his right wrist to the frame once he opened the door and rolled the window down.

"Sorry about this," said Cobb. "Can't have you getting to Baker before I do."

Cobb walked away from the car, his boots clomping against the pavement, the keys to the car and handcuffs still in his coat pocket. The detective just stared, watched him leave, unable to believe what he had just learned. He was suddenly willing to believe that what Halloway had told him was true, and that somehow there was more to the world than just cause and effect, that cold logic was less important to the world than it had been a few hours ago. Casey, or whoever he was, represented something terrible, something in the world that defied science and explanation.

LeGrasse sighed as he wondered how long it would be before he could get out of there. Even though he was able to sit in the driver's seat the fact that his right hand was cuffed to the door would make it hard to just shut the door, not to mention drive. Someone had to pass by eventually, though, and maybe he could shout them over. The detective sighed again and shook his head. Katharine's meatloaf was going to seem awfully tame when he finally got home.

CHAPTER 12

▼

Cobb sucked in a breath as he stood outside the Lone Star Bar and Grill, hidden in the shadows of an alleyway while he loaded one of his Schofields. It was nearly two in the morning. Some asking around had turned up the fact that Wes Baker was a regular at the Lone Star, and that he liked to stay out all night. Pretending to be a potential client had gotten Cobb far in only a few hours, and now it was time for the payoff.

He holstered his pistol and pulled his coat over his gun belts, and then crossed over to the Lone Star. With a grave expression he walked in through the heavy wooden door as a drunk staggered by him. The inside of the tavern was much the same as any such place, with beaten wood planks for a floor, a long bar, some glasses hanging over it, and several tables hidden in shadows. Only a few people were left at that time of the night, and those that could turned to look at Cobb, who kept his face turned low. In the darkness of the interior it would be difficult to see his disfigurement, but Cobb wasn't going to make it any easier.

Cobb crossed to the bar and waved a gloved hand at the bartender, who wandered over less quickly than Cobb would have liked. "What can I get you?" He asked.

"Whiskey," said Cobb. The bartender poured him a shot, tried glancing at his face. Cobb kept the brim of his hat low, though. The bartender seemed to lose interest and went back to wiping down the bar. Cobb sipped his whiskey, ignored the painful sting as it met the raw tissues of his lips. "I'm looking for someone," he said, just as the bartender turned to leave. "I hear he hangs out here."

"He got a name?" The bartender asked.

"Baker," said Cobb. By way of reply the bartender nodded and pointed across the bar at a table in the corner. Turning, Cobb saw that he was indicating a skinny blond man slumped over the tabletop, seemingly unconscious.

"Passed out about ten minutes ago," said the bartender, indifferent. "He does that some nights, especially when he's in the chips."

Cobb smiled and downed his whiskey. "Thanks," he said, and he dropped a fin onto the bar before walking over to the table. As he drew closer he could see that Baker was a small man with a rough complexion. He was breathing deeply, completely unconscious.

In the chips, was he? Cobb would teach him the foolishness of taking money to mess with someone like him.

A slight nudge to the sleeping man got nothing but a soft mumble. After deciding that there was nothing else for it, Cobb grabbed Baker by the back of his shirt and threw his inert body over his shoulder. Cobb turned back to the bartender and asked, "Know where he lives?"

The bartender wrote an address on a napkin. "It's a rat-trap about a block from here," he said as he handed it to Cobb.

The bartender, nor anyone else for that matter, made any move to stop Cobb as he walked out with Baker. He must have been a pain if no one wanted to stop a strange man from walking off with him, Cobb reasoned.

The bartender's estimation of Baker's place was reasonably accurate. Situated above an automat just around the corner, the apartment was a small room with cracked walls, diseased carpet, and a single bed with a stained mattress in the center. Cobb threw Baker onto the mattress and started checking things over. There was little to go through. The kitchen had a few cupboards, and there was a closet but no bathroom (that was down the hall. Cobb had nosed it out coming up).

It was in the closet that he found what he was looking for. There was a box on the floor, and inside Cobb found a clump of wiring and some explosives. With a smile Cobb pulled the box out of the closet and dragged it over to the bed.

Baker was still unconscious on the mattress, so Cobb decided to help him wake up. He went to the kitchen and filled a pan with water, and then unceremoniously splashed Baker on the face. The bomber was awake in a second, his eyes red as he thrashed about on his mattress, clearly trying to figure out where he was. His eyes fixed on Cobb, and all at once he tried rolling off the bed, but the big man was too fast for him and he grabbed Baker by the sleeve as he dropped onto the edge.

"Hold on a minute, Wes," said Cobb, his voice heavy with malice. "You're not going anywhere."

"I don't know anything," spat Baker, his words slurred. "I didn't do anything."

"That's not true and you know it," argued Cobb with a grin. "You blew up a guy named Cobb outside of the Monarch Hotel, didn't you?"

"Never heard of anyone named Cobb," Baker replied, fear in his eyes. "You've got the wrong guy."

Cobb whipped off his hat and let Baker get a good look at his face. The little man choked on the scream that tried shooting up his throat, his eyes wide.

"I sincerely doubt that," said Cobb, and he reached under his coat and slid out his Bowie knife. In the half-light of the apartment the blade gleamed wickedly. He turned it slowly in front of Baker, who went rigid at the sight of the huge instrument. "Just tell me who hired you to do it."

"I'm telling you," Baker insisted, nearly paralyzed with terror. "I didn't do anything. I'm straight now."

Cobb pulled out a paper-wrapped stick of dynamite from the box. "I don't think so," he said casually, and he put his hat back on. He brought the tip of his blade closer to Baker's face, sweat on the blond man's forehead. "Now tell me who hired you or I'll hang you up to dry like a deer."

"He'd kill me," Baker cried, and then he clapped his hand over his mouth. Cobb smiled.

"I'll kill you first," he said. "Now out with it."

Only an idiot would have been unable to tell that Cobb was serious, and as stupid as Baker could be he turned out to be smarter than that. "He said his name was Fletcher," he admitted. "Paid me two hundred bucks, gave me the make and license number on your car, told me where you were staying."

"He tell you why he wanted it done?"

"I didn't ask any questions. The guy was plenty queer, and I didn't think he'd like it. I just took the money and did the job."

Cobb thought for a moment. "Where is he now?" He asked.

"I don't know," said Baker. Suddenly he perked up. "He gave me a phone number to call him, though, if something went wrong. Maybe it still works."

"Perfect," whispered Cobb. "Let's make a phone call."

The call to Fletcher had to be made from a phone down the hall, set into the wall, Cobb providing the dime. He was happy to see that the number did work, however, and that Baker apparently made contact with Fletcher, who was none too happy if Baker's reactions could be read properly. It took some haranguing, but eventually Baker was able to convince Fletcher that there was some sort of problem and that he needed to talk to him right away at his apartment. When the call was finished Baker hung up the phone and looked at Cobb, sheepish.

"When?" Cobb asked the question gruffly as he ushered Baker back to his apartment. The little man walked quickly, his voice trembling when he answered.

"About an hour," said Baker as they went back to the apartment. He sat down on the bed as Cobb pulled out his knife from the concealing folds of his coat.

"Thanks," said Cobb. Baker smiled.

"You're done with me, then?" He asked.

Cobb grabbed Baker by the scruff of his neck. "Not a chance," he said. "I need you here for when this Fletcher shows."

"I can't," Baker pleaded. "Please, just let me out of here. I promise I'll be straight after this. No more contracts, I don't need this kind of shit."

"Just until he comes," Cobb reassured. "Just distract him for a second and I'll take care of the rest. Then you don't ever have to see me again."

Baker seemed to consider this. "All right," he said. "You promise you won't let him get me?"

"No."

They said no more about it, and once he put Baker on the bed Cobb set about to waiting for Fletcher. He toyed with the idea of rigging a bomb to the front door of the apartment, a poetic way of dealing with the man who had hired Baker to blow him up, but he decided against that. He wanted to interrogate this Fletcher person. He knew who was trying to kill him but now he had to know why. As far as he knew he'd never met anyone named Fletcher who would have any reason to come after him.

So Cobb resolved to simply wait. He pulled a chair up behind the door and sat down, his eyes locked on the nervous Baker. Just to remind Baker that running would be a bad idea he checked his pistols, his knife on his lap. Baker stared at the big six-guns with dread while Cobb sighted down the barrels and turned the cylinders. Once he was finished he put them away, but the impression had been left in Baker's mind.

The sun was poking through the curtains when Cobb heard the heavy footsteps in the hallway. Quickly he got to his feet and gently moved the chair away from him. Baker swallowed, nervous, and Cobb flattened himself against the wall, his knife ready. As the footsteps approached, Cobb could feel the presence of something more than human getting near, his strange, otherworldly senses lighting up as the man he knew had to be Fletcher walked towards the apartment. Cobb's lips pulled back from his teeth, he was growing anxious. Fletcher wasn't human. He could already sense it.

Fletcher knocked three times. Cobb waited, holding his breath, then nodded to Baker.

"Come in," Baker called. The door opened slowly in reply, Baker's eyes widening.

"Hi, Mr. Fletcher," he said, his voice shaking as he stared at the man that Cobb couldn't see. "Come on in."

Hidden by the door, Cobb edged forward, ready to act the moment he saw Fletcher. After a moment Fletcher entered, and from his angle Cobb could see that he was huge, bigger than Cobb, with broad, powerful shoulders and a thick head of curly black hair. He was dressed in a simple shirt and trousers, his sleeves rolled up to expose a pair of massive, hairy forearms.

Cobb wasn't one to be intimidated, though, even if Fletcher was big and inhuman. He moved with surprising grace and slid his left arm under Fletcher's while bringing his knife to the man's throat. Fletcher froze, the steel a hair's-breadth from his skin.

"Don't move," said Cobb. "We're going to talk."

The answer he got was definitely not what he wanted. Fletcher merely grunted, grabbed Cobb's right forearm, shifted his bulk, and somehow managed to throw Cobb over his shoulder. Cobb's feet scraped along the ceiling as his body hurtled across the apartment, and smashed into a wall, shattering its surface. After he flopped to the floor Cobb had only a moment before Fletcher kicked him in the ribs. The force of the blow sent him onto his back and suddenly Fletcher had picked Cobb up by the front of his shirt. Dust and splinters of plaster and brick ran off him.

"Shit," Cobb muttered, just as Fletcher lifted him into the air and sent him crashing through the nearby window. Outside was a two-story drop, and Cobb fell the whole way. With an enormous crunch he landed on the sidewalk, blood spurting from his mouth. Passers by looked at him, horrified, people on their way to work shocked by the sight of the mangled man dropping out of the sky.

For a moment Cobb lay on the sidewalk, shifting slowly from side to side, trying to get his head together. Everything hurt. He turned onto his stomach and pushed himself up, his Bowie knife and his hat a few feet away, his mangled, misshapen features exposed.

Someone screamed, and it took a second for Cobb to realize that it was coming from the open window he had just fallen out of. He turned his face up towards it, just in time to see Baker's broken body flop out. It landed alongside him, and Cobb saw the empty eyes that stared back at him, Baker's face streaked with blood. His head had been twisted almost completely around, the neck destroyed. A quick glance revealed that the arms had been similarly ruined, Baker's hands turned backwards at the ends of his arms. There was no doubt what order the injuries came in. Fletcher did the arms first. He hurt Baker before he killed him.

Cobb would waste no tears for the assassin, and no sooner had he managed to clamber to his feet than Fletcher came out onto the street. Cobb heard him bellow a challenge, and he turned towards him in time see him barreling forward like an enraged bull. Cobb took the full force of the charge, Fletcher's shoulder in his stomach. The onslaught launched Cobb through the air, and he hit the pavement a second time like a sack of wet cement. His head smacked the black surface with a disgusting slap.

Someone from the group of shocked onlookers tried to stop Fletcher, but he grabbed this man by the head and smashed it down onto the sidewalk to crush his skull like a grape. The would-be hero's body flailed once in its death-throes and then went still while Fletcher turned his attention back to Cobb.

"Come on, Cobb," shouted Fletcher, his voice like a thunderclap. "Get on your feet and fight me."

Cobb pushed himself up, his mouth and nose wet with blood, and looked at Fletcher, finally seeing the huge man's face. Fletcher was ugly, with chubby cheeks and a turned up nose, almost like a snout. His beady eyes looked black from Cobb's distance.

"Who the hell are you?" Cobb demanded. Fletcher snorted, a peculiar sound.

"I am the first," he barked, angrily. "Most honored of the Great Pig, and though you have imprisoned his body his spirit can never die."

Suddenly Cobb understood. Yulgo Kharan had his acolytes, brainwashed humans whose minds would gradually return to their proper state once Kharan went dormant, but this Fletcher person was something else. Cobb wasn't sure how, but it seemed that Kharan had somehow managed to give him power, probably physically warping him in addition to working on his mind. That explained Fletcher's vaguely porcine features, not to mention his great strength. Kharan had imparted some of its own qualities to its servant, and in the process had made its mind control permanent.

That's why Fletcher had arranged the car bombing. It was revenge. Obviously he didn't know enough about Cobb's condition to know that blowing him up wouldn't kill him, but that wasn't a shock. Few people knew much about him at all.

"I don't know how you survived Baker's bomb," said Fletcher as he stalked towards Cobb, his head low, "but it doesn't matter. Killing you with my own hands will be better."

"Come on," dared Cobb. He was in a great deal of pain, but he didn't care. Yulgo Kharan had fallen, so would this idiot. Fletcher had caught him by surprise before, it wouldn't happen again. "Come get me."

Fletcher roared and came at him, but was immediately stopped by the blasting of Cobb's Schofields, plucked lightning-fast from his hip holsters. Fletcher staggered back as Cobb pummeled him, the bullets tearing great holes in his torso. Looking almost peaceful Cobb emptied his revolvers into Fletcher, the most favored of Yulgo Kharan.

As soon as the guns started firing the onlookers broke and ran, leaving Cobb and Fletcher relatively alone.

The shooting stopped and Fletcher wavered, but he did not fall. His shirt was sticky with his blood but he still moved forward, his close-set eyes locked on Cobb. Cobb, in the meantime, lowered his pistols, tall and straight on the street.

"Had enough?" He asked as Fletcher shambled. "Maybe you should just lie down and die."

"My god is my strength," muttered Fletcher. "Through his power the world shall be cleansed, and all will bow low before him. He is the ancient and unchallenged."

With a sigh, Cobb holstered one of his pistols and reloaded the other. He did this without urgency. Fletcher wasn't hurrying. Then he clapped the revolver shut, pointed it, and fired. The bullet went through Fletcher's left eye and exploded out of the back of his skull. Yulgo Kharan's favorite servant stiffened before he toppled like a felled tree onto the pavement to lay there, motionless.

Cobb looked away from Fletcher's body and reclaimed his hat and Bowie knife. He was still in pain, but he was getting better. He'd have to clean the grit and detritus from his naked tissues, but by morning he'd be fine.

Cobb couldn't help but feel a twinge of sympathy for Fletcher. He had probably been a normal man until coming across Yulgo Kharan, who had infected him with its essence and turned him into a loyal juggernaut. Cobb wondered if Fletcher had a family, and if they were still alive or if a willing supplicant had offered them up as sacrifices. The forces of the unknown had raped Fletcher, just as they had raped Cobb, and there was nothing that could be done about it. One could merely roll with the punches as they came.

The sound of approaching sirens hit Cobb's ears and he realized that he was still out in the open, several bystanders back from their hiding places now that the shooting had stopped. Wasting no more time Cobb ran off and disappeared down an alleyway just as the police arrived.

Two police cars rolled onto the street, the officers inside expecting to find a pair of men engaged in a brawl, one of them apparently armed. What they got, however, was a bizarre description from a half dozen witnesses of a severely burned man in a long coat and a victim of multiple gunshot wounds which, as one of the officers noted with disbelief, was still alive.

CHAPTER 13

▼

Cobb staggered down the street wildly while he tried to ignore the fact that his left leg was being extremely uncooperative. The drop onto the street had damaged more than just a few things but he knew he had to keep moving. If he didn't get away from the immediate area the police would be all over and he didn't want to spend the rest of the day back at the police station trying to explain his guns or his appearance. That was just a pain he could easily do without.

The street he was on had a few people walking by, some stared at him openly while some others tried to do it with a bit more subtlety. He grew conscious of his strange appearance and damned both Fletcher and Baker for causing him all this annoyance with their stupid bomb. He had to get out of the open, he decided, and lumbered towards the building on his right, into the church that seemed to loom over him as he threw open its huge double doors and let in the light of day.

The doors slammed shut behind Cobb and he felt the comfort of isolation press upon him. He seemed to be alone. His boot heels clicked against the tiled floor as he walked further into the church, the sound loud and intrusive in the solemn silence. Out of some half-remembered sense of ceremony Cobb removed his hat and held it in front of him in a gesture of respect. The pews were thankfully all empty and with slow steps he walked to the altar, his eyes on the huge statue of Christ that hung on its cross. With a flat, emotionless expression Cobb stared at the statue. Candles burned beneath it, bathed the area in soft yellow light.

Carved of wood, the statue was painted all of the necessary colors, Jesus crowned with thorns and looking to His right. Faint spots of blood were visible on the forehead and the eyes were half-open to suggest benevolence. Cobb just looked up at it, strangely apathetic. Once in his life he had been a loyal follower of this figure, a frequent visitor to places such as this, in a time that was far more simple and innocent. Once a church would have been a sanctuary and a place of hope to him, but not anymore. Now it was just a place to hide from the eyes of the regular folk, a place to stay while the police searched outside.

"Can I help you, my son?"

Cobb spun to his right, a hand going to one of his Schofields, but he relaxed once he saw that the speaker was a simple priest, barely visible in the dark doorway to the rectory. Quickly Cobb pulled his coat over the pistol, but he knew the priest had seen it. The priest, however, seemed more interested in Cobb's face, and he stepped forward without fear, squinting, apparently uncertain if he was seeing properly.

For a moment the two men appraised each other. Cobb was covered in dust, fragments of glass, and blood, while the priest was dressed in his simple uniform, all black with a square of white visible at the collar. He was an older man, probably in his fifties, with white hair and spectacles, a Bible clutched in one hand.

"God have mercy," whispered the priest in response to Cobb's features. "What happened to you?"

His eyes bulging, Cobb shrugged. "Fell down some stairs, father," he said. The priest frowned, and Cobb turned towards the door. "I'll be on my way."

"One moment," said the priest. He moved closer with one hand held out. "You look like you need some help."

Cobb shook his head and a quiet chuckle escaped his wet lips. "None that you can give me, priest," he said, his voice low. "Don't worry about me."

"Please, sit a moment, catch your breath."

For a moment Cobb was going to just leave, but he looked at the priest and realized exactly how tired he was. It wasn't physical, more mental, and besides he needed a few minutes to recover from the beating that Fletcher had dished out to him. So he dropped onto the nearest pew, his hands on his thighs and rested his hat alongside him.

The priest walked towards him. "What on earth did this to you?" He asked, after a moment.

"An accident," he said. "Don't worry, I'll be better in a couple of days."

"I doubt that," replied the priest, slowly. "Such injuries are usually permanent, aren't they?"

Cobb smiled. "Usually," he said. "But not for me. I heal pretty fast."

There was a pause. "My name is McAllen," the priest said. "Father McAllen."

"Sebastian Cobb."

The priest smiled and reached out a hand. Cobb looked at it for a moment, and then shook it. "Nice to meet you, Sebastian," said Father McAllen. He sat down a foot or so from Cobb, still smiling, and Cobb started to relax, his natural distrust for people starting to wear away. The priest seemed friendly enough, and he certainly didn't seem to mind that Cobb was in his church.

"Tell me about yourself," said McAllen. Cobb shrugged and took in a breath.

"Not much to say," he replied, understating himself immensely. The priest was dubious, however, and just stared at him. Cobb felt a little uncomfortable under that gaze, old habits crawling back up from under the weight of time. He remembered the minister of his province, a man named Perkins. He had been a friend of Cobb's once, but he had a stare that could shrivel a doorknob. "I'm from a few miles outside of the city," he said, keeping his answer as general as possible. "How about you?"

"Born in Boston," said the priest. "Stayed there until I was ordained, got sent here."

The priest shifted slightly. "Are you a Christian, Sebastian?"

Cobb looked up at the statue again, his eyes wide. "I used to be," he said. "A long time ago. Why do you ask?"

Father McAllen shook his head. "Just wondered," he answered. "Something made you come through those doors."

"I don't think you'd like the real reason if I told you," said Cobb, quietly. "A long time ago I used to believe in God."

"And now?"

Cobb's expression was cold as he turned and looked at the priest. "Now I believe in the devil."

"But not God?"

"Never met Him."

The priest remained composed. "You might have," he offered, "more times than you think."

Cobb shrugged. "If I have," he said, "then I feel sorry for you, because He's a lot different than you think."

This time the priest laughed. "I'm willing to admit to that possibility," he said, looking up at the statue of Christ. "But what's important is to remember that Christ died for us, He gave His life so that His followers can inherit the kingdom of God. I think that's pretty special, don't you?"

"I suppose," replied Cobb as he moved his eyes to the floor. "But sometimes truth is more important than sacrifice."

McAllen looked at Cobb, his eyes hard. "You're running from something, aren't you, Sebastian?"

"The gun help you figure that out?"

With a slight nod, the priest smiled. "A bit, but I think it's your attitude that really tipped me off. What are you running from?"

"Right now, or in general?"

Glancing back over his shoulder at the doors, McAllen thought before answering. "Either one," he said, eventually.

"Time," Cobb answered, choosing the latter option.

"Time?"

"Time."

Both men were silent for a moment. The priest waited for Cobb to continue, perhaps to even clarify, but he said nothing. "Care to explain?" McAllen asked.

"No," said Cobb, flatly.

"So what are you running from right now?"

Cobb slumped down. "The police," he said. "They're outside, looking for me. I killed a man in the street a block from here."

The honesty of the answer was a surprise to the priest, even more than the actual answer. "Why did you do it?" He asked.

Cobb chuckled. "Is this confession?"

"It might be."

"All right then, I killed him because he was the unclean servant of a heathen god," said Cobb, a bit mockingly. "Does that make it all right?"

"Not really, no," said McAllen. "And I doubt that's why you did it."

"Well, it's part of the reason. Mostly I killed him because he needed it, but I guess you could say it was self-defense."

"Did he do this to you?" McAllen indicated Cobb's face. Cobb nodded. "Then I understand why you did it, but it was still the wrong thing to do."

"It wasn't the wrong thing to do," said Cobb, a bit irritated, "and you don't understand why I did it. There's things in this world that you wouldn't believe, priest, evil that's worse than anything you've read about in that book in your hand. Your devil is a piker compared to some of the things I've seen."

"Evil comes in many forms," McAllen replied. "The Bible warns us of that. Trust in God, my son, and everything will be fine."

That statement sent a quiver of anger up Cobb's spine, the ignorance of the priest to his situation wearing on him. He got to his feet and slapped his hat back on while the priest also stood. "You're a fool, priest," he said. "Hide in this hole for the rest of your life, read from that book and be comforted, but remember that you're still going to die and the things that I know exist will be there waiting for you. If you can avoid them fine, but don't think that you're going to stand a chance at being saved. If salvation exists it isn't for people who really need it."

Cobb turned and started for the doors. McAllen followed, one hand out. "Wait," he called. Cobb paused, but did not turn. "Don't go yet. I know there're things you don't want to hear, Sebastian, but don't turn your back on God. Turn your back on me, fine, but not on God. He loves you, Sebastian, even if you don't."

Slowly, Cobb turned and looked at McAllen. His eyes were narrow, his raw lips pressed tightly together. "You sure of that?" He asked.

McAllen nodded. "Listen," he said, "if you need a place to stay for a little while I have a cot set up in the storeroom, I use it sometimes for naps in the afternoon. You know. If the police are looking for you."

"Shouldn't you turn me in?" Cobb asked, dubious.

The priest shrugged. "Maybe," he answered, his Bible held out before him, "but I think that somehow that wouldn't do you or the police any good. Rest here if you like, I'll get you some food."

The priest hesitated a moment, as if to make sure that Cobb wasn't going to run out the door as soon as he left, and then went back towards the rectory. Alone, Cobb laughed softly and looked first at the floor and then at the statue of Christ.

He couldn't shake the feeling that the statue was laughing at him.

CHAPTER 14

▼

"Here he is, detective."

Doctor Carlsbad turned up from his patient and saw LeGrasse nod a thank you to the nurse as he entered Fletcher's room. The huge bandaged body on the bed was immobile while LeGrasse looked around at the white-walled hospital room.

Carlsbad smiled to the detective, who stared at the spots of dark red visible through Fletcher's cloth wrapping. Carlsbad followed his gaze and saw Fletcher's huge chest slowly rise and fall, the sound of his breathing loud in the quiet room. The top half of his head was wrapped in bandages, a large wad of folded gauze over his eye.

There was no way that this man could be alive. Carlsbad knew that, and so did the detective. Identified by his driver's license as Jeremy Fletcher, he had thirteen bullet wounds through his lungs and stomach and that included one very large hole drilled through his eye and out the back of his head. He had to be one tough bastard to live through all of that.

Judging by his size, thought Carlsbad, he probably *was* one tough bastard. About a dozen people had seen him brawling on the street with another man, a fight that had eventually come to shooting. Fletcher was comatose, about as close to death as he could be.

The funny thing was that the driver's license listed Fletcher as being 5'8" and 157 pounds, but the man in the bed was much, much larger than that. Maybe the license was stolen, Carlsbad mused, and the man in the bed was not Jeremy Fletcher.

LeGrasse cleared his throat and the doctor looked at him. "I'm Dr. Carlsbad," he said. "Are you working with Mr. Greene?"

LeGrasse shook his head. "No," he said. "Detective Greene is from a different precinct. I'm here because the man who shot Fletcher here might be a suspect in one of my cases. Greene was here?"

Carlsbad nodded. "About an hour ago. Like I told him, though, I hope you're not hoping to talk to Mr. Fletcher, because I don't think he's going to make it through the night."

LeGrasse looked back at the body on the bed. "I'm surprised he's alive at all," he said. "He's taken some serious heat."

"People have been talking," said Carlsbad. "It's rather impressive."

"Any idea why?"

Carlsbad shrugged. "Could be a mixture of things," he replied. "Mr. Fletcher's a big boy, his muscle mass is almost ridiculous, I'm sure that has something to do with it. The human body's a strange thing on any day of the week, detective. Some people just live through things."

With a nod LeGrasse thrust his hands in his pockets. "Thanks, doc," he said, and he walked out of the room, back into the hallway. Carlsbad shook his head at the policeman's abrupt departure, and then went back to his work.

Moving with practiced ease, Carlsbad made sure that everything was as it should have been for Fletcher. His explanation to LeGrasse had been the best he could come up with for Fletcher's living through injuries that should have killed him, and in his mind it was probably the closest thing to the truth. Some people lived through injuries like Fletcher's, others died from much, much less. It was just the way of things.

A bit of movement caught Carlsbad's eye, and the doctor realized that Fletcher's left hand had twitched. He frowned and checked Fletcher's pulse, one of his eyebrows rising when he felt the strength of it. Was it possible, he wondered, that Fletcher would wake up? As unlikely as it was it was certainly possible in the grand scheme of things, but still unlikely. No, thought Carlsbad, it was more likely just a muscle spasm, even if the pulse was strong. Few people lived long after being shot in the head with a .45 caliber bullet.

Carlsbad turned, his intent on walking out of the room, when the dying man on the bad made a noise.

"Hu…"

The doctor froze, his breath seizing in his chest. After a moment he turned around, looked down at the huge man, his eyes going first to the bloody bandages and then to his gaping mouth.

"Hun…" the dying man grunted. Carlsbad took a cautious step forward.

"Mr. Fletcher?" He asked, unable to believe that he could be awake. The damage to his brain should have been enough to keep him from ever waking up, much less talking. Combined with the damage to his other organs it just wasn't possible. "Mr. Fletcher? Can you hear me?"

Fletcher's eye opened. Carlsbad flinched as it moved from side to side, looking about quickly, the owner trying obviously to figure out where he was. Sweat dripped from Carlsbad's forehead and he reached up to wipe it before he walked over to stand where Fletcher could see him. The eye locked onto him as soon as he came into view. "Mr. Fletcher," said the doctor, "I'm Dr. Gordon Carlsbad. Can you understand what I'm saying?"

Fletcher nodded slightly while his tongue worked strangely over his bottom lip. "Good. You're at Mercy General hospital, do you know where that is?"

Again Fletcher nodded, breathing quickly. He tried lifting his head and one giant hand reached towards the bandage on his eye. Carlsbad stopped him gently. "No, you don't want to touch that," he said calmly, oblivious to the glare of Fletcher's intact eye. "Your eye has been destroyed, Mr. Fletcher. I'm sorry, but it's gone."

Fletcher's eye closed and he looked as if he were about to cry, a strange expression on the man's face. Carlsbad tried to console him. "You're very lucky to be alive, Mr. Fletcher," he said. "By all rights you should have died. Try to take comfort in the fact that you didn't."

"Cobb," whispered Fletcher, getting his voice back. The word meant nothing to the doctor.

"I'm sorry, what did you say?"

"Cobb," Fletcher repeated, clearly going through a great deal of effort to get the word out. "Where is Cobb?"

Carlsbad shook his head. "I don't even know who he is," he said. "Try not to talk, you're still very weak."

"My god is my strength," Fletcher muttered, the doctor thinking that he meant the Christian God. He smiled, pleased that Fletcher was taking comfort in his beliefs.

"Is there something I can get you?" He asked. "Something that you need? Some water, perhaps?"

"Food," said Fletcher. His eye turned up towards the doctor. "Get me food."

"Certainly," said the doctor. "I'll have something sent up right away."

As he turned towards the door Fletcher leapt up from the bed, and grabbed him with his massive hands tightly about the shoulders. Carlsbad let out a strangled yelp as Fletcher threw him onto the bed, his teeth bared, staring with his one good eye like a hideous demon.

"Get off of me," Carlsbad shouted, but Fletcher clapped one hand over the doctor's mouth to stifle his cries. While Carlsbad struggled in a futile attempt to escape, Fletcher yanked the fountain pen from the doctor's coat pocket and stabbed him with it, drove the metal point into Carlsbad's chest. The doctor screamed beneath the hand as he felt the pen pierce his breastbone and then withdraw, only to come slamming down a second time. Again and again Fletcher stabbed him with the pen while blood sprayed from the shallow holes it made. Finally Carlsbad's strength left him and he went silent in a shocked stupor on the bed, soaked in red.

Fletcher muttered something but Carlsbad was too out of it to hear. He could dimly see the giant standing over him, could almost hear the soft grunting of his breath. Why wasn't anyone helping him? There had been some talk of putting policemen outside of the room, but Carlsbad had convinced them that Fletcher wasn't going to be any trouble since he was comatose. There were no guards.

"…luck, doctor."

Carlsbad tried to focus, tried to listen to Fletcher's guttural voice. He couldn't do it, though. He was too hurt. When Fletcher spoke again he only caught a word here and there.

"…Kharan…" Fletcher said. Carlsbad assumed he heard the word wrong. "Few…meal…chosen…"

Suddenly Fletcher's meaty hand closed over Carlsbad's mouth again, the doctor too stunned to care. What he did care about, though, was the fact that a moment later he felt Fletcher's teeth sink into his arm. Even through the shock he felt the pain of his flesh tearing, and he tried screaming, but his jaw locked and Fletcher's hand kept it in place. His weak attempts to break free were pointless and futile. Fletcher just kept ripping into him with gargantuan bites to the forearm.

It was a mercy when Carlsbad went under. He stopped feeling any pain, drifted away on black waves into nothingness. He died there on the hospital bed, food for the servant of a god he'd never even heard of.

CHAPTER 15

▼

The moon burned brightly overhead, a titanic silver sliver hanging in the black sky, as a carriage rolled up to the front of a large, white-walled manor, the care-free sounds of music and laughter seeping out from within. Giant willows rose up out of the ground around the manor, their low tresses muffled the noise a bit and shook almost in appreciation.

Before the carriage pulled to a halt, the side door opened and Sebastian Cobb jumped out onto the cobblestones, a smile on his lips as he looked up at the house. He wore his finest suit—a matched set of black trousers and stockings, a blue waistcoat, white shirt, and black coat. His hat held in one hand, his thick, curly brown hair exposed.

After a huge breath of air he smiled, exhaling as the carriage stopped and the other passenger disembarked. She turned towards him and he walked over to her.

"Really Sebastian," said Mary, her long brown hair in delicate curls around her face, "you can be so foolish sometimes."

"Nonsense, dear," said Sebastian as he put his arm around her waist and leaned in close. She smelled like lilacs. "All in good fun."

"There'll be plenty of that inside," Mary chided, and she straightened the folds of her white dress. "So wait for it."

She broke free from him and headed up the steps to the front of the house, the open door letting out a swatch of yellow light. In the light she looked back at him and, with a slow, deliberate movement, reached up to blow him a kiss. Sebastian laughed and started towards her, only to pause a moment at the sound of a strange scraping coming from the road. He turned and saw a tall man dressed as a laborer, digging into the road with a shovel.

For a moment Sebastian stared. There was something strange about the man he was looking at. It was as if he didn't belong somehow, as if Sebastian was remembering something that he couldn't quite understand, and that this man did not belong where he was standing. The cobblestones had been pulled up and the laborer's spade jabbed into the soft earth beneath with regular, hypnotic motions.

Sebastian opened his mouth to speak, but then remembered his wife. He pushed the improbable thought that he knew the laborer from his mind and bounded after her, the heels of his shoes clomping against the wooden steps.

"Good evening, sir," said a butler, meeting the couple as soon as they entered the doorway. "And you are?"

"Sebastian and Mary Cobb," said Sebastian. He reached into his coat and pulled out their invitations. He shifted, noting that the tear in the shoulder of his coat was showing a bit. Mary's impromptu sewing from only an hour before hadn't completely covered it up. He turned as he handed the butler his invitation, trying to prevent the servant from seeing it.

"Very good, sir," said the butler, after examining the invitation for a moment. The couple nodded past and entered the party. The house was huge, much bigger than theirs, filled with beautiful furnishings and lit by colossal candelabras that burned all around. A magnificent chandelier hung overhead, completing the scene. Elegantly dressed men and women mingled back and forth, and servants moved between them with platters of wine and food.

As they stepped into the hall, a pair of young women in blue dresses descended upon Mary, laughing as they pulled her away from her husband. Sebastian watched her go off, knowing that the Martin sisters were old friends of Mary and that she would undoubtedly spend the next half hour listening to them giggle and gibber.

"Sebastian!"

On his left, Sebastian saw a man in a black and red suit walk up. A powdered wig was perched perfectly on his head and a group of hangers-on followed him. They looked Sebastian over with condescending eyes but he paid them no mind and instead focused on the man who knew him.

"Good to see you, Henry," he said, grasping the man's hand tightly. "Thank you for the invitation."

"Nonsense," said Henry, and he clapped a welcoming hand on Sebastian's shoulder. "It's not a party without my oldest and dearest friend and his lovely wife."

Sebastian nodded, a bit embarrassed by the statement. "Thank you," he repeated. The hangers-on smiled and nodded to Sebastian, apparently deciding that it was all right now that the man had been identified.

Sebastian continued to ignore them. Henry Wagner was a good man, and he and Sebastian had been friends since childhood, but sometimes his choice of guests left something to be desired. Of course, that was the price one paid for wealth, Sebastian decided. That was something he didn't have to worry about.

"Come on," said Henry as he pulled Sebastian to his side, "there are some people I'd like you to meet."

The "people" turned out to be a small group of three dour-faced men, all dressed conservatively, who were sitting in large chairs on one side of the hall with snifters of brandy in their hands. The men looked up at Sebastian and Henry, nodding as the two approached. Introductions were quick, with the three men being identified as Edward Thompson, Benjamin Fisk, and Robert Urich. According to Henry, they were all newly arrived businessmen from Pennsylvania.

"Gentlemen," said Henry, his arm still around Sebastian's shoulder, "this is Sebastian Cobb, himself a gentleman, and someone who once saved my life."

"Henry," said Sebastian, quietly. Henry ignored him.

"That's right," he continued, "this man saved my life. It was during the war. Those redcoats put up one hell of a fight at Yorktown, but General Washington was in the front, pulling us behind him. I was shot in the first charge, but Sebastian here pulled me to safety. The field surgeon was able to clean my wound pretty well, but I probably would have been killed if not for this man."

Sebastian blushed a bit. He spoke in a hushed voice, his embarrassment growing. "That's not how it happened, Henry, and you know it. I was wounded too."

"So what?" Henry asked with a laugh. "What's the point of remembering something if I can't change it a little?" He looked seriously at Sebastian, his eyes hard. "I mean it, Sebastian, you saved my life, and I'm never going to forget it."

The businessmen called Urich cleared his throat and Henry looked at him. "Forgive me, gentlemen," he said, his smile returning. "A bit too much wine and suddenly I'm as solemn as a schoolmaster." He looked again to Sebastian. "I wanted you to meet these men because they have come to me with a business proposition. I wanted you to be a part of it."

Sebastian shook his head. "I don't know, Henry," he said as he bit his lower lip. "Mary and I have Elizabeth to look after, we don't have a lot of money as it is."

"I know. That's why I want you to be a part of this. You'll make quite a bit, you won't have to worry anymore."

"If I may," said Urich, his voice deep and well formed. "We are putting together a trip, Mr. Cobb, an expedition, if you will."

"An expedition? To where?"

"Africa," said the second man, the one called Fisk. "We plan to head into the central part of Africa."

"Why?"

Henry laughed. "Think about it," he said. "There are whole parts of that continent that haven't been mapped out, whole areas ripe for exploration. Think of what we could find there, think of what treasures we could bring back."

Sebastian thought for a moment. "How much do you need?" He said.

"I'm putting up ten thousand dollars," said Henry. "But I wouldn't expect you to have that much available. Maybe a thousand?"

With an apologetic smile Sebastian shook his head. "I can't," he said, politely. "Mary would never forgive me. I'm sorry."

"Now wait a moment," said Henry, walking over to stand beside the three men. "You haven't heard everything. Robert here is a qualified explorer, formerly of the English army, and he's going to be leading the expedition. He's got a group of men that he chose himself, all able-bodied and well trained. Men of science, as well as action."

Sebastian shrugged and scratched the back of his neck. Henry was pressing the point and he was becoming increasingly uncomfortable. "I'm sorry Henry," he said, "and I mean no disrespect to you, Mr. Urich, but I can't. I really can't afford it."

"Fine," said Henry, flatly. "Forget I ever brought it up."

Sebastian could see the disappointment in his friend's face, and the sight of it hurt him deeply. "Please, Henry, don't be angry about it. You know I have a child now, I can't take foolish risks."

"It's all right," said Henry, but clearly it wasn't. "If you don't mind, I've got business to discuss. Enjoy the party."

It was clear that Henry wasn't willing to discuss the situation any further, so Sebastian walked away and began to move into the crowd. After a few steps, he felt a strange tingling awareness that began in the back of his neck. He turned, looked through the crowd of people, and saw that Henry and his three companions were staring at him wide-eyed, motionless as statues.

"This isn't right," he whispered to himself. "This isn't what happened."

He started to turn back towards the four men but was suddenly stopped by a cold hand that wrapped tightly around his wrist. The owner, he saw, was a beautiful, red-haired woman standing alongside him, dressed in a rich gown of green and black. She looked up at him with dark, luxurious eyes, her full red lips pulled back in a wicked grin. Beautiful as she was, her breath reeked of the stench of an open grave.

"Dance with me," she commanded, and pulled him into the crowd, the music growing louder. Sebastian struggled against her, but she was too strong. She yanked his body backwards and forwards in a sadistic mockery of a dance. Sebastian tried to focus on Henry and his friends.

"This isn't what happened," he told himself again, dimly aware that something was very, very wrong. He remembered what was supposed to be happening, already knew what should have come next. Henry should follow him after his refusal, trying to convince him, until it was he who grew angry. Sebastian would then collect Mary and the two of them would leave while Henry called anxiously after them.

It was just as well too. The expedition was going to be an utter failure. The whole team was going to disappear into the African wilderness and never came back. Inquiries will be made, but no one will ever find a real answer. Some will say that the natives had taken them, others that the French did it, but no one will ever found out. Henry was going to lose all of his investment, as well as a great deal of his pride, in that venture. Sebastian would lose a lot more if he committed.

The red-haired woman yanked Sebastian hard to his left, and he ignored her as he wondered why he knew what was going to happen. How could he know that the expedition was a failure? And who was this woman that was throwing him around like a rag doll? She seemed familiar, but he couldn't place her face. There was a wanton quality to her that Sebastian found attractive in a vulgar way, but he was devoted to his wife, he would never consider dishonoring her. He certainly didn't want this woman abusing him so. Where was Mary? Shouldn't he have gone after her by now? Why wasn't Henry badgering him?

"Look at me," the red-haired woman whispered as she pulled Sebastian closer. She placed his hands forcefully onto her hips while her lips brushed the side of his face. Sebastian could smell her hair and the perfume she was wearing. It was some flowery odor that almost masked the distracting smell of her corpse-like exhalation. No one else was dancing like this, Sebastian thought to himself looking around, yet no one saw the impropriety with which this woman was behaving. Surely Henry hadn't invited her. This woman's manners were more fitting to a prostitute than a gentlewoman.

Her hands came up and grabbed Sebastian by the sides of his face and he shuddered at the cold touch of her flesh. He wanted to run but found that he couldn't. He just kept staring at her eyes, kept feeling the coldness of her on him. The room around was spinning, as though the pair of them were standing in place while the whole world went mad around them. He felt dizzy, felt like he wanted to vomit. His guts heaved within his torso and he pulled himself away, thrust out a hand to throw the woman off him. She laughed and disappeared into the crowd as the world stopped.

And he was back at the party. He stood in the crowd of dancers, bent over at the waist. Sweat trickled off his forehead and he choked for breath as though he had just run from one end of the city to the other.

"Is something the matter?"

The man who spoke was a short, blue-coated man with black hair. A woman stood at his side and they both stared at Sebastian with concern. Sebastian straightened, his vertigo fading, and grabbed the man by the collar.

"What year is it?" He demanded. A few nearby people noted his roughness. "The day, year?"

"Unhand me, sir," the short man began, but Sebastian ignored him.

"What year is it?" He almost shouted.

"1785," the short man in the blue coat answered. "May the 13th, 1785."

Sebastian released the man and staggered away like a drunkard. "That's not right," he muttered as he wiped sweat from his pale face. "That's not right. This already happened, this is finished, I've already done all of this."

"Dance with me, lover," said the red-haired woman, reappearing out of the crowd like a second thought. She drifted towards Sebastian, arms outstretched. Her dark eyes gleamed. "Dance with me."

The sight of the woman brought a cry from Sebastian, and he staggered backwards to crash into a tall, thin man. "Mary!" He cried and turned away from the red-haired demon. "Mary!"

"I'm here, Sebastian," said Mary, her voice coming from right in front of him. He blinked and saw her in her white gown, only inches away.

"Mary we need to go," said Sebastian. He looked around frantically for any sign of the red-haired woman but saw nothing. "We have to go home."

"Is something wrong, dear?" Mary asked as she reached up to smooth her husband's hair. Sebastian's eyes widened and he was suddenly aware that he hadn't seen her in a long, long time.

"Mary," he whispered. He put a hand to the side of her face. "Oh God, Mary." He kissed her firmly, surprising her slightly. "Mary, I've missed you so much."

With that he swept her up in his arms, pressed her body tightly against his. He couldn't quite remember, but he was certain that he hadn't seen her in more than a lifetime. How long had it been, ten or twenty minutes? A decade? He couldn't be sure, but he knew it was longer than that. For some reason he felt like he'd been away from her for longer than anyone should have to endure.

"I love you, Mary," he said, putting her back on the ground. She smiled at him as he kissed her again and pulled back to look at her with childlike wonder. He had forgotten how perfect she was, how beautiful. He remembered the first time he met her. Her family had lived on a farm; Sebastian had gone there with his father to deliver some flour and had been smitten with her from the first moment he laid eyes on her. "I love you so much."

"I love you too, Sebastian," replied Mary, bewildered, as if she couldn't understand why her husband was behaving in such a strange way. She kissed the side of his face, her hair falling to one side. Sebastian eyes welled with tears and he felt as if his heart was going to burst with the joy he was feeling.

Then the woman with red hair reappeared.

She came out of the crowd behind Mary, grabbed her by the shoulder and the hair, and yanked her head to one side. Sebastian felt his limbs go limp, all feeling leaving him as the red-haired woman laughed, her eyes catlike and crimson.

"Wonderful," said the red-haired woman, and then she turned her face towards Mary and ran her tongue up the length of his wife's neck. "Delicious."

"No," whispered Sebastian, unable to help his wife. He felt weak, useless. "Stay away from her."

She pulled back her perfect lips to reveal a pair of long, wicked canines that sank into Mary's soft flesh and punctured her jugular. Mary screamed and her husband matched her cry.

On his cot at the church, Cobb cried out and flailed madly as he jerked from sleep. He flopped onto the wooden floor of the storeroom, the hard slap waking him fully.

For a moment he laid there while his mind returned to him. Memory came back like a splash of icy water.

It was August 12th, 1934. Mary had been gone for almost 150 years and he was a monster.

On the stark, wooden floor, with a rare feeling of vulnerability upon him, the monster began to weep silently. The sight of his wife's perfect face was still framed in his mind. In all of the decades since she died, he had never thought of her so clearly as he had just dreamt, had never seen her in such a height of her happiness. The pain of being jerked from so pleasant a memory was like a cold spike of steel in his heart, and the last image of her being victimized only added to his misery. Why had he dreamt that?

The visions started to cloud over as his dreams often did. He was beginning to forget. But he didn't want to forget, at least not everything. The dream had been so real. Even seeing Henry's face had been welcome. There were times when he missed Henry almost as much as his family.

He only wished it had been real, and that all the madness and the horror and the death that had followed was the dream. Why did he have to wake up? Why did it have to be a dream? Wasn't there any way to go back, to keep the nightmare from ever beginning?

CHAPTER 16

▼

Cobb didn't have much motivation that day. The memory of his dream came back every few minutes and sent him into an episode of lethargy that took several more minutes to climb out of. He spent a great deal of time sitting on the edge of his cot with his head in his hands, trying to forget. It bothered him that he hadn't remembered his wife clearly until the dream. Her face had been brand new to him, as if he had been seeing her for the first time. The argument might be made that a memory fading was natural, especially to someone who had lived almost two hundred years, but Cobb still felt like a heel for it.

Father McAllen showed up at around 10 in the morning with a breakfast tray in his hands. Cobb had already started in on the whiskey, sitting with his back against the wall. He hoped it would help him to forget what he had seen, or at least why what he had seen bothered him so much.

"You shouldn't be drinking that this early," said McAllen as he set the tray on the end of the cot. When he had entered, there had been a moment of unease when he saw Cobb's mangled face. "It's not good for you."

"I'll be fine," Cobb replied.

"I suppose," McAllen shrugged. There was a folding chair set against the brown brick wall, and McAllen set it up in front of Cobb and sat down, looking over at Cobb's open trunk. The trunk had been retrieved from his car during the night, Cobb felt better having it close.

The priest's eyes wandered over the weapons and odd trinkets sitting in plain sight, and for a moment Cobb thought about kicking it shut, but then he decided that there was little point. The priest had already seen what was inside.

"You need all of those?" McAllen asked.

"Most of the time."

"There's a lot there."

Cobb looked over at the trunk. His Schofields gleamed on top, wooden grips poking from the holsters. "I suppose," he said, and then he was silent.

A smirk appeared on the priest's face. "You ever read the Bible?" He asked. Cobb shook his head.

"Not for a long time," he said as he took another pull off his whiskey.

"There's a passage in the Book of Revelations that you just reminded me of. It talks about Death riding a pale horse."

"I don't own a horse."

"No, probably not. I'll bet the rest applies, though."

Cobb wasn't interested in that line of conversation, and he made it clear by saying nothing.

McAllen coughed once. "So, what's bothering you today?"

"What?"

"You're not very hard to read, Sebastian," McAllen said. There wasn't any sarcasm or mockery in his voice. "You have too much honesty in you."

That almost struck Cobb as funny, since most of the time he used fake names and stole money from people he killed. "I had a dream," he said. Being elusive was too much effort, he decided.

"What kind of dream?" McAllen asked.

Cobb looked down at the tray of food the priest had brought him—two pieces of buttered toast and a fried egg. Cobb picked up a slice of toast and nibbled at the corner, more to be polite than from appetite. "I saw my wife."

McAllen's eyes widened. Cobb had told him nothing of his family. "Your wife? Is that a good thing?"

The silence that followed McAllen's question was barely broken by the sound of Cobb lifting the bottle to his lips. He took a long swallow while he stared straight ahead. McAllen just waited.

"I suppose it should be," said Cobb. "I suppose I should be happy that I saw my wife. I'm not."

"Where is she now?"

"Dead."

McAllen nodded, sympathy in his expression. "I'm sorry, my son," he said, and a slight twisting of his expression showed that he realized how hollow the words sounded. "What happened?"

Cobb closed his eyes. "She was murdered, along with my daughter."

If McAllen had any words for that, he kept them to himself. Another silence followed while McAllen clearly tried to figure out what to say. Cobb wished he would stay quiet.

"There doesn't seem to be any limit to the horror that men can visit on each other," the priest said, finally.

Cobb chuckled and McAllen looked at him, uncertain. "You're right about that," said Cobb as he shook his head. "Definitely right about that."

McAllen hesitated before speaking again. "How did it happen?" He asked. "If you don't mind me asking."

"I don't mind you asking, I just might not answer very well," said Cobb, ignoring the priest's look of confusion. "There were men in black robes," Cobb explained, "the kind of men that you warn people about on Sundays. They took my wife and daughter and they killed them."

"Why?"

Cobb shook his head. "I don't know," he said. "It was a ritual, I think, some kind of Black Mass. I don't remember what happened very well."

McAllen opened his mouth to speak but promptly closed it, confused. "You see why I believe in the Devil so much," said Cobb.

"I think I do," McAllen replied. A soft grunt popped from Cobb's throat. "It's a terrible thing to lose someone close to you," the priest went on. "A terrible thing, indeed."

The tone of the priest's voice caught Cobb's ear. He was talking from experience. "You know something about it?"

McAllen nodded. "I had a younger brother," he said, slowly. The fact that he used the word "had" was not lost on Cobb.

"What happened?"

"He was a stockbroker. When we were kids he would always run everywhere, just loved moving fast. Whenever we went to the swimming hole near our house, he would have to get there first. I was never much of an athlete. He always won. I used to love to hear him laugh, though. He laughed whenever he ran."

His voice grew distant and his eyes lost focus in the way that often happens when someone speaks of old memories. Cobb listened patiently while McAllen worked through them. "Dad was really proud of him when he made it to Wall Street," he said. "We all were. I knew our parents couldn't understand why I became a man of God, but they had always supported me. Jaime, though, was going to be somebody, and that was something we all got behind.

"For a while it looked like Jaime couldn't be stopped. He was buying and selling, doing everything that such people do. I never understood it. Jaime would get so worked up when he told me about it, but I never understood."

"Me either," said Cobb. McAllen glanced at him. "I knew someone in the market," he continued with a shrug.

"So you must know something about what happened in '29."

Cobb nodded. "It was terrible," said the priest. "Jaime told me that things couldn't be better. That was in October. He cashed in everything to take advantage of it. By the end of the month it all changed. I read in the newspapers how the market lost billions of dollars in one day, or some such nonsense. I never understood it. It just didn't seem possible."

McAllen removed his spectacles and wiped his eyes. "It was terrible," he repeated in a shaking voice. "Jaime lost it all. There were a few days where it looked like things might get better, but it was too late. He'd run too fast."

Cobb reached out and offered McAllen the bottle. The priest hesitated, and then he took it and lifted it to his lips. He only drank a little, though, before he went on.

"The last time I talked to Jaime he told me not to worry. He said he would be all right. I should have known better," he said, giving the bottle back. "I should have heard it in his voice. I should have listened to his voice, not his words."

There was no doubt in Cobb's mind where this was going. "His wife found him in their basement. He had tied one end of a rope to one of the beams in the ceiling," said the priest. The next words came slowly, McAllen nearly choking on each one. "He hanged himself from the other end."

Now it was Cobb's turn to be uncomfortable. He had suffered, yes, but at least he had been allowed the luxury of revenge, if even a small amount. He had killed the men that had victimized his family, and there was still the hope that he could find whatever had turned him into the creature he was, but McAllen didn't have that. McAllen couldn't blame anyone but his brother, unless he wanted to go after the New York Stock Exchange and everyone who contributed to the crash. In the end, though, it was Jaime's own impatience that had caused him to scramble after the brass ring too soon and McAllen had to know that.

"I performed his service," said McAllen, heedless of Cobb's thoughts. "I said words over my baby brother's coffin while my mother and father cried in the front row. I had to think about the Church's condemnation of suicide, about how I was supposed to think that he was burning in hell for what he had done. None of my friends, none of my priest friends, said anything about it, but I could tell they were thinking it."

"Must have been hard," said Cobb.

"Very," McAllen replied. "I like to think that he got away, though. I like to think that he ran all the way to Heaven. Jaime was a very good runner."

A small smile appeared on McAllen's face, and Cobb returned it. Again silence filled the room. Both men stared off into space, their minds lost in the past.

It was Cobb who broke the calm. "I was an only child," he said. "No brothers or sisters. My parents had a daughter, but she died of consumption before I was born."

"Were you lonely?"

Cobb shook his head. "No," he said. "My parents were always there for me. I had to help my father from the moment I could walk. My father was a hard worker."

McAllen took the second piece of toast and bit into it. He chewed for a moment, thoughtful. "Your mother?" He asked.

"A very hard worker," Cobb answered. "She made most of my clothes, kept the house clean, cooked our meals. She never complained, though. She and my father loved each other very much."

"That's good," said McAllen. "My father passed away about a year ago. He was never the same after Jaime died. I think it weakened him, to be honest. He was sick most of the time afterwards."

"You miss him?"

McAllen leaned back in his chair. "Of course," he replied, his voice quiet. "But I also think it was a mercy. Mother cared for him as best she could, but it wore her down. I helped as much as I could, of course, but she insisted I stay here in Manhattan. Wouldn't let me come back to be nearby. She's a proud lady, that's for certain."

Cobb's smile widened as he thought about his own mother. She had been a proud lady, too. There had been so much strength in her, more than enough to raise him and maintain their home. His father had always said that she was the stronger of the two of them.

"Tell me about your daughter," said McAllen, suddenly. Cobb looked at him. "I'm curious to hear about the child of this man who sits before me."

He started slowly. "Her name was Elizabeth," he said. "She was beautiful, just like her mother. She had long brown hair, just like her mother. Chestnut, I think it's called."

"Did she frown a lot?" McAllen asked. Cobb's brows crumpled together in confusion. "Her father does, I wonder if she took after him."

The joke finally registered and Cobb laughed, some of his black mood fading. "No," he said. "She didn't frown a lot. Neither did I back then. She was full of life, full of spirit. I saw a lot of my parents in her, a lot of my wife. She had the best of them in her."

"And the best of you, I'm sure," McAllen said. "I'm sorry about what happened to her."

"So am I."

"When was it?"

Cobb answered so fast he didn't have time to realize the effect his words might have. Both the alcohol and McAllen's innate affability had relaxed him. "1787," he said.

McAllen started. "What?" He asked, incredulous. Cobb grimaced.

"Forget it," he said. "It was a long time ago, let's just leave it at that."

McAllen seemed like he wanted to go further, but he changed his mind. "All right," he said, patiently. He looked back at the breakfast tray. The food was getting cold. "You're not going to eat any more of this, are you?"

Cobb shook his head and dropped his toast onto the tray. "No. Thanks, though," he said. "I guess I'm not hungry."

"I understand," McAllen replied, getting to his feet and picking up the tray. "I have some work to do," he said as he turned towards the door. "If you need anything, Sebastian, please ask."

"I will."

The priest walked towards the door and paused before passing through. "One more thing," he said, over his shoulder. "We are tested often in our lifetimes, Sebastian. Sometimes we win. Sometimes we lose. It's how we deal with both eventualities that determines our worth in the eyes of God."

Cobb sat alone in the storeroom, the priest's words turning in his mind. It was a common enough aphorism, but at that particular time it was something that he needed to hear. So what if his memories of Mary had faded? He had her face in his mind again; brought to him by the dream, as clear as the day he had met her. That alone should have been enough to make him happy, at least for a moment.

Cobb chuckled, first at his own thoughts and then at the priest's words. His mood lifted a bit, and he sat forward, putting the whiskey bottle on the floor. He was going to put aside his self-pity, he decided, and get on with things. His conversation with McAllen had reminded him that he still had hope. It was often mingled with rage, but it was still hope. He could still dream of something better. It might not be much, but it was better nothing.

CHAPTER 17

▼

The door slammed loudly as LeGrasse thundered into his office, his face contorted into an angry snarl, a set of papers in his tight fist. He dropped these onto his desk and ran a hand through his thin black hair, tried to calm himself down.

How could this be happening? He asked himself. What was going on? It was bad enough that a man was blown up outside of a Broadway Street hotel, worse that this man seemed to still be alive, but now the only suspect in the bombing, someone who should also have been dead, walked out of Mercy General hospital the day before after eating half of his doctor. Yes, the forensic people had yet to identify the exact reason that Dr. Carlsbad's arms had been stripped of flesh, but they had said at first glance that it looked like the bones had been gnawed on, and that was good enough for LeGrasse. He was even more willing to believe it because of the bizarre nature of everything he had dealt with since hearing about Jack Casey.

And there was more evidence than just Carlsbad's shredded corpse, Fletcher's car had been found about a block from Baker's apartment and the contents of his trunk had left little doubt as to Fletcher's dietary habits. Again the forensic people weren't sure, but it appeared that the skeletal remains of five or six people resided in the trunk, the bones blackened and caked with dried blood and the remains of tissue. So that made Fletcher some kind of sadistic cannibal. Wonderful, thought LeGrasse, considering his size. LeGrasse sighed when he thought about it. If the newspapers found out they'd have a field day.

The detective dropped into his chair and looked up at the ceiling, tried clearing his head. What did he have? First he had Fletcher, who probably hired Baker to hit Casey, who was in town for no particular reason that he had been able to discern yet. Baker screws up, doesn't kill Casey, so Casey kills Baker and then almost kills Fletcher. Fletcher survives in a manner just as improbable as Casey's own survival, and then kills his doctor and escapes from the hospital, climbing out the window and disappearing onto the street even though he was probably covered in blood.

That was it. That was all LeGrasse had and none of it came to much. This whole thing was giving him an ulcer. What was going on in his city?

Maybe in a couple of days he would know more about Fletcher, he thought, something that could explain what he had been doing at Baker's place and why he had been fighting with Casey. It was possible, the detective reasoned, that Fletcher was the man who had hired Baker to bomb Casey, but that still didn't explain how Casey survived the explosion. That was something that LeGrasse was more interested in. Who was this Casey? How had he survived? What were he and Fletcher that they seemed invulnerable? Something big was going on, Casey himself had said as much, and LeGrasse wanted to know what it was.

Almost as importantly, LeGrasse wanted to get his own back. Casey had left him shackled to his car and he had been there the entire night before the morning shift came in. Sleeping on the back seat had been humiliating enough, but knowing that Baker was dead because of him irritated him even more. Baker should have been arrested, should have gone to jail. Casey and Fletcher should be in jail, too. The whole sick lot of them should have been, at that very moment, rotting in cells. LeGrasse should have put them there.

There was a knock on the door. LeGrasse looked up and thought long and hard before he answered. Only bad news seemed to come through that door. "Come in," he said, after a moment. The door opened and a short, pudgy man entered, a folder in one hand. LeGrasse recognized him as Sam Chalmers, one of the forensics boys. He perked up a bit, wondering the obvious. "Have you got something?"

"I might," said Chalmers, seemingly unconcerned by the lack of a greeting. He checked his file, hummed to himself. After a moment he found what he was looking for. "It's not much, yet," he began, "but it might be interesting. I got a look at those slugs the doctors pulled out of Fletcher, and they might be a match for a multiple homicide that Jenkins and the state boys are working on."

"Which one was that?"

"The Kilroy killings," said Chalmers. LeGrasse nodded. He'd heard about that one, another strange case, though not nearly as strange as his. "Seems most of the victims were shot with .45 caliber rounds, just like Fletcher."

LeGrasse shook his head. "It's a common bullet, Sam. Thugs use it all the time."

Chalmers conceded the point with a motion of his head. "Call it a gut instinct. You get me a gun and I can match them to it."

"I'll let you know."

Chalmers came all the way in and looked around quickly, as if making sure there was no one in the office to hear what he was saying. "Look, detective," he said, bent slightly, his voice low, "I know you're working on something strange. Everybody's talking about it."

LeGrasse's eyebrow rose. "Talking about what?"

"Cannibals eating doctors, people being blown up and not dying. It gets around."

"Well it shouldn't," muttered LeGrasse. Keeping a lid on things was the only way to get a case solved without interference, it always bugged LeGrasse to know that cops were gossiping like schoolgirls. Chalmers went over to LeGrasse's desk, put one hand on its surface and leaned in closer.

"But this Kilroy thing got me thinking," he said, seeming to ignore the fact that LeGrasse didn't appear interested. "There was all kind of weird shit at the house, like secret rooms and stuff like that. It looked like Kilroy was operating some kind of underground cathouse. It had been cleaned out by the time the police got there, probably by Kilroy and his accomplices, but there was even weirder stuff downstairs."

Something in Chalmers' tone sparked LeGrasse's interest, and though he wasn't into rumors he listened further. "The bodies were found around a circle burned onto the floor," Chalmers went on. "And there were some books left in the library about black magic, real voodoo stuff. Jenkins shipped them off to the university and found out some of them were really old and rare."

LeGrasse looked hard at Chalmers. "So what?" He asked. "You think they were casting a spell or something? Honestly, Sam, that's the dumbest thing I've heard in a while."

"They never tracked down Kilroy," added Chalmers. "No one's seen him since the killings. Now I'm not saying I believe in magic, detective, but what if they were trying something like that? You know how rich folks are sometimes, they get bored."

"I don't know how rich folks are," said LeGrasse quickly, "and neither do you."

"Maybe not, but I know a few things. I know that some of the dead people at Kilroy's house were from out of town, and some of them were suspects in some weird cases."

"Like who?"

Chalmers shook his head. "There was a guy named Smythe," he said, "I think his name was Smythe. Smith? No, Smythe. He'd been arrested about year back for killing a whore in Denver. Cut her heart out, apparently. He got cleared for lack of evidence."

LeGrasse leaned forward, started to get into the story. "Go on."

"And there were two brothers named Brighton," said Chalmers. "Twins, identical. They did some time for robbing graves in Arizona back in '28, and they didn't steal just the valuables, detective, but the *bodies*. That's about all I can remember, but I think that everyone they found dead had been arrested or suspected of something strange at least once."

A hand to his chin, LeGrasse thought about this. "So what are you saying, Sam?" He asked, after a moment.

Chalmers shrugged. "I don't know, detective," he said. "But what if there's some kind of weird witch thing going on around here? What if we've got some kind of coven on our hands?"

"Where the hell did you get that word?" LeGrasse asked. "'Coven?'"

"I read a lot."

LeGrasse looked at him for a moment, and then he laughed and shook his head. It just wasn't possible. "That's bullshit, Sam," he said. "There's nothing like that going on. It only happens in dime novels, which, incidentally, I think you should stop reading."

"If those bullets match, what then?" Chalmers challenged. "What if the guy who shot Fletcher is the same guy who shot up the Kilroy place?"

"Then Jenkins and I will be working together," replied LeGrasse, casually. "It's a good lead, Sam, check it out. Just try not to let your imagination get the better of you, okay?"

Chalmers nodded, seemed to take the detective's advice. "Sure thing, detective," he said. "I'll let you know if I find anything."

Chalmers walked out of the office and left LeGrasse on his own. The detective leaned back in his chair again, took in a huge breath and held it. Chalmers was a good man, but a little melodramatic at times. They had to deal with hard facts if they were going to find out what was really going on, even if the facts didn't always make sense right away. There was always a rational explanation for everything.

LeGrasse exhaled and got to his feet. He needed to get out of the office, needed to look at some things. To that end he threw on his hat and walked out, intent on checking out the scene of Fletcher's shooting again. Maybe he'd missed something around Baker's apartment, or maybe he just wanted to walk around the place again, if only to be close to the scene of the crime. It helped sometimes to actually be there. It made things much easier to visualize.

The trip to Baker's apartment didn't take long, just a little over ten minutes. LeGrasse parked his car on the side of the road, near the area where Fletcher had actually been found and got out. The afternoon sun washed down on him as he looked around, people walking back and forth on the sidewalk, the occasional truant child laughing and running where he shouldn't. By the sight of it no one would believe that someone had died there less than 48 hours ago.

Heading over to the spot in front of the automat where Fletcher had been found, the detective looked up at the broken windows of Baker's apartment. A square of sidewalk was cordoned off, protecting the chalk outline of Fletcher's other victim, some poor bank employee named Killian. Witnesses said that the shooter had fallen out of the window and dropped two stories to the street, only to get to his feet and gun Fletcher down as he came out. Killian tried to get in the way and got a crushed skull for the trouble.

Of course the shooter was Casey, LeGrasse knew, and surviving a thirty-foot drop onto pavement was no less miraculous than living through a firebombing. Whatever Casey was eating to make him so impervious to harm LeGrasse wanted a steady supply of it.

He thought about the witness reports and wandered onto the curb, looking at the automat. Apparently Casey had run off as soon as he heard the police coming, and he had headed east. A search of the area had come up with nothing. The man had just disappeared.

LeGrasse whistled softly while he walked down the street that Casey had taken, glanced around as he tried to deduce where he could have gone. People didn't just vanish, after all.

As he looked down a side alley, LeGrasse thought to himself where he would go if he were Casey. More than likely he would just keep moving, only stopping in one place long enough to be certain that he hadn't been spotted. That would be the smart thing to do.

A hot dog vendor was parked on a nearby corner and LeGrasse sidled up and bought himself a snack. Katharine, his wife, would have snapped at him for getting a dog with kraut only a few hours after lunch, but LeGrasse liked to eat when he thought and chomped away while he took in the details of his surroundings.

There was a newspaper stand across the street, a cabstand near that, and then a block of what looked like low-rent apartments. An easy place to lose someone, thought LeGrasse. On his block there was a Jewish deli and a church. LeGrasse laughed a bit at the irony of such strange neighbors.

LeGrasse finished his hot dog and walked towards the church, hands in his pockets, the heavy weight of the food in his belly. He liked churches. They were always such peaceful places. It was a Catholic church and being of French ancestry LeGrasse was himself Catholic, so he decided to go in to relax for a moment, away from the outside world, or maybe even to pray a little. It couldn't hurt.

The first thing LeGrasse saw when he walked in was the statue of Christ above the altar. LeGrasse crossed himself and walked through the huge hall, glanced at the lone figure of an old woman sitting on one of the pews. A kneeling priest was the only other inhabitant, his head bowed as he prayed before the altar. The priest looked up, smiled at LeGrasse, and climbed to his feet.

"Hello," said McAllen, quietly. "The afternoon service starts in half an hour if you'd like to wait."

LeGrasse smiled. "No thanks," he said. "I'm just here for a little soul-searching, if that's all right."

McAllen returned the smile. "Certainly," he replied. "If there's anything you need, please let me know."

LeGrasse ran a hand through the side of his hair. "Well, actually," he said, quietly, "I was wondering if maybe you'd seen anything strange in the past day or so." He pulled out his badge and showed it to the priest.

McAllen hesitated. "I already talked to the police once," he said.

The priest's reaction lasted only a split second, but it was enough. A faint trembling of the breath, a flash in the eyes, and LeGrasse knew that McAllen was trying to hide something. "I'm aware of that," he said politely. "I was just wondering if maybe you remembered something you might have forgotten. You were here all alone, I'd hate to think that you were at any risk."

McAllen laughed, a vindicating action, only this time it was too little too late. "This is a house of God," he said, and he turned towards the candles around the altar. "No one would bring violence into such a place."

LeGrasse couldn't help but marvel at the priest's naïveté. "Are you so sure of that?" He asked as he took a step towards the priest's back. "Let me tell you something about the man I'm looking for."

"Please do."

"His name is Jack Casey, at least that's the name I know."

"Never heard of him."

LeGrasse smiled. "That's good," he said, "because the man I'm after is a vicious, cruel lunatic. He tried to kill a man named Fletcher about a block and a half from here. Put a gun to my very own head, too."

The priest paused and put one hand on the altar and his voice trembled when he spoke. "This man, Fletcher, what kind of man is he?"

"Well," started LeGrasse while he looked up at Christ, "Fletcher is...something else. I don't think you want to hear the details."

"And Fletcher is still alive?"

"Maybe," replied LeGrasse. "But I doubt it. He escaped from his guarded hospital room yesterday. Killed his doctor first, though. His injuries were pretty severe, I doubt he made it through the night."

McAllen turned back towards the policeman, his eyes hard. "I'm sorry," he said, "but I can't help you. I don't know the man you're looking for."

Taking his eyes off the statue, LeGrasse looked at McAllen, and all at once he knew he had found what he was looking for. McAllen was hiding Casey, or at least had helped him on his way. He wondered if Casey was listening, if he knew that LeGrasse was there, if he could hear him talking to the priest. "Like I said, that's good," he said. "If you change your mind about that you be sure to call me."

"Of course," replied McAllen. "Now if you'll excuse me I have to get ready for the afternoon service."

"Sure thing," said LeGrasse. "Take care of yourself, padre."

"Thank you, my son," said McAllen, and he walked quickly through the door to the rectory.

LeGrasse smiled; he had Casey. The priest's sudden departure could only mean that Casey was still somewhere on the premises. Without a second thought he left the church and headed into the deli next door, nearly breaking into a run.

He had a call to make.

CHAPTER 18

▼

McAllen nearly kicked the door to the storeroom in, and the loud bang of it flying open caused Cobb to jump to his feet, revolver in hand.

McAllen saw the gun and froze, his face pale and sweaty. Cobb saw that it was only the priest and lowered his weapon. He was dressed in his customary white shirt and black trousers, but he had also wrapped a black vest around his torso.

"Sebastian," said McAllen, quickly, "someone was just—"

He paused, his eyes wide and Cobb looked at him, his eyes hard. "What?"

"Your face," said the priest. "Your face looks much better."

"It speeds up as it goes," shrugged Cobb. He'd seen himself in the mirror that morning and knew that he looked almost normal. Only faint scars decorated his flesh, like the remnants of bad burns received during childhood. "By this time tomorrow I'll probably be completely healed."

"It's a miracle," McAllen whispered. Cobb sneered.

"Not really," he said. He was feeling physically better now that he had skin again. When he had interrogated LeGrasse every movement had brought burning pain from the exposed nerve endings. "What was it you wanted to tell me?"

McAllen stiffened. "There was a policeman here," he said, the words spilling out of his mouth. "He was asking questions, wondered if I'd seen a man named Casey."

"LeGrasse," said Cobb. He smiled at the fact that the detective was still looking for someone named "Jack Casey." Cobb's gun belts were on the cot, he holstered the revolver and tossed the belts into the trunk.

For a moment he considered the idea of visiting LeGrasse, to scare him off the trail for good. It was for his safety, really. Policemen had no business messing around in Cobb's affairs. What could they do besides get themselves killed or worse?

"What'd you tell him?" He asked.

McAllen shrugged. "I told him I'd never met Jack Casey, which isn't a lie, really."

"Think he believed you?"

The priest was silent, which was enough of an answer for Cobb. "Then I guess I'd best be on my way," he said.

"Wait—" McAllen started, but Cobb cut him off.

"If I get out of here there's no more problem for you," he said. The lid of his trunk slammed as he shut it. "You'll be better off."

McAllen frowned. "That's not what I'm trying to tell you," he said. "The policeman said something else, something about someone called Fletcher."

That got Cobb's attention. "What about him?" He asked before he picked up his coat and folded it over his forearm.

"He said that Fletcher escaped from the hospital yesterday," said McAllen. "Said he killed his doctor."

Cobb absorbed this, his eyes narrow. Fletcher's survival was news to him. More important, though, was the fact that he was on the loose. Oh well, thought Cobb. He'd just have to kill him again. "Thanks," he said, and he put on his hat and grabbed the handle on the side of his trunk. "For everything."

Without waiting for any further goodbyes Cobb was on his way. He rushed from the rectory and out through the hall of the church, his trunk by his side. He glanced up at the statue of Christ, a forgotten sense of comfort working through him for a moment as he headed towards the huge main doors. No sooner had he thrown the doors open, though, than the feeling evaporated like smoke in the wind, his flickering impression of safety vanishing when he saw what lay beyond.

The police were there, waiting for him.

Cobb counted the cars quickly—there were four of them, arranged in a semi-circle around the entrance to the church to form a barricade about thirty feet away at the center. Uniformed officers stood ready behind the vehicles, shotguns and pistols ready, and near the center of the barricade, behind the front of a car, stood LeGrasse, a cigar perched in his mouth, a bulletproof vest protecting his chest, and a pair of .45s in his hands. He looked up when the doors flew open and smiled when he saw Cobb.

"Jack Casey," he called as he placed one of his pistols on the hood of his car and plucked the cigar from his mouth. "Put down your weapons and give yourself up."

"Shit," whispered Cobb, and then he reached up quickly and slammed the doors shut again, closed the police out. With practiced ease he opened his trunk and yanked out his gun belts. It took him only a few seconds to get them on. Father McAllen entered the main hall just as Cobb pulled his long gray coat around his shoulders, eyes on the inside of the trunk.

"What is it?" He asked.

"Police," said Cobb as he reached into the case and pulled out his cut-down Stoeger. He loaded this quickly with a pair of white-paper cased shells stuffed into the hungry barrels before he clapped it shut. He'd grabbed those shells on purpose, he realized, and a handful more went into his pocket. The familiar weight of his Bowie knife reassured him from one of the gun belts as it rested against the small of his back.

"What are you going to do?"

As he looked at the shotgun in his hand, Cobb realized that he really wasn't sure how to answer that question. He didn't like the idea of shooting at policemen. They were just doing their jobs, after all, and nothing they could do would really hurt him. But they would delay him, and the last thing he wanted to do was end up back at the morgue. Besides, if the cops started shooting they would no doubt destroy the church trying to get him, maybe even killing McAllen in the process. Cobb didn't want that on his conscience—the old man deserved a better reward than that for helping him out.

"I need to get out of here," he decided. "Is there a back way?"

"Yes," said McAllen. "Out the other side of the rectory, it leads to the garden."

In seconds Cobb was running towards the back way out, his heavy trunk bouncing alongside him. McAllen followed, nervous, praying under his breath and probably hoping to God that he was not about to witness his own little Armageddon. As they approached the door to the garden, however, it suddenly opened and a uniformed officer revealed himself. LeGrasse had apparently had the foresight to send someone to check for escape routes.

"Hold it!" The cop shouted as he aimed his revolver. Cobb was quicker, though, and he had his shotgun pointed and fired before the cop could react. The explosive report was nearly deafening in the narrow hallway. The cop flew out of the doorway, screaming like a wild animal. Cobb ignored him and ran out into the garden, his shotgun held out protectively.

McAllen had covered his ears and dropped down when the shot was fired, and once the sound had faded he rushed into the garden and went immediately to the policeman's side as he thrashed about on the grass. The cop clutched at his reddened face and the torn cloth covering his chest.

"You shot him," said McAllen, horrified, and then he looked at Cobb. "I can't believe you shot him."

"He's fine," said Cobb while he replaced the spent shell. "Take a look."

McAllen complied, and after a moment he saw that Cobb was right. Buckshot at that range should have torn the policeman open, but it hadn't. Instead his skin was blistered and streaked with red and the policeman, though wailing in agony, looked as though he would be all right.

"Rock salt," said Cobb as he glanced at the wall that surrounded the garden. It would only be seconds before the police figured out where the shot came from and descended on their position. "It won't kill him but it hurts like hell."

The priest shook his head and stood. "That's a damn humane weapon you've got there," he said.

"Not really," replied Cobb. "It works on ghosts sometimes. That's why I carry it."

McAllen looked about to say something when the sound of footsteps came echoing down the hallway from the rectory. Without hesitation McAllen ran to the door and slammed it shut, pressed his slight body against the wood. "Get out of here!" He barked. Cobb was prepared to fight, but the priest pointed towards the other side of the garden and Cobb turned, saw the gate leading out. "Run!"

Cobb took one look at the priest and realized that he wouldn't be able to hold the door shut once the police got to it. With a tip of his hat to the priest he made up his mind and bolted for the gate, his boots clomping on the moist earth as he escaped. He crashed past the gate and out onto the street, all the time hoping that McAllen would be all right.

It was him they wanted, though, and the priest was nobody. While he raced away from the church, Cobb assured himself that LeGrasse would probably take the priest in but it wouldn't go much further than that. No, he told himself, the old priest was someone that people would sympathize with, even if he had aided a fugitive. Cobb was the one he was after. LeGrasse wouldn't concern himself with McAllen.

At least that's what he hoped.

CHAPTER 19

▼

Anyone looking in the drainage pipe under the old Fern Brothers Chemical plant in Dutchess County, New York on August 15th, 1934 would have been quite surprised by what he or she saw. Sequestered in the darkness where the pipe met the open air, no longer funneling waste water into the river as it flowed by, there was a huge, hunched shape that shifted every now and then, moving back and forth while it watched the sun go down through a glittering eye. Anyone looking would have been in dire straits, to say the least.

As the nighttime spread over his part of the world, Fletcher thought about what his next meal should be. There were rats, of course, but they weren't nearly enough for someone of his particular needs, not unless he managed to eat twenty or thirty of them, and that would take all night. No, it was time for him to go out and hunt for something a little more substantial.

He was hiding in a desolate, abandoned part of the state, human beings were few and far between, and that's what Fletcher was after—a taste of human.

With a grunt, Fletcher leapt out of the drainage pipe and landed hard on the ground below, one foot splashing in the edge of the river. His clothes were in tatters, most of them never really fitting him anyway since he had stolen them from people much smaller. They were crusted around the chest with dried gore from his earlier meals. He squinted as the sun sank below the horizon, his one good eye like a black bead, the other a dark pit. There was a road nearby. That would be the first place to go and from there he could find his way to the small town of Brandenburg, only mile or so away.

As he trudged towards the road, Fletcher thought about everything that had happened to him recently. The wounds were healing, albeit slowly, but he had lost an eye and that would never come back. Only Yulgo Kharan could return that to him, and his god had been immobilized. Kharan could be revived, at least in theory, but the techniques to pull off such a miracle were beyond Fletcher, and he didn't have a clue as to who could help him. No, his god was frozen in time until the stars chose him to awaken, and Fletcher would have to learn to live with that.

The Great Pig still spoke to him in dreams, though, still whispered his thoughts into Fletcher's mind while he slept, and it was for that reason that Fletcher looked forward to each morning, when he could sleep the day away and speak with his lord and master.

One of the worst things was that Fletcher was now the only one who heard the Pig's voice. All of the other followers, the inferior ones, had fallen from the fold, returned to their human lives as if they never knew that they had stood next to the divine. They returned to their old religions, their smoke and mirror shows that promised and promised but gave nothing.

How many people in the synagogues or mosques or churches had actually stood in the physical presence of their living god, felt his hot breath on them, saw his terrible face? How many of them heard his voice inside their minds, telling them the secrets of the universe and asking only their loyalty in return? How many of them had touched the iron-hard skin of their god and felt the heat beneath? None, thought Fletcher. No one could say that they had done that if they had not been a follower of Yulgo Kharan.

The thought of the ignorant masses that followed false gods made Fletcher's temper rise as he stepped onto the side of the road, his huge arms swaying back and forth and his massive feet slamming against the pavement. How dare they build their temples to their illusions? Who were they to turn a blind eye to the power of the Pig? Had he not given Fletcher the gift of power? Had he not transformed him from a small, ineffective man into the giant that hobbled towards Brandenburg, opening his mind at the same time to the true nature of things? Yulgo Kharan was Life, the embodiment of the way of all things, ever hungry and unstoppable, a force for destruction as well as creation. Through his power Fletcher had left his mundane life behind and had become like his god, strong and boundless.

His family had been the first to see the new Fletcher, his wife and children becoming food for both him and his god. They would be with Fletcher and Yulgo Kharan for all eternity because of that, and if Fletcher stopped to think about it he could almost feel them within him, their spirits part of his now and forever.

Cobb was next on Fletcher's list, not because he wanted to honor the infidel but because it was the only way he could be sure that Cobb was dealt with. He needed to pay for his desecration of Yulgo Kharan's sacred form, needed to suffer for what he had done to the Pig's servant. Fletcher would simply eat Cobb, steal his soul and his strength and keep it inside him. But Fletcher wasn't ready yet to fight Cobb. His wounds still weakened him and he wasn't quite used to the lack of depth perception that having only one eye caused. Cobb wasn't even a fair fighter. The heretic used the weapons of man, used technology instead of his own personal strength and that was an insult. The Pig fought with his hands, therefore only the honorable did so.

Cobb was no mortal and Fletcher knew that now. Cobb had strength but he didn't use it. This was only one more reason to despise the infidel.

First Fletcher would regain his strength and then he would take his revenge, for both his god and himself.

The pains of hunger ran through him more acutely than they had before, and Fletcher paused, a hand to his belly. The doctor had not lasted long. Of course he hadn't had enough time to eat all of him, and the woman he had caught the day before had been too skinny for a really full meal. He needed something better. As he continued he salivated, teased by the thought of a nice, meaty farmer or shop-keeper.

A strange scent hit Fletcher's nostrils and he stopped, suddenly aware that he wasn't alone. His massive head shifted from side to side, but he saw no one and there were very few places to hide. Around him were simply low hills and bits of scrub brush, not the easiest place to find concealment.

As he searched about, Fletcher noticed the scent grow stronger. It smelled sort of human, but not really. There was a musty dryness to it. He waited, crouched low like a gorilla, and noticed that the smell was mixed with a flowery, sweet odor. A smile appeared on his face and he became aware of a presence behind him. He spun about suddenly, his mouth wide.

The woman stood only twenty or thirty feet away, her long reddish-blonde hair blown to one side by the slight breeze, porcelain features only barely visible in the nighttime darkness. Dressed in men's trousers and a button-down shirt, she looked at him, not a trace of fear in her eyes as he leered in her direction.

How she had appeared and why she was out on a back road at nighttime were irrelevant issues. As far as Fletcher was concerned this was a lucky victim, some-one who had happened upon him and was ripe for the taking. All that mattered was his hunger. He charged, shouting. Unfortunately Helena was quicker than he could comprehend and his attack met nothing. The woman disappeared from sight as he approached.

Fletcher came to a screeching halt, confused. Where had she gone? He could still smell her perfumed mustiness, but didn't see her anywhere. He turned around several times, his eyes wide.

Helena attacked quickly. She reappeared at Fletcher's left and slammed him in the chest with the blade of her hand. The giant flopped onto his back, more than a little shocked by the force that the small, lithe woman commanded. As he scrambled to his feet Helena kicked him in the stomach and he buckled, the wind knocked out of him.

"You might want to stay down, big man," said Helena, her eyes red. She leered viciously, her face pale and her lips pulled back to reveal her fangs. "I'm here to collect you, not kill you."

"Then die and feed me," Fletcher growled and he sat up and swiped one big fist at her. The blow caught Helena by surprise, smashed against her jaw and threw her backwards. She stumbled and fell to one knee while Fletcher climbed to his feet.

Right before Fletcher's eyes Helena's face contorted horribly, her beautiful features shifting into an almost wolfish aspect—the face of an angered vampire. Blood dripped from her bottom lip as she moved. Without bothering to stand she hurled herself forward, literally flying at Fletcher, her arms outstretched.

Fletcher tried to catch the charge, but he was simply too slow. She drove her clawed hands into his chest, sliced open his tattered clothing and ripped wounds into his flesh. He winced, the woman practically flowing up to his torso to grab his shoulders with her talons, and then following up with a knee to his groin. Fletcher was strong and tough, but Helena was too fast. He dropped to the ground, clutched at his wounds with frantic hands.

Apparently Helena wasn't finished yet, and she grabbed Fletcher by the hair and twisted his head painfully to one side, exposed his jugular. He grunted when she bit into it, felt her suck out his blood.

She stopped almost instantly, though, and turned her head to spit the fluid onto the dirt.

"Disgusting," she choked out, looking ready to vomit. Fletcher laughed. Did she think him so easy a target? The Pig protected its servants better. Helena wiped her chin clean and walked away from him while he put a hand to the wound on his neck.

"Now stay down," She commanded. "I don't want to have to kill you."

"What do you want?" Fletcher asked while he tore a patch of cloth from his rags and pressed it to his neck.

"I want to help you get revenge," she replied, her face back to normal. Fletcher shuddered, a sudden pressure against his temples. He blinked quickly, tried to ignore the rush of memories that had filled his mind. "I want to help you get Cobb."

"What do you know about Cobb?"

Helena's dark laugh resounded through the night. "I know that you got your clock cleaned the last time you went against him," she chided as she took a step towards him. "I know that if you try fighting him again you'll just get killed. Next time he'll make sure you're dead."

"Next time I'll be ready for him," grumbled Fletcher. "Next time he'll be mine."

"You can't kill Cobb," said Helena. "Not like a regular person, you can't. Cobb's immortal. Really immortal."

"I don't care. I'll eat his flesh and grind his bones to dust, and maybe I'll eat that, too. Then we'll see how immortal he is. He can go on living inside my belly for all I care."

"You'll never get the chance," argued Helena. "He's too smart for you, my dear. Sorry to break it to you."

"And what can you do?"

The woman knelt and put a hand gently on Fletcher's cheek. He pulled away, stared through his single eye. "I can hunt him," she said, "the same way I hunted you. I know what hurts him, and I know what he thinks. My husband can trap and weaken him and then I will take his blood while you get his flesh. The three of us will take his power from him and make sure he dies for good. That's what you want, isn't it?"

Fletcher smiled as he thought about this. "I get his flesh?" He asked. Helena grinned and put her hand back on Fletcher's face. This time he didn't pull away.

"You get his flesh," she said, "I get his blood, and my husband gets his soul."

Flying was very new to Fletcher and he allowed himself a moment of childlike wonder as Helena carried him through the air, her hands under his armpits. He laughed as the wind whipped across him. Beneath him the ground moved steadily by, plants and rocks much smaller than they had once appeared.

They traveled about a mile before Helena descended, and Fletcher saw a car parked by the side of the road, its lights off. As his feet touched the ground he felt Helena release him and he stumbled a bit before he found his footing.

The sound of Helena's booted feet on the gravel in his ears, Fletcher squinted as the car lights flared to life and the passenger side door opened. A man stepped out, and once Fletcher's eyes adjusted he made out the form of a tall, smiling man standing a few feet away.

He'd never seen Philip Farwell before, and so had no knowledge of who he was or what he was doing there, but his encounter with Helena had convinced him that acting with restraint was probably the best way to go for the moment. Philip didn't look like much, though, standing there in his black suit, hands in his pockets.

"This is my husband, Philip," Helena told him. Fletcher grunted.

"Another vampire?" He asked, though he already knew the answer. Philip smelled like a human.

"No," said Philip as he looked over Fletcher with distaste. Fletcher paid it no mind, not caring in the slightest that he was dressed in filthy rags or that he stank like a slaughterhouse. In fact he liked it.

"Has Helena explained things to you?" Philip asked. Fletcher nodded.

"Yes," he said. "You have some sort of plan?"

"Indeed I do. We need to lure Cobb into a trap. Think you can handle that?"

Fletcher was dubious. He didn't like this little man and he certainly didn't like the tone of his voice. "What kind of trap?" He asked.

"The kind where we surprise and kill him."

This brought a laugh from Fletcher. "Very well," he said. "So what do we do first?" Philip scratched his head and Helena smiled.

"Cobb's still in New York," said Philip, "at least he was a few days ago. He was hiding in a church near where he fought you."

Fletcher frowned. "How do you know this?" He asked.

"I saw it in his mind," Philip replied. "That's how I found out about you."

Intrigued, Fletcher glanced first at the vampire and then back at the husband. "Can you hurt him?"

"Nothing physical at this distance. I might be able to affect his waking perceptions if he were closer."

"That should be worth something, I think," said Fletcher, a hint of venom in his tone.

Philip glared. "And what good do you think you'll be?" He asked. "You've already proven that you can't handle Cobb alone. He nearly finished you."

"Watch your tongue," spat Fletcher as he loped towards Philip. "Or I'll eat it. I am the favored servant of Yulgo Kharan, whose glory cannot be measured. I alone in all the world have been blessed by his sacred essence, implanted in my body by the Great Pig himself."

"I'm sure it was very romantic," said Philip quickly. Fletcher growled and nearly attacked when the vampire stopped him.

"Don't worry about Philip," said Helena. She walked over to stand by her husband. "He can hold his own in this."

Fletcher regarded them both thoughtfully. He knew that the woman was strong. She had proven that much, though he was certain that he would have been able to defeat her eventually. The man, on the other hand, seemed so thin and weak. Fletcher could have snapped his spine with one hand. If Helena had faith in him, however, there must have been something he was good at.

He decided to trust the vampire. If worse came to worse he could always eat them both. He wondered what the vampire would taste like.

"I'm sure," he said.

"So we should head for the city," said Philip. "Once we're there we can track Cobb down and take him back to Rhode Island."

Fletcher's eye narrowed. "Why Rhode Island?"

"Because that's where we live. I have to perform the rituals there if we want to weaken Cobb. You didn't think we'd just do it anywhere, did you?"

Fletcher shrugged and looked back at their car. "We go to New York. Then what?"

"Once we get to the church we can figure out our next move," answered Philip. He seemed to lose interest in Fletcher and started walking back to the car. "The most important thing is that we take him by surprise. If he knows we're coming he'll put up a very loud fight and then we'll have to deal with the police. I don't know about you but I don't want that."

"Forget them," called Fletcher after Philip. "They mean nothing."

"Don't be an idiot," said Helena. "Do you want to have to fight both them and Cobb?"

With a grunt Fletcher took the point. His stomach rumbled and he was reminded of his more immediate needs. Helena and Philip were both getting into their car and he shambled after them.

"I still need food," he told them. "We need to find someone for me to eat."

CHAPTER 20

▼

Around midnight Cobb realized he was drunk.

The Anchor wasn't a bad place, even if it was clearly on its last legs, but that only added to its charm. Formerly a speakeasy until Prohibition was repealed, the Anchor catered to all sorts of people and usually had some sort of local jazz musician handy on the piano wedged into the corner. That didn't do much for Cobb. He wasn't much of a jazz fan, but some people seemed to like it.

By midnight he'd been drinking for almost four hours, thinking almost the entire time about his earlier escape from Father McAllen's church, wondering if the priest had been all right. He hoped that nothing had happened to McAllen, since he had been responsible for one of the first real acts of kindness that Cobb had received in a long time.

When he thought about it, though, he realized that LeGrasse probably wasn't the kind of person to take out his frustrations on a clergyman. He was a policeman, not a thing from hell like Cobb was used to. He wasn't going to hurt McAllen. He might make him uncomfortable for a bit, but he wouldn't hurt him.

That had been three days ago, anyway. The priest had probably only been in the tank for a day, sweating things out before LeGrasse decided he didn't know anything and released him. It was more or less true. Apart from his real name Cobb had told him very little.

For now Cobb was just trying to get out of New York. He'd spent too much time in New York. He learned a long time ago that moving around was the best thing for him, and that if he spent too much time in one place and he started to draw attention to himself. Having LeGrasse looking for him was annoying enough. He didn't need anyone else getting into the mix and if he stuck around that was going to happen sooner or later.

He supposed he could have just killed LeGrasse since scaring the cop off was probably going to be impossible, but Cobb didn't kill people that he didn't think deserved it. LeGrasse was doing his job, like Cobb, he wasn't someone that Cobb was just going to shoot. No, it was better if he just left, forgot about Fletcher and LeGrasse for a while. If he ever needed to he'd come back once the heat died down.

Fletcher was going to be a problem, though. He was the kind of person that would follow Cobb to the ends of the earth. He didn't have any jurisdictional boundaries like LeGrasse. He just had the insult of losing his god to push him along, and not many people got over that.

In a way this actually suited Cobb. Let Fletcher do all the work and come to him, he thought, and then he could make sure that the zealot was dead. If that meant he had to chop off Fletcher's head and burn his corpse then so be it. Cobb would make the time.

That was all for later, though. At that moment Cobb was drunk in the Anchor, his hat and a half-empty bottle of whiskey on the bar next to him. It was his second such bottle that night. The bartender had been reluctant to serve him after the first, but Cobb's lack of any signs of drunkenness seemed to convince him, probably out of a desire to see how much Cobb could actually drink more than anything else. When he got near the end of the second bottle Cobb was as drunk as a normal man would have been after half of one, his eyelids drooping and his cheeks pink. He felt warm and his fingers tingled. His concerns seemed irrelevant, and that was how he liked them.

"Get you something, honey?"

Cobb looked up at the sound of the voice and his eyes fell on the painted whore standing next to him. She was about thirty-five, probably, and by her appearance Cobb could see that she had been around the block more than once. Her face was lined, her eyes drenched in blue. She stank of cheap perfume and sweat. A tangled mess of brown hair sat on top of her head, and she was dressed in something that had probably been a nice dress once. But, like its owner, it had seen too many summers, and was now worn and rough. She smiled at Cobb, her teeth yellow from smoking.

"No thanks," said Cobb, his voice low. The woman, however, wasn't going to be put off so easily.

"Come on, sugar," she said as she put a hand on his shoulder. "You're all alone, and no one needs that."

"I do."

The woman shook her head and rubbed Cobb's shoulder a bit. "I see you up here, burying yourself in your drink, trying to be a tough guy," she said. "Don't worry, I won't tell."

The urge to wave his knife in the woman's face was pushed down almost immediately, but the thought made Cobb chuckle. "No thanks," he said again. "I'm just trying to be drunk."

"Well you've got that down," said the woman, glancing at the half empty bottle. Cobb wondered if she'd seen him empty the other one. "But that's no good for you. I've got something better."

Cobb eyed her up and down and grinned. "I doubt it," he said. "But thanks for the offer."

That seemed to do the trick. The woman shrugged and walked off, headed to a table nearby and struck up a conversation with a tattooed laborer sitting there. Cobb shook his head, turned back to his drink and forgot about her. That was just bad news; that he could do without. After a hundred and fifty years he still took his marriage vows seriously.

Suddenly Cobb's left hand twitched. He stiffened on his stool, realized very quickly that something wasn't right in the area. Cobb could sense the presence of something, something that wasn't part of the human world. There was something nearby, and after a moment he realized that it wanted him to sense it. The feeling he was getting was being thrown out to him intentionally.

Cobb turned and looked around. There were only a few people in the bar, most of them having been there since before Cobb arrived, and back then he had sensed nothing.

The bar's front door opened and Cobb glanced at it but there was no one there. As the door swung on its hinges, though, Cobb saw that there was someone behind it, staring at him while the door opened and closed. Who it was Cobb couldn't tell, all he saw was a humanoid silhouette with a glaring eye visible when the light from the bar hit it. Cobb knew that he had found his presence, though, and whatever it was that he was sensing was looking right at him. Cobb grabbed his hat and nearly ran from the bar, intent on figuring this out.

By the time Cobb got out of the Anchor the street was empty, no strange person around. Cobb could still feel its presence, though, and he looked around quickly as he put his hat back on, the chill night air moving around him. He swore.

A sound from his left caught his attention and Cobb turned in time to see a shadow slip around a corner. Without a thought he ran after it, reached under his coat and pulled out his Bowie knife. Whatever this thing was it was playing games and that irritated him.

As he rounded the corner he saw the figure standing only fifteen or twenty feet away, a black shape against the pale moonlight. Cobb took a cautious step forward, tried to figure out what he was looking at. It was shaped like a man, the eyes glittering as it just stood there and looked at him.

"Who are you?" Cobb asked, his Bowie knife at his side.

The thing gave no answer. Instead it chose to rush at him, making a sound like steam escaping from a teakettle. Cobb had only a moment, but it was enough. He slashed at the thing's middle with his knife, sliced clean through from one side of its waist to the other, split it in half like it were made of cloth. The top half flew over Cobb while the legs ran past and as Cobb swung around he saw the halves of the monster rejoin. The whole monster turned and stood before him. Cobb frowned. This thing was going to put up a tougher fight than he expected.

After it emitted its strange battle cry the shadow spun forward, whipped its legs out like a dervish and struck Cobb across the jaw with both feet, the one after the other. Cobb staggered back, tasted blood on his tongue, and the thing followed up with a blast to his chest. Cobb's boots scraped on the sidewalk as he tried to keep his balance, but he fell. He crashed onto the ground, his knife clattering out of his hand.

"Damn it," whispered Cobb just as the shadow melted into an indistinct, amorphous shape and slid onto him. He thrashed about and tore at the black stuff with his great hands. The texture of it was like molasses. A chill ran up his spine when he realized that the thing was trying to get into his mouth and nose, trying to enter his body for whatever strange reason that it had. Cobb growled, turned over onto his stomach, and tried to press the shadow between his body and the pavement. With a hiss the creature disengaged to slide away and pool off to Cobb's right. Cobb rolled away and grabbed his knife before jumping to his feet.

"Come on," he goaded, breathing heavily as the shadow reformed into its anthropoid shape and stared at him. "Come and get me."

The beast's eyes flashed red and it launched forward, its claws raised. Cobb howled and sliced at its neck, hacked its head clean from its body before he brought his huge knife around and slashed it from one shoulder to the opposite side of the waist, leaving it in three bizarre pieces. These quickly rejoined but Cobb kept cutting. He hacked off a leg, a hand, chopped it in two, but the fragments kept coming back together as the pair spun in their weird dance on the street. As easy as it was to cleave through the creature, Cobb realized, he wasn't having any luck keeping it in pieces. It was like trying to cut water in a pan.

Finally, Cobb played his trump card. With a snarl he drove the point of his knife into the shadow's face, transfixed it for an instant while he thrust his left fist into its chest, buried it to the wrist in the black body.

And then Cobb began to feed.

He didn't want to have to do it but he saw no other option. Clearly the creature was composed of no earthly matter and no amount of hacking or chopping was going to kill it. He didn't know what it wanted with him but he didn't care to find out, either. When it had had him on the ground it had been trying to get inside him, and that was enough.

A moment after Cobb began to draw the essence out of the shadow, something very strange happened. The creature had no energy to drain! Cobb realized it quickly, waiting for the ghastly sensation of taking something foul into his body and soul accompanied his feeding, but it never came. In fact, nothing happened. The beast slid from Cobb, pulled away and stood before him, staring. It didn't attack. It just looked at him.

"You're nothing," said Cobb, slowly. He'd guessed the thing's secret. "You don't exist."

The shadow took another step back, the glittering eyes locked on Cobb. With a sigh he let his knife fall to his side and the shadow started stalking in a half circle before him. "You're a figment," Cobb went on. "A vision."

And then, the shadow vanished.

Cobb reached up and touched his lip where the monster had struck him. There was no blood. No sensation of numbness as there had been before. He didn't even taste any blood on his tongue. Everything it had done to him had been an illusion, a phantasm that he had supported with his own belief. Once he had tried to eat its essence, however, the illusion had been dispelled.

"Wonderful work, Cobb."

The voice spoke inside Cobb's mind, but that didn't stop him from suddenly coming on guard, his knife back up. It was the same way demons spoke. "I wondered how long it would take you to figure it out."

"Figure it out?" Cobb asked aloud. A soft chuckle answered him.

"The shadow was just to get your attention," the voice said. "It wasn't capable of really hurting you."

"Who are you?"

"We've met before," the voice replied. It was a man's voice. "I was at the Kilroy house the night you murdered him."

"That wasn't murder," said Cobb, irritated. "He got what he deserved."

"In all likelihood. It doesn't really matter, though."

Cobb's eyes narrowed. "What do you want?"

"You," the voice replied. "Just you."

"Fine. Tell me where you are and I'll come."

The sound of laughter entered Cobb's mind again. "I'm sure you will. My name is Philip Farwell. I'm in Providence. Come find me here."

"You can count on it," said Cobb with a sneer. He sheathed his knife.

"One more thing, though," said Philip's voice. "In case you get the idea of burning my house down while I'm in it or anything unsporting like that, you should know that I have a friend of yours with me."

Cobb's head tilted. "Who?" He asked.

"He says his name is Father McAllen. Does that sound familiar to you?"

Cobb swore and Philip laughed. "I see that it does," he said. "He's comfortable enough, but I don't know how long he'll remain so. That means you'd better hurry, Cobb. And remember one thing—come after dark."

"I'll be there," said Cobb just before the presence vanished from his mind. Hands balled into fists, Cobb tried to think of who this Philip Farwell was. Silently he berated himself for being so sloppy with the Kilroy affair. How could he have let anyone get away? If he hadn't been so intent on getting a look at the demon Kilroy summoned he would have just done what Farwell had suggested— burned the house down and shot everyone as they rushed out. Then no one would have escaped. But Cobb wanted to know what he was, and his pursuit of that goal sometimes led him into situations like the Kilroy one. It had gotten him into trouble before and now it looked like it had again. Only this time the trouble had snatched up someone else, too; someone who had tried to help him.

There wasn't any question about his next course of action. Cobb had to go to Providence and meet this Philip Farwell. The fact that he had invaded Cobb's mind and set his shadow creature to humiliate him was bad enough but he had also kidnapped McAllen. For a moment Cobb wondered how Farwell had known about the priest, but then he realized that if Farwell was able to communicate with him mentally he was probably capable of pulling information right from his brain. But what did he want? Why was he after Cobb?

Cobb hoped he'd remember to ask Farwell all of these questions before he killed him.

CHAPTER 21

▼

Helena Farwell woke just after sunset, wrapped in black sheets and her husband nowhere to be seen. She sat up, her naked torso slipping out from the covers, and looked around.

The bedroom was as it was supposed to be, with its bare hardwood floors and pale blue walls. There was a vase of fresh flowers on the nightstand, a gift from Philip. Helena smiled and sniffed their petals, her sharp senses picking up every nuance of their odor.

Things were going well, that's why Philip was being romantic. He always was when a plan neared success. There had been some difficulties with their ritual a few nights before, but Helena had come out fine. She knew that her husband would feel guilty about that for a while, though, no matter how little harm she actually suffered. He was so protective of her.

Helena got out of bed and bathed in the adjoining washroom. Hot water and soap always made her feel more comfortable. Modern plumbing was a miracle as far as she was concerned, remembering a time when something like hot water was considered a luxury. Submerged in the ornate tub, Helena ran her hands on her skin, a smile on her face. She wanted to stay there for hours but she knew that was impractical.

Cobb was coming and she had preparations to make.

Thoughts of Cobb swirled in her head. There was so much fire in him, so much rage. It was sad, in her opinion. The man had more power than others could dream of and he didn't use it. He relied on human weapons and his own brute strength, ignorant of the vast potential that he possessed. She had seen his memories, had seen him fighting a thousand different things, and yet he had never once tried to understand what he killed. At least not in any way that Helena saw.

The vampire climbed out of the bath and got dressed, still thinking about Cobb. What would happen when he arrived, she wondered. Would he really try to save the priest, or would he just focus his awesome energies on killing her and her husband? These things weren't really that far apart, she decided as she pulled on her clothes. She had decided a pair of trousers and one of Philip's undershirts would suit her fine. She wasn't going anywhere special, after all.

Back in the bathroom, Helena looked at herself in the mirror and set about pinning her long red hair up. Pausing for a moment, she looked at the hair, at its color. It hadn't always been this color. In fact the woman that she saw in the mirror was very different than what she remembered. She remembered black hair and eyes, less angular features, heavier breasts, and a flatter nose. She had still been beautiful of course; the terrifying queen of a vast empire, but standards had been much different.

Her empire. It was so long ago but still so recent in her memory. The millennia had wiped it from human history, but she still held it in her heart. Not a day had passed that her subjects did not quake in horror as the sun went down, knowing that their ruler would rise from her crypt to slake her thirst on their blood. Her armies marched from her cities and put her enemies to the sword, crushed resisters under sandaled feet, all in her name. Mortal men satisfied her desires at a mere clap of her hands, offered up their bodies for her pleasure at a whim. She could still see her statues at the city gates, their eyes jewels that stared out over the walls and struck fear in fools who considered violating the peace that her rule guaranteed.

It was all gone now. The beautiful gardens of B'harak, the Temple of the Queen, the fabled Street of Ki'tai, they were gone, washed away by time and jealousy. No more did the fires burn at the foot of the Statue of the Old Queen, no one traded in Merchant Square, and no one spoke her name in hushed silence, fearful that the wind would carry their voices to her ears.

For a moment Helena lost herself in the past. She heard the voice of her High Priest. What was his name? Jarak. He had been the last of the Old Queen's priests and Helena's first. It was Jarak who had instructed her in the ways of her new station, who had shown her what it was to inherit the mantle of power.

"You are queen, now," he had said. "Your word is law."

How she had loved the sound of that! Her word carried the torment of whole cities, raised towers out of sand, and howled triumph to the heavens. She feasted on the throats of slaves and nobles, draped priceless treasures on her body, and saw her face in gold sculptures that decorated the walls of her crypt.

All it had taken was the abdication of the Old Queen. Helena allowed herself a small laugh when she thought about her. Her name was forgotten even before her rule ended, she was simply called "Majesty." Now that had been a woman who understood power. For nine hundred years she ruled, turning her small collection of provinces into the empire that Helena would later control. As beautiful as she was terrible, the Old Queen had been the template that Helena had followed during her first years of rule.

Helena's legacy would have eclipsed the Old Queen's dread domination if she'd been given the chance. She had only two centuries to spread her influence versus the Old Queen's nine. Her fist clenched when she thought about the end. How dare they defile her temples? How dare they murder her servants? Who were these bastard children that ran wantonly through her cities and came for her with fire and steel? They were her subjects, hers to defile and punish, hers to command. They should have known their place better.

She relaxed and opened her fist. It was best not to obsess over the past when the future lay stretched out before her. She had Philip and he had promised to make her more of a queen than she had ever been. She would not rule just a single empire but the entire world, she would stand at his side and there would be no limit to what she could have or do.

Her spirits rose and she finished pinning up her hair. The dark-haired terror of ten thousand mortals was gone, replaced by the thin, auburn-topped lady that lived with Philip Farwell. She was content with that.

But she still had things to do. To that end, she went down to the first floor of the house, walking at an easy pace, and there found Father McAllen. They had tied him to a chair in the dining room, his white hair in need of combing and his eyes filled with fear.

The priest looked up at her as she entered the dining room, standing on the other side of the long wooden table before him. She could smell the terror in his sweat, her predatory instinct aroused.

"Hello, priest," she said. Her luscious red lips pulled back to reveal her long canines. "I trust you're feeling well?"

McAllen swallowed nervously. He seemed extremely agitated by Helena's presence, and she wondered if it was because of her vampirism or her femininity. From what she understood about his order they were not allowed contact with women and while this had amused her at first she gradually started to think about the effect that had on a man. It sounded so unhealthy.

"Please," said McAllen, "let me go."

The honest simplicity of the words made Helena laugh. "You know that's not possible," she said. "You're here to make sure your friend Sebastian plays by the rules."

"But why?" McAllen implored. "What do you want Sebastian for?"

Helena crossed over to the priest and pulled his chair back from the table. "Don't you worry about that," she said, whispering the words into his ear. Then she circled around in front of him and squatted down by his shins, her hands on his knees. "You've got enough to think about as it is."

McAllen went rigid. From his chest Helena could hear the pounding of his heart, speeding up when she touched him. He looked straight out, kept his eyes off her.

"My husband has told me many things about your God," she said as she ran her hands slowly over his knees and calves. "A simple carpenter nailed to a cross. How quaint."

"He is our shepherd," said McAllen, his voice monotone. "He watches over us in times of darkness."

"The dark is your friend," said Helena, still whispering. "Darkness is safety. Why do you choose to follow a God that would keep you frightened of your own shadow?"

"God strengthens us and gives us courage," said the priest. "He sends his angels to protect us."

Helena looked around the room. "I don't see any angels," she said. "Is he choosing not to protect you now?"

"The Lord is my shepherd. I shall not want."

Helena squeezed the inside of the priest's thigh gently and McAllen went silent, sucked in a quick gasp of air. "You do want," she said. "You want very, very much. Imagine, a virgin at your age. I can see inside your mind, priest, you've been a very good boy."

"Please." McAllen's voice was barely audible. "Please leave me alone."

"Look at me."

The priest didn't move. "Look at me," Helena commanded again, more forceful. McAllen's head swiveled towards her as if it were acting of its own accord and heedless of its owner's wishes. Helena's eyes flushed crimson and she put a hand to her neck. "Am I not beautiful," she asked as she ran her fingertips slowly across the pit of her throat and towards her chest. "Am I not the very incarnation of magnificence?"

"Yes," whispered McAllen in awe. "You are beautiful."

"You want me, don't you?"

McAllen said nothing, but Helena ignored that fact and moved her hand to the fabric between his legs. She felt the unmistakable bulge of an erection. "I see that you do," she said as she laid the side of her head against his knee. The act was almost childlike. "You can have me, you know. I can give you anything you want. I can make you young again and show you pleasures that you have denied yourself for far too long."

There was only a moment of hesitation before the priest spoke. "No," he said, his voice quiet and frail. "You are beautiful, but empty. Your soul is dead."

Helena's transformation was instantaneous. Where she had been seductive and enticing she was suddenly boiling with anger and indignity. She jumped to her feet and slapped a hand around his neck, McAllen's heart thundering. "What do you know of my soul, shaman?" She barked. Her eyes were such a deep red they looked almost black. "You are an ignorant child in a sea of madness. You are blood and bones and meat, a bag of trash that I could tear to pieces if I wished it. How dare you refuse me? Whole cities have been eradicated for less. Have you any idea who I am?"

"Helena."

It was Philip's voice. She released McAllen and spun around, saw her husband standing in the kitchen doorway, his hands in his pockets. "Helena," he said, patiently, "leave him be."

The enraged vampire snarled, her lust for blood almost overpowering. Philip just stood there, smiling. She thought for a moment about gutting him, but then realized what she was doing and calmed herself. Her eyes reverted to normal and she sucked in a deep breath, forcing herself to relax.

"He insulted me," she said, a hand on her forehead. "I'm sorry."

"Don't worry," said Philip, and he walked over to her and put his hands on her shoulders. "You'll get your chance."

Suddenly Helena pushed her head forward and kissed him, her lips pressing tightly against his. He lowered his hands to the small of her back and for several seconds they held each other, kissing. McAllen looked away.

Eventually they disengaged. Helena felt her lusts on her, first aroused by the idea of tempting McAllen and then by her blinding desire to kill him. Now Philip was holding her and she wanted nothing more than to throw him down and take him. In fact the thought of doing it in front of the priest made her even more excited. If he didn't want to experience it she would make him watch it, make him see what he was missing.

The look in Philip's eyes, however, told her that she would have to wait. "Fletcher's out back, in his burrow," he said. "Please make sure he knows what he's supposed to be doing when Cobb gets here."

Helena nodded and took one last look at the priest before she left. He was staring at her, his face livid. Philip was right, she would get her chance at him, but for now she'd have to be patient. That was fine. She was almost five thousand years old. She could wait.

Fletcher's "burrow" was a small space between some trees at the edge of the back yard where Yulgo Kharan's favorite had strung up a tarp as a sort of roof, the space below it left open. He liked sleeping outside, apparently, and was fine on the hard ground without pillows or blankets. Helena found it almost as obscene as she found Fletcher, being used to comfort like she was.

The porcine giant was hunched down beneath his tarp, sitting cross-legged, his eye closed and his forearms on his knees. Helena walked up to him, her vampire eyes piercing the darkness. His strong reek was even stronger to her sensitive nose, and her face screwed up as she approached. She could see blood-crusted bones littering the dirt.

He gave no indication that he heard her as she walked over, her bare feet on the grass.

"Fletcher," she said. "Are you awake?"

"Of course I am, woman," grumbled Fletcher. "Come to make sure I'm ready?"

"Yes."

"Don't bother," he replied. "Once Cobb arrives I'll be waiting."

"He doesn't know you're here," said Helena. "That's your best weapon."

Fletcher opened his eye and stared at her. "Don't lecture me," he said. "I know all about surprise. Just stay out of my way."

"You should be more polite," Helena warned. She still smarted over McAllen's refusal and the last thing she wanted was to suffer Fletcher's attitude.

"You should be more respectful," Fletcher countered. "A woman should keep her mouth shut."

That did it. Helena flashed forward and kicked him in the chest with enough power to kill a normal man. Fletcher flopped onto his back, but in a second he was up and facing her.

"I should kill you for that," he spat, hands clenched at his sides. "You and your bastard husband."

"You ever touch Philip and I'll take your eye out and feed it to you."

Fletcher smiled. "That's what I like to hear," he said. "You and I are not as different as I thought."

That really insulted her. "Don't you ever say that," she said. "You and I are nothing alike."

Fletcher's laugh boomed off the trees. "You think so," he asked. "We are both the same, we both use humans for sustenance and take what we want, when we want it. How are we different?"

Helena fumbled for a moment, tried to come up with something that made sense. "You're an animal," she said finally. It was all she could think of. She remembered the taste of his blood. It had tasted polluted, diseased. "You're disgusting."

Again Fletcher laughed. "And you're not an animal?" He asked. "Think about it, little vampire, we are not so different. We may wear different faces but you and I are both hunters. We are like sharks in a sea of human prey. We are the same."

Helena thought about what she said to McAllen and how Fletcher's words echoed hers. It horrified her.

"Just be ready," she commanded. Arguing with Fletcher wasn't going to get her anywhere, so she decided to stop. She ignored his continued laughter while she stormed back into the house, walking past Philip without a word and running upstairs while her husband watched her, suddenly concerned.

Back in the bathroom Helena ran the faucet and splashed her face with water. She knew that Fletcher was wrong, but something about what he said bothered her. Was she like him? She couldn't accept that. She was regal, a former queen. Fletcher was a pig-faced cannibal man. How could they be alike?

She looked in the mirror and saw the beautiful face staring back. No, she told herself. She and Fletcher were nothing alike. She took solace in the fact that Fletcher wouldn't live long after they had conjured up the spirit of the house and given Cobb to it. She would make him eat his own guts and smiled when she thought about it. He would regret his words. Regret that he crossed her.

Still, though, as she went back downstairs, cool and composed to reassure her husband that she was all right, a small part of her still worried that Fletcher was right. She tried to ignore it but it was there, as real and as potent as a guilty conscience.

CHAPTER 22

▼

It took Cobb two days to get to Providence.

He arrived just after sunset, a quick check of the city directories telling him that Philip Farwell and his wife, Helena, were living at 1128 Halfpenny Lane, about a mile out of the city. It was ten minutes later that he arrived, the dark all around him, out on Halfpenny Lane.

He parked his car about a hundred feet from the house and loaded up. The Schofields were in his holsters, his knife on his belt, a bandolier of shotgun shells slung across his chest and the sawed-off Stoeger in his hands. Under his coat dangled a bundle of dynamite. They said to come after dark but the never said to come unarmed.

The house loomed ominously as he approached, a single light burning in one of the windows on the second floor. His hands worked on the shotgun while he stood across the road from the front of the building, contemplating what was about to happen. A slight breeze ran over him, the trees behind rustled softly. His coat whipped around his calves, his eyes glared from beneath the brim of his slouch hat.

Something was in that house. Something was waiting.

Cobb could almost taste it on the breeze, the presence that lingered in that house. It couldn't have been Philip—this was something different, something that set Cobb's supernatural senses on fire. Something old and powerful waited, hungry, and it could sense him. It knew that he was there, just as aware of him as he was of it.

Something touched the back of Cobb's head, just behind the ear, and he froze.

"My turn, Casey."

Cobb almost laughed when he heard LeGrasse's voice. He turned his head slightly and saw the fat policeman standing to his left, a .38 revolver held up to Cobb's ear. LeGrasse was pale in the darkness, his eyes wide. "I knew you'd show up eventually," he said.

"What the hell are you doing here, LeGrasse?"

"Waiting for you," the policeman answered. "I cooked your preacher friend for a few hours before I realized he didn't know where you went, then I let him go. I figured you'd come back to him eventually, so I had his church watched."

Cobb listened attentively. "Then what?"

"Then he got kidnapped," said LeGrasse. "The boys I had watching the place said that he was taken out of the church by a guy and a woman, looked like they had him pretty screwed up. I thought they might be friends of yours, but they assured me that this couple didn't look too friendly to McAllen. They got the license number of the car and I checked it out. It led me here."

Cobb's grip tightened around his short shotgun. "They didn't try to help him?" He asked, his tone accusing.

"One of them did," said LeGrasse, grim. "He's dead. His partner said the woman snapped his neck like a damn twig. He stayed clear to make sure I knew what happened."

Cobb nodded. "So what are you doing here?"

"I wanted to find you," LeGrasse answered. "There's too many damn questions I need answered, I didn't want any Rhode Island cops getting to you before I did."

"You knew I'd help the priest."

LeGrasse nodded, a strange glint in his eyes. "Damn right," he said. "I've been in those trees for three days now, watching the house every waking moment, waiting for you to get here. So what's going on, Casey? These people old partners of yours that you double-crossed? Or are they just working for some other mob boss?"

"Damn it," muttered Cobb, "first of all, stop calling me Casey. My name is Cobb. Second of all I don't work for the fucking mob."

"So what, then? You a bank robber?"

"A long time ago," said Cobb. "But not anymore. You should go home, LeGrasse. This isn't anything you can help with."

"Oh no," said LeGrasse. "I'm not walking away from this one. I've probably already given up my job just being here and ignoring jurisdictions and professional courtesy. But I don't care. So far I've got two assholes who don't die when they're supposed to—one that eats people, I should add—and a woman who, by all reports, is smaller than my sister but can twist full-grown men's heads around with her bare hands. You think I'm just going to forget about all of that?"

"You would if you were smart," Cobb replied, looking back at the house. The presence within was waiting for him and he was getting impatient to meet it. Suddenly a thought struck him. "The woman," he said. "What does she look like?"

LeGrasse shrugged. "About five-two, 110 pounds, pretty. Reddish hair."

"Damn," Cobb whispered, finally understanding. That was how Philip Farwell knew him and that was who the vampire that attacked him was. She was Helena Farwell, the name he had read in the city directory. At least now he knew why Philip had insisted he come to the house after dark. It was so his wife would be up and around.

What had Helena said to him? "We have such plans for you." She had said after drinking Cobb's blood and he remembered not liking the sound of it. Cobb realized that he was in for more of a fight than he thought.

"You should go," he told LeGrasse. "The woman can snap your neck with her bare hands, and she probably will. If you're lucky."

LeGrasse lifted his gun away from Cobb's head. "You know who she is?" He asked.

"I do now," Cobb replied. He looked at LeGrasse, his eyes hard. "Do you believe in God, LeGrasse?"

"Sure," said the policeman. "Why?"

"Because He's not in there," said Cobb as he pointed at the house. "But there are things in there that will make you think God is a madman. You think you can handle that?"

"Yes," he said, after a moment.

"You sure?"

"I told you I can't just walk away from this."

"Good," said Cobb. "Then let's go back to my car."

"Why?"

"You need more than just that gun," answered Cobb.

The pair them went back to Cobb's car and the policeman watched while Cobb dug around inside his trunk. Weapons glittered in the moonlight, and after a few seconds of searching Cobb found what he was looking for.

"Here we go," he said, pulling out an old, single action Remington .44 revolver. "You ever fire one of these?"

LeGrasse took the pistol, looked at it. "No," he said. "But it can't be much different than most guns."

"It's not," said Cobb, and he handed LeGrasse a box of bullets. "Put as many of these in your pockets as you can," he said. LeGrasse complied and Cobb went back to the trunk, got a long knife that he handed to the detective. LeGrasse stuck it through his belt and put his .38 into a pocket, the big .44 in his hand.

Cobb closed his box and then the trunk. The slam was loud in the quiet night, LeGrasse jumped a bit. Cobb looked him in the eye, his coat flapping in the breeze. "Now look," he said, his voice rough, "we're about to go into hell. I don't know exactly what's in that house, but I know it's not like anything you've ever seen. If you're serious about this then I guess I owe you as much of an explanation as we have time for."

LeGrasse nodded.

"First off," started Cobb, "the red-haired woman is a vampire. Her husband is something else, probably a magician of some sort."

"What, like Houdini?"

"No," answered Cobb, "like Merlin. Anyhow, the vampire is the real problem. If you see her, shoot first and scream later. Forget that she's a woman, and forget that she's pretty. She can move very fast, and she'd kill you without hesitating. Don't make eye contact with her if you can avoid it. If you do get a chance to shoot you should aim for the head or the knees. The more you can get her to bleed the better. You can't kill her with that gun, but you can slow her down, and that's all you can hope for. Just get away.

"Secondly, you should know that I'm one hundred and eighty-two years old, and that I spend most of days hunting and killing things like vampires. If anything happens, or if you think something is about to happen, fire off a shot. I'll come running. And if you see me getting cut up or otherwise hurt don't you dare try to get in the way. You know I can't be killed easily so don't waste your time trying to save me."

LeGrasse looked at the ground. "You know that I don't believe in any of this," he said. "What you're saying just isn't possible."

Cobb's reaction was quick. "I didn't say you had to believe me," he said. "I just said I wanted you to know what's going on. If you have trouble believing in this sort of thing then just focus on this: inside that house is a priest that's being held hostage, and right now you and I are the only ones that can help him. We can't call anyone else. The Farwells know I'm here and they're waiting for us."

This statement had a visible effect on the detective, and he nodded, lifting his pistol so that it rested near his shoulder, pointed up. "All right," he said. "Let's go."

Cobb reached out and clapped LeGrasse on the shoulder, smiling. "That's the spirit," he said. "Just keep your head down and your gun up and you'll be fine."

They walked quickly to the house, their weapons in their hands, their feet crunching against the bare pavement. Cobb decided to head in the front door, a frontal assault what he was best at, but he told LeGrasse to hunt for a back way in. If the policeman could get in unnoticed while Cobb made noise from the front, maybe they could find the priest without much trouble. That was LeGrasse's job—to find McAllen as fast as possible and get him out. Cobb would take care of the fighting. On the edge of the road the two nodded at each other and LeGrasse disappeared into the trees that surrounded the house, Cobb turning towards the dimly lit front door. Shotgun in hand he walked up to it and unceremoniously kicked it in, the door banging on the hinges.

"I'm here, Farwell," he shouted, looking into the open doorway. "Come get me."

No sound answered him, but the lights came on. Cobb squinted while his eyes adjusted and saw that just past the door was a large entryway, a doorway to the rest of the house on the right and to his left a set of stairs heading up. His boots thudded on the wood planks of the floor as he stepped carefully inside.

He walked over to the stairs and looked up, saw no one at the top. The strange presence was like ice in the air.

Something moved to Cobb's right, in the open doorway to the living room. In a flash he pointed his shotgun and turned his head, but there was nothing there. It hadn't been his imagination, though. Cautiously he stepped into the doorway, his shotgun ready.

The living room was a narrow, slightly cramped room, filled with photographs, lamp tables, two chairs, a sofa, and a grandfather clock, a brown and red rug on the floor. After checking to both sides Cobb entered the room, getting impatient. He didn't like waiting games. Beyond the room was another doorway, which led to what looked like the dining room.

Cobb searched the living room briefly, checked under the tables and sofa, and then walked into the kitchen. For a moment he remembered being attacked by Helena in Kilroy's kitchen and a sensation of déjà vu came over him. It was a similar room, with white cabinets, a stove, sink, and everything else that a kitchen should have. To the right was a door that looked like it led to the back yard, to the left a doorway to the dining room.

Suddenly, Cobb felt something brush by his ear. He jumped, turning, and saw nothing. Still, though, he felt almost as if something was in the air around him, like the air was moving slightly in tiny whirling motions around him. He blinked, reached up and wiped his chin. The cold presence was getting stronger, he noticed, and it was starting to annoy him.

"Cobb."

The voice was a whisper, and Cobb realized quickly that it was LeGrasse, standing in the doorway to the back yard. He had managed to open the door just a crack, and was staring through the tiny aperture. The fact that he had managed to open the door without Cobb hearing bothered him a little. It meant that the presence was distracting him more than he thought.

A finger to his lips, Cobb moved quietly to the door and pushed it open slightly. LeGrasse looked at him, huge revolver ready.

"It's queer out here," said the policeman in hushed tones. "Like we're being watched."

"We probably are," answered Cobb, and he looked back into the kitchen. "Have you seen anyone moving around?"

LeGrasse shook his head and Cobb replied with a slow nod. "I'm going upstairs," he said. "You keep an eye out down here."

Cobb stepped away from the door and the policeman entered and shut it behind him. Quickly, yet as quietly as possible, Cobb went back to the entryway, noted that the front door was still hanging on its hinges, and looked back up the steps. There still wasn't anyone there.

Cobb ascended the stairs in a few bounds, boots thudding on the carpeting, and looked down the hallway that led from the top. The second floor was smaller than the first, simply a long hall with two doors on both sides and a window at the end. Cobb stared down the quiet, empty corridor, the heavy presence almost a physical thing now. Something was in one of those rooms.

Slowly, deliberately, Cobb walked down the hall, his hands firmly on his shotgun. Keeping his eyes on the hall he tried the knob on the first door on his left, turned it slowly, the sound of the latch loud and intrusive in the oppressive silence.

The door opened with a slight creak, the room inside dark, and the light from the hall cutting a swath into the blackness. With a frown Cobb pushed the door completely open and let in as much light as possible. The room looked to be a bedroom of some sort, probably a guest bedroom since the room was sparsely furnished and the bed looked like it hadn't been slept on in ages. Light fell across the mattress, a yellow rectangle that only slightly illuminated the surrounding area. Cobb's eyes darted around the bedroom, and then he turned away from the open doorway, convinced that what he was looking for wasn't in there.

Cobb headed to the second door on that side, repeated the procedure of opening it slowly while keeping his eye on the hallway. For a moment as the doorknob turned he wondered if LeGrasse was all right downstairs. The latch clicked and Cobb held his breath as the door opened. He didn't know if he would see a hideous monster on the other side, but he was starting to wish he would. Anything would be better than the silence that was pressing on his ears.

Like the first room this one was dark, but this was no bedroom. Cobb saw in the hallway light that he was looking at Philip Farwell's study. Facing him on the other side of the room was a long wooden desk with a chair set behind it. Paintings of rural scenes were on the walls, interspaced between filled bookshelves. Cobb took a guarded step into the study, his curiosity rising. Perhaps some clue as to what Farwell wanted with him was in this room, he thought.

A switch was on the wall next to the door. He reached out and flicked it, bathed the study in yellow light. Cobb relaxed slightly and headed towards the desk, checked it over for anything interesting. Besides some papers that looked like mundane correspondence he saw nothing.

After a moment's searching he realized that he had people to kill and he went back to the hallway. He could sift through Philip's possessions later at his leisure. Right at that moment he had a priest to rescue and a married couple to butcher.

Cobb looked back towards the stairs. As he did his eyes caught a flash of movement from the open door to the guest bedroom and he stiffened. Something had definitely ducked into the bedroom as he came out of the study, he was certain of it. He shut the study door slowly and crept back towards the guest bedroom, his eyes narrow. He could feel his heart pounding in his chest as his anticipation started to build. He couldn't be certain of what he had seen, only that it moved into the bedroom as soon as he appeared.

Cobb reached the edge of the doorway, twisted his head around the opening and peered inside. The room looked the same as it had been, a yellow rectangle bisecting the bed, the rest of the room dark. Cobb's eyes moved from side to side.

And then he saw it. Nestled to his right, in the corner on the other side of the bed near the headboard, something was standing in the darkness, looking at him.

Cobb froze. It was standing perfectly still, a pair of eyes that glittered in the hallway light, only about four feet tall. As he strained to discern the details, Cobb slowly became aware of what he was looking it.

It was a girl, a young girl.

She couldn't have been older than eleven or twelve, dressed in a long, lacy nightgown, the color of her hair impossible to tell in the lack of light. Her skin was gray in the darkness, her lips an indistinct, black line under the shadows of a nose. Cobb couldn't tell but it almost looked like she was swaying slightly from side to side.

"Hello?" Cobb asked, keeping his voice quiet. Stepping into the doorway, his huge shadow intruding on the yellow rectangle, he knew there was something wrong with what he was seeing but he couldn't ignore the possibility that he was looking at a real child.

The girl smiled. Cobb felt a sickening sensation of dread come upon him as the girl's black mouth twisted up at the sides. She looked maniacal.

Then, the girl laughed. It was a cold, tittering sound, quietly rattling from the corner while Cobb stared. His lips pulled back, baring his teeth, unable to lose the feeling that something just wasn't right.

And then something hit him. It landed on his back, crashed into him from behind and knocked him forward, snarled like an enraged tiger and beat at him with frenzied limbs. Cobb swore and he fell across the bed. The mattress frame snapped under the massive impact of his weight and whatever it was that tore at him with sharp claws. Cobb threw his right elbow out, trying to hit the thing on his back while twisting over onto it. It pulled away, slipped off the foot of the bed and onto the floor. Cobb scrambled towards the headboard, trying to get a look at his attacker while pointing his shotgun at it.

Suddenly he realized that he had moved alongside the little girl. She was standing on his right, not more than a foot away. He turned and looked at her, then back to the thing at the foot of the bed. The thing that had attacked him was getting to its feet, a black humanoid shape in the shadows.

"Get out of here," he barked, deciding that if she was an actual child she needed to escape. The girl stared right at him, still grinning strangely.

"Boo," she said, and then she leaned forward and the flesh melted off her face. She stared through hollow eye sockets, her bare skull exposed, a death's head that grinned worse than before. Cobb swore in surprise and took a swing at her. His fist struck nothing, though, and the little girl giggled as his arm passed through her.

The thing at the foot of the bed leapt at Cobb, who turned his attention away from the spectral child and kicked out one foot. His boot heel smashed into the thing's face with a loud crack and Cobb was pleased that it was solid. The thing squealed as it was deflected towards the doorway and into the light. Blood, almost black in the hall light, struck the wooden floor just before the creature did.

In the light, Cobb could see what he was fighting. It pushed itself up, looked at him with hate-filled eyes. It looked a great deal like a man, with neatly combed hair, and dressed in a blue shirt and tie. Its face, however, was a lined, almost wolfish horror, the eyes red and the mouth filled with jagged fangs. The nose was a deformed mess, broken by Cobb's kick, blood ran down its chin as it let out a low, menacing growl.

Cobb knew what it was. It had once been a man. He couldn't quite remember the proper name, but it was a species of vampire, and one that he should have expected. Some people, he knew from his conversation with the vampire Matthias, became vampires from drinking vampire blood. They were like Helena and Matthias, the higher species of vampires who could pass as humans when they wanted. Some people, however, when they were bitten by those higher vampires became like this creature after they died, animalistic and savage. These feral vampires were used as foot soldiers and slaves by the higher, more sophisticated caste. It had a name, but Cobb couldn't remember it.

Whatever the creature was called, he tried to attack again, raised his claws and jumped forward. This time, however, Cobb pointed his shotgun and fired both barrels. The blast shook the windows and the feral vampire took the impact in the abdomen. The force of it threw him back against the edge of the doorway, off which he bounced and landed back on the floor. Cobb reloaded quickly while the vampire reared back up, the flesh of his stomach and chest ripped apart.

The entire time the little girl kept tittering.

"Shut up," grumbled Cobb, and he fired again. The load of buckshot knocked the vampire out into the hall. Cobb leapt up off the bed, reloading, and kicked the vampire in the head as he tried to right himself on the floor of the corridor. The vampire sputtered, his face a bloody mess, and flopped onto his back, stunned.

With a quick, efficient motion Cobb slid out his Bowie knife and slashed downward, hacked into the vampire's throat while dropping onto one knee. Blood spattered onto his face and he started sawing back and forth, his powerful muscles forcing the blade deep into the esophagus. The vampire struggled, gurgling and clawing at the air. It took several seconds, but Cobb managed finally to silence the creature, its throes ceasing once his blade reached the spine. Placing a knee on the barely-moving vampire's chest, Cobb struggled to push his knife through the gap between the individual vertebrae, cut through the spinal cord and severed the head completely from the body.

Once this was finished Cobb became aware that he was kneeling in a very large pool of blood. His left hand and knife were drenched in it.

Behind him, the little girl still giggled. Cobb jumped to his feet and swung around, an angel of red-spattered wrath. She stood in the doorway, completely visible in the light, her face complete again. She had shoulder length brown hair and her skin was pale, but her grin was no less maniacal.

"Who the hell are you?" Cobb demanded, realizing that the girl was slightly transparent.

The girl said nothing. She just stopped laughing. Staring at Cobb with her big eyes she reached up with both hands, as if expecting him to pick her up. He didn't, however. He simply looked down at her, tiny flecks of blood on his face, his bloody knife in his left hand and his shotgun in his right. After a moment the girl became disappointed and frowned. The sight of it would have been heart-breaking if it had been a normal child. She wasn't, though, and this was made even more evident by the fact that she was gone a second later, vanishing as if she had never been there.

And then Cobb remembered what the vampire was called. Upuir. That was the word; at least that's what Matthias had told him. The higher species were vampir, the lower were upuir. They were inherently weaker than the vampir but still more than capable of ripping apart the average human being.

He looked back at the dead upuir, at the jagged stump at the end of its neck. This one had probably been young but it had still survived four 12-guage-shotgun shells at close range. Cobb shrugged. He was probably just some poor bastard that the Farwells had taken one night, murdered and transformed for the purpose of fighting Cobb, one more person that the Farwells owed vengeance to.

From downstairs there was a loud gunshot, and Cobb remembered LeGrasse. Boots thundering against the floor, Cobb ran to the steps, only to halt as he saw another grinning upuir standing on the staircase. This one was a woman, with long, scraggly blonde hair, her lined face streaked with dirt. There was no waiting for the creature to make its move, Cobb just shot her in the face and burst her skull apart like a warm melon. The vampire twitched horribly, her arms waved about in the air, and then she toppled down the stairs to land in a heap at the bottom.

Cobb leapt down the stairs as another shot from LeGrasse's .44 resounded from the kitchen. He sheathed his knife and slapped another pair of shells into his Stoeger, and then ran into the kitchen.

Two more upuir menaced the policeman, their backs to the door. It looked as though LeGrasse was holding his own, though, even if his face was white as a sheet and he looked absolutely terrified as he waved his big revolver at the pair of monsters. One of the upuir was clutching its left shoulder, a huge exit wound on its back.

"The head, LeGrasse," barked Cobb, and he grabbed the wounded upuir by the hair, "aim for the head!" He brought his shotgun down on the upuir's skull with a dull thud. The thing wailed in protest and LeGrasse fired, this time shooting the second upuir through the eye. It fell backwards, blood and brains pouring from the back of its head.

Cobb slammed his flailing vampire against a nearby cabinet and pressed its head against the wood. He looked at LeGrasse.

"Shoot that one again through the head," he ordered, pointing with his shotgun. "Make sure it's finished."

While LeGrasse walked over to the fallen upuir Cobb shoved the barrels of his weapon against the side of his vampire's skull and stepped back, eyes narrow as he unloaded. A cloud of wood splinters and blood burst around him as the shot shattered the skull and the cabinet door. The vampire slid onto the floor, silent.

On the other side of the room LeGrasse was standing over his vampire, pistol pointed down at its head. He was hesitating. Cobb frowned at him. Hardened police detective or not, apparently LeGrasse wasn't the kind of person who could just shoot someone in cold blood, and even though this was a hell-spawned thing that had been trying to kill him it was now lying inert on the floor, one shot already through the head. The feeling was something that Cobb remembered from his early days. Shooting it again seemed like overkill.

"Do it," he ordered. "It might not be dead."

LeGrasse looked at him, at the hardness in his eyes, at the faint streaks of red on his face and the tears in his clothes. Cobb wanted him to understand that this was what he did. This was how he spent his days. Everything he had told him outside was true, and if the cop wanted to survive he had to go on automatic, had to fight and kill out of instinct. There was simply no other way.

"Do it," Cobb repeated. "Do it right now."

Intimidated, LeGrasse looked back at the vampire and pulled the hammer of his revolver back. It looked like a corpse, a pool of red beneath its head, broken fragments of bone and chunks of shredded meat visible in its hair.

Then the thing twitched.

It was only a tiny, almost invisible movement, but Cobb saw it and it was enough to make LeGrasse fire out of reflex. The bullet punched through the vampire's head and slammed into the tile beneath, more gore showering the floor. After a moment LeGrasse looked at Cobb, his breath coming in heavy gasps.

"Forget about law and order," said Cobb, flatly. "This is a completely different thing."

The detective nodded, and Cobb glanced around the room while policeman swung open his revolver and replaced his spent shells. "There's got to be a basement," he said. "Maybe that's where they're hiding. I don't know how many of these things there are," he kicked the dead upuir at his feet, "but there might be more. Keep your eyes open."

Without waiting for a reply Cobb headed into the dining room. It was a simple place, with a long brown wooden table, a small chandelier, and hardwood floor. A pair of silver candlesticks rested on the middle of the table. Cobb felt a chill as he entered the room, but ignored it and focused instead on the matter at hand.

The silence that permeated everything seemed strange after all of the shooting and shouting of the past few minutes, and Cobb could feel his adrenalin pump through his veins. Now that the action had started he didn't want it to stop, he just wanted to keep going.

He stooped slightly and glanced under the table, saw nothing.

When he straightened, however, he saw that he was no longer alone. Where there had been no one now stood eight people, all in a line on the other side of the long table, looking at him. Cobb frowned, recognized one of the onlookers as the little girl he had seen upstairs. All of them were dressed in their nightclothes, but those of a style that suited Cobb's original century rather than the 1930's. The oldest of the eight were a man and a woman, side by side in the middle, both probably in their mid to late forties. On the woman's opposite side stood two young girls and a boy, three more boys by the man. The little girl that Cobb had met upstairs was right alongside the woman. The oldest of the children couldn't have been more than fifteen or sixteen. All of them had mournful, almost sardonic expressions on their faces.

"Hi," said Cobb, a bit uncertain. Like the little girl had been upstairs, all of them were semi-transparent in the light. "What's your story?"

"I built this house," said the old man, his voice hollow. The words came slowly. "I built it for my family."

"We lived in this house," said the woman, chiming in as soon as the old man finished. There was an almost singsong quality to the way their voices flowed together. "We lived here for each other."

"Now we live for the house," said the little girl that Cobb had met before. She giggled and the woman reached over to stroke her hair, smiling down at her. "We live here because it wants us to."

"I don't think you're alive at all," said Cobb. His knuckles whitened on the shotgun. "I think you've been dead for a long time."

One of the boys laughed. Cobb looked at him, suddenly wishing he'd brought his rock salt. The boy had thick black hair and appeared to be around twelve or thirteen. "You can live here with us," said the old man. "Stay here for the house. It wants you, too."

"No thanks," Cobb replied. The old man frowned.

"You will stay with us," he commanded. "You will stay here forever."

The rest of the family started spreading apart, came slowly around the table towards Cobb. "Stay here forever," the old man repeated.

"Forever," the rest of the family droned in unison. Cobb backed off as they started to get near.

"You can play with us," said one of the boys. "We know all of the best games."

"There will be no more nightmares," said the mother. "Only peace."

"We can be the family you have lost," said the second girl. "You can love us like you loved them."

Cobb knew that there wasn't much he could do against ghosts, so he turned to run. Unfortunately as soon as he had his back to the table he felt the icy touch of several hands grip him tightly by his hands and shoulders. A yelp of protest shot out of him and Cobb was yanked off his feet and thrown across the table. The candlesticks went flying and his gun followed suit. He rolled off the table and crashed onto the wooden floor.

"Stay with us!"

The entire family yelled at once, their voices angry. Cobb pushed himself onto his knees, looking around for his shotgun, realized after a moment that the spectral people had vanished even though he felt as though they were still in the room. The table lurched once, as if to prove that they were, and then toppled over. It crashed into him and he threw it away, his patience exhausted. The wood cracked as it landed on its side.

Cobb felt the temperature of the room drop even more, just as he spied his shotgun lying a few feet away, near the entrance from the kitchen. He rolled forward and scooped up the gun just as one of the candlesticks picked itself up off the floor and hurtled at him. It missed his head by a fraction, embedding itself in the wall with bone-crushing force. Glancing at it, Cobb looked up and saw that there was a door set into the opposite wall. He leapt to his feet and jumped over the sideways table, grabbed the knob and flung open the door. The power of his arm popped one of the hinges so that the door hung at an angle. Without a second thought he bounded through the opening. He simply wanted to get away from the specters in the dining room.

Cobb found himself on a staircase headed downward, and he went through the doorway so fast that he almost stumbled and fell down the steps. It took a moment to regain his balance, and then he hurried down towards the door at the bottom, illuminated by a single bulb that hung from the ceiling. In his ears Cobb could still hear the strange tittering of the little girl—he tried ignoring it, clomped down to the basement door.

Pausing before the door, he took a breath, his shotgun ready. He knew that Helena and Philip were probably just beyond, the priest with them, all of them waiting for his arrival. He would have to move quickly if he were going to keep the vampire from harming McAllen. She was top priority. Philip could be dealt with later.

Like he had so many times before, Cobb pushed all thoughts of mercy or pity out of his mind. McAllen needed help and there wasn't any room for error. He nodded to himself, reached out and took the doorknob in his big hand, ready to do what had to be done. The dark presence that had surrounded the house was stronger in the basement, but Cobb took no notice. He had to forget about it, at least until he was ready to deal with it. McAllen's safety came first.

Cobb pulled the door open, expecting to see Helena and Philip menacing a bound and gagged McAllen, but what he got was entirely different.

What he got was a huge beast of a man stooped just past the door, grinning while one eye glared down at him. It took a moment, but he recognized the giant.

"Fletcher?" He asked, dumbfounded. What was Fletcher doing with the Farwells?

Knowing full well that the answer didn't matter, Cobb pointed his shotgun into Fletcher's chest, but the giant swatted the gun away before it could be fired. It clattered out of Cobb's hand, into the basement. Cobb kicked Fletcher in the shin, but the blow wasn't enough to keep the giant from punching Cobb across the jaw. Cobb was knocked backwards and he tripped onto the stairs, flopped onto his back. His skull bounced painfully off the edge of a step.

Fletcher gave Cobb no time to shake off the disorientation that overtook him. He loped forward and clutched Cobb's shirt with one enormous hand, pulled him up from the steps. The giant balled his other hand into a fist and smashed Cobb's face, first once, then a second time, and then a third. Cobb's body went limp. Blood ran from his nose and mouth and his eyes were barely open.

Smiling maniacally, Fletcher lifted Cobb a bit higher and then smashed him against the stony wall. A patch of red marked where Cobb hit as Fletcher, still smiling, pulled him back.

"It's good to see you again," said Fletcher. Cobb managed a slight smirk of defiance. Saliva trickled from his drooping jaw. "I've been waiting for this chance."

Cobb wanted to say something in response, but it just seemed like too much work. Besides, Fletcher just hit him against the wall again anyway, an audible crack resonating through the air. Cobb felt his consciousness slipping—he thought that his skull might be breaking or broken. All he wanted to do was close his eyes and rest for a while.

Fletcher dropped his enemy on the steps, his eyes filled with contempt.

"For my god," said the giant under his breath, and then he stomped on Cobb's stomach. Cobb spat up a mouthful of blood, his body buckled as something inside him ruptured. Fletcher took a step back, his pig's face beaming with satisfaction. Cobb squirmed a bit, still awake.

"Wonderful job, Fletcher," said Helena, appearing at the top of the steps. Fletcher looked up at her, his eye narrow.

"Now I eat him," snarled the giant. "Now his flesh is mine."

Helena came down a step. "Not yet," she said, raising a finger. "First I get his blood, but before that Philip gets him."

Fletcher seemed to accept, and Helena came down to stand over Cobb in a low crouch. "Hello again," she said. Cobb recognized her from his dream, but there wasn't much he could do with that at the moment. She touched the side of his swollen and distorted face with a long, slender finger and wiped a bit of blood onto the tip. Slowly and deliberately she brought the finger to her mouth and kissed the blood from it while Fletcher watched, silent. "I'm so glad you could make it," Helena explained with a smile. "Philip and I weren't sure that the priest would be enough to get you here."

"He didn't come for the priest," Fletcher said. "He came here to kill you. He doesn't care about hostages." He may as well have been on the other side of the city, for all Cobb could tell. He was losing consciousness, Fletcher sounded like he was miles away.

"It makes no difference," said Helena as she adjusted her hair, pulled back into a tight bun. "He's here now, and that's all that matters."

With that, the vampire put her hands on the sides of Cobb's head and twisted. His neck snapped with a sickening crunch, sending him into oblivion.

CHAPTER 23

▼

It took a long time for Cobb to realize he was awake.

It was dark and that was the first problem. He wasn't even able to tell that his eyes were open at first, and by the time he sensed that he was actually conscious he didn't know how long he'd been that way. The second problem was that he felt like he was floating—his limbs were almost numb—and that was something that he usually associated with sleep.

It was only when he tried to move that he realized why he felt like he was floating—he was hanging in the air, his arms were pulled straight out to the sides, and something was gripping his wrists and ankles tightly. That was why his limbs felt numb; the circulation was being cut off.

His awareness sharpened and he looked around, trying to remember what had happened.

It all came back. Fletcher had surprised him and Helena had finished him. That was it. He hadn't expected Fletcher. Even if it had been a possibility that the Farwells somehow knew the last scion of the Great Pig, it seemed unlikely that they would work together. Their attitudes were much too different for them to get along, but Cobb supposed that a mutual hatred was enough to conquer all adversity. It was almost a compliment to his abilities that he could bring them together.

Cobb wondered how long he'd been out. He couldn't remember the exact moment when Helena put him under, but he remembered that it involved breaking his neck. That was a favorite technique of hers and it may have kept him unconscious for a day or two.

Cobb tried to figure out where he was. The air smelled musty and he became aware of the floor under his feet. It felt like dirt. Cobb supposed he was in the basement of the house. He also realized in that moment that his feet were bare, and it didn't feel like he was wearing a shirt. He was definitely wearing pants; he could feel the cuffs against the top of his feet.

Cobb was feeling very disoriented due to the darkness and the fact that he was hanging suspended in the air. He wondered if LeGrasse had managed to escape the house, or if he was even alive. If Fletcher or Helena caught him it was likely they would kill him without a second thought. That was how they worked. Helena would drain his blood and turn him into an upuir whereas Fletcher would simply eat him. Cobb wasn't sure which was worse.

"Are you afraid?"

The voice was so soft from the darkness that Cobb wondered if he actually heard it. He couldn't tell where it had come from.

"Are you afraid?" The voice asked again, a little louder or perhaps it was just closer. Cobb thought it was a female voice, young, but not the singsong child's voice of the little ghost girl he had met before. It was stronger than a child's, but not quite the full voice of an adult.

"No," said Cobb, deciding to answer the question. The sound of his voice seemed loud.

"I'm not, either," said the voice, with the tone of any youth trying to impress an adult. "What's your name?"

"Sebastian," said Cobb. "What's yours?"

"Rebecca," said the voice, definitely closer now.

"What are you doing here, Rebecca?"

"I like it down here," the girl answered. The sound came from somewhere to Cobb's right, but no more than a foot or two away. "I like the dark."

Cobb frowned. "Do you live in the house?" He asked. "With the Farwells?"

There was a pause before an answer came. "I don't like the Farwells," said Rebecca. "They make noise and turn the lights on."

"I don't like the Farwells, either," Cobb said. He pulled at his restraints. His hands felt like they were ten feet away. "If you can get me out of here, I can make sure they don't bother you again."

"You could stay here," said Rebecca and a cold breath of air on Cobb's ear made him flinch. "With me. I get lonely sometimes."

Damn, thought Cobb, another one of the house's ghosts. How many of them were there? "I can't, Rebecca," he said. "I'm sorry."

"Please, Sebastian?"

The room suddenly filled with light, and Cobb reflexively shut his eyes. After a few seconds, they adjusted and he could open them again.

A man was looking at him with a smile on his face and his hands in his pockets. Tall and thin, dressed in plain trousers and a gray shirt, Cobb guessed that he was looking at Philip Farwell. He had an air of confidence about him, almost smugness, really. And why shouldn't he? He had managed to capture the terrible Sebastian Cobb, after all.

Cobb looked at Philip's face. He was rather normal looking, with his hair neatly combed, but something about him was very, very familiar. Cobb seemed to remember seeing him before, but he couldn't place where or when. He didn't even know if he actually had seen him before, or if he was just confusing Philip with someone else. In the face of things, however, Cobb realized that it hardly mattered.

In the light, Cobb could see that he was in fact in the basement. It looked like the same basement that he had seen just before Fletcher had pounded him into a bloody pulp. A quick glance at his arms showed Cobb that he was bound with chains, pulled tight from fixtures bolted into the walls. They all looked recently installed. His back and shoulders ached from the strain of his arms being pulled for so long, but he was good at ignoring pain.

"Glad to see you awake, Sebastian," said Philip. "I was afraid we'd killed you."

"Not likely," replied Cobb, his voice low. Philip laughed.

"Yes, I imagine that'd be quite a task. Fletcher said that he even blew you up and you managed to survive it. That's quite a trick."

"Just wait until I get out of here. I'll show you a better one."

Philip shook his head. "I don't think that's something I need to worry about," he said. "You're not getting out of here, at least not in any way that you're going to enjoy." He started pacing back and forth in front of Cobb.

"You see, Sebastian, there's something that lives beneath this house. A power that I'm sure you've already felt, and it likes you. I was hoping that it would, because I'm betting that if I can work the right sort of rituals, I can get it to give me its power in exchange for you. Or maybe it'll just give me yours. It's an old, old thing, Sebastian, and as you know old things are usually the strongest things."

Cobb's top lip curled back, the muscles of his thick torso bulging. "That's what this is all about?" He asked. "You want to use me as bait to get your demon out?"

"It's not a demon," Philip said quickly. "It's from another world, another part of the universe. It came here millions of years ago and was trapped. Now it's asleep, but it comes close to waking up every now and then when the right people live in this house. It hears dreams, listens to desires, and feeds on emotions. That's why it likes you, because of your pure hatred, of your single-minded lust for vengeance, and your immortality. You have power, Sebastian, and power always attracts the powerful."

"That's the stupidest thing I've ever heard," replied Cobb. "And it's bullshit. If you wanted this thing to get out of the ground so badly, you'd use your wife, or Fletcher. You don't need me."

Philip suddenly went rigid. "Don't you ever talk about my wife," he ordered, pointing a finger, his voice rough. "You have no idea what she is."

"She's a vampire," Cobb goaded, seeing that he'd managed to push one of Philip's buttons. "She's immortal and powerful too. Just tie her to an altar and cut her open."

"Shut up."

Cobb ignored the instruction. "You have to admit," he said, "she's a lot prettier than I am. That would probably get your big monster's attention. Just put her in a corset and a pair of stockings and see what happens."

Philip stepped forward and punched Cobb across the jaw. Cobb took it smiling. He'd been hit a lot harder. Philip straightened his shirt and cleared his throat as he regained his composure.

"You have to watch that mouth," he said. "What I'm going to do to you can be very painful or it can be easy. It's up to you."

Cobb grunted. "What can you do to me?" He asked.

"I can rip you into pieces," said Philip, a strange gleam in his eye. "I can take you apart and scatter you to the wind. I can take out your soul and let Helena and Fletcher have the body. I can tear your soul apart and give it up to the thing beneath the house. What do you think about that?"

"I think you're full of shit."

Philip laughed. "Wonderful," he said, showing his teeth. "Keep thinking that. You know I can do what I claim. I've already been inside your mind. I have seen your memories and your thoughts. I know all about you, Sebastian, at least as much as you know about yourself."

Cobb's face went livid and he strained against the chains pulling his arms. He remembered the dream he'd had about Mary and that night in 1785, remembered the strange man digging in the road, and now he remembered why Philip looked familiar. They were the same man—the laborer in the dream who had been digging into the cobblestones and the man who stood before him now were the same.

"You were in my dreams," growled Cobb as his temper rose. "You broke into my fucking mind."

"Indeed," chuckled Philip. "It wasn't easy, I assure you. I had to use the link that Helena had with you after drinking your blood, but even that was rather weak and you have a very confusing mind."

"Bastard," whispered Cobb.

"Since we were talking about wives, I rather liked yours," said Philip, his turn to goad. "Pity she came to such a bad end."

Cobb jerked against his chains again, causing Philip to glance momentarily at the bolts holding them in the wall. They held. "I saw your daughter while you were dancing with my wife," Philip continued. "So pretty, wasn't she? She would have made a fine woman if she'd been given the chance."

"You're a dead man, Farwell," Cobb snarled. He had reached his limit. He wanted to snap the skinny man's neck in his hand and feel the bones crack and pop. The intrusion into his thoughts and memories was more of an insult than he could bear. "A dead man."

"Not if I get my way," replied Philip. "I don't really see the problem here, Sebastian. I know that you want peace, an end to these centuries of existence. Why fight me?"

"I'm not going out that way," Cobb answered. "I'm not going to be beaten by someone like you."

"I saw a lot of things inside your head, Sebastian. I saw you meet the Sioux medicine man in 1892. What was his name?"

The memory came back like a shot. "Runs-in-Wind," he said, almost without realizing it. He hadn't thought about that night in almost ten years. "His name was Runs-in-Wind."

"That's right. What did he tell you?"

Cobb thought back. The night Philip was talking about had been like a nightmare, when Cobb fought off a horde of horrors conjured by the rogue medicine man in South Dakota. Runs-in-Wind was trying to take revenge for the wrongs perpetuated on his people by the White Man, a noble aspiration if misguided. Butchering children and women wouldn't bring back the land his people had lost, nor would it keep them from losing more. Cobb had been forced to kill Runs-in-Wind, even though he had tried every other option, hoping that the withered old man could be reasoned with. In the end, however, it was not to be. But before he died, he said something to Cobb that had haunted him many nights afterward. Cobb could still see the old man's face. He could feel his hand on the Bowie knife in the medicine man's stomach.

"These things you kill," Runs-in-Wind had told him, coughing the words out, "they still live inside you. The black spirit possesses you, and until it is gone you will never be free."

Philip could see that Cobb remembered; the look in his eyes clear enough. "I can take it out of you, Sebastian," he said. "I can remove the black spirit and set you free."

For a second, Cobb wanted to believe him, to give in and let Philip do what he wanted. It only lasted a moment. He thought of Philip rooting around inside his head and his anger came back.

"Fuck yourself," he spat, his body tensed. "Where's McAllen?"

The tall man smiled. "I was wondering when you'd ask about him," he said. "He's fine, we're holding him upstairs now. I think he's starting to like it here."

"You've got me, let him go."

"Perhaps. We'll see what happens. I find it amusing that you came here to rescue him. I really wasn't sure that you'd show up. After all, we went to the church to find you, but you had already gone and the priest was there."

"What makes you think I care about him? I came here to kill you, the priest means nothing."

Philip snorted. "You think that's going to make me let him go?" He asked. "Really, so transparent a trick isn't suited to either of us. We're better men than that."

"Maybe not," said Cobb.

Cobb's impertinence was starting to wear on Philip. The look in his eyes was proof enough of that. "You think killing people like me makes you human?" He asked, nearly spitting out the words. "You think you're the same man you were a hundred and fifty years ago? I know everything about you, Cobb, everything that you know about yourself. You're no better than the demons and monsters you hunt and kill. If your wife and daughter were here now they'd run from you in terror."

As much as he would have liked to deny it, the words affected Cobb. The same thought had occurred to him on more than one occasion. How would Mary and Elizabeth feel if they could see him? Philip was right. They would have fled.

Cobb looked down at the floor. Defiance was still on his face, but it was tempered with a hint of despair. "You're pathetic," said Philip, turning and heading toward the door. "It's a pity you can't be reasonable," he said over his shoulder. "I was really hoping we could be civil. No matter."

He walked out of the basement, the door shutting behind him with a muffled thud. Cobb stared at it, a mixture of emotions running through him. The old sadness he had felt after having the dream about 1785 came back, and there was still the memory of Runs-in-Wind floating in his mind.

That actually helped, though. Runs-in-Wind had been a powerful Indian medicine man, a force to be reckoned with. Philip didn't seem to be half the sorcerer he thought he was. Runs-in-Wind had failed to stop Cobb, so naturally Philip would fail, too. It was only a matter of time.

But the fact that Philip had gotten inside his head still bothered Cobb. He was an extremely private man, his mind was his own, the thought of someone like Farwell poking around inside made him angrier than most things could. And he wasn't fooled by Philip's attempts to make it sound like he would be doing Cobb a favor by splitting up his essence and sacrificing it. What Philip was talking about was the utter destruction of Cobb's soul and that was far worse than death.

Now that he was alone, Cobb took in the layout of the basement. He was facing a long, wooden table set against the opposite wall, covered in strange-looking odds and ends, and a large object covered in black cloth sat in the middle of it.

"He's gone, isn't he?"

Rebecca's voice came from behind Cobb, from just against the wall. He turned his head as far as he could, but she was outside of his field of vision.

"Please don't look at me," the girl asked, her voice desperate. "Please."

"I can't see you," said Cobb, gently. There was something pathetic about Rebecca's tone—it tugged at the part of Cobb that had once been a father, now awakened by the memories that Philip had stirred. "Don't worry."

"I hate the light. I don't like it when people look at me."

"It's all right," said Cobb, facing forward. "I won't look at you."

"You promise?"

"I promise."

"Is it true that he's going to hurt you?" Rebecca asked. Cobb shook his head.

"I don't know if he can," he answered, "but he might. He wants to take something from me, Rebecca, something very important."

"And you had…a daughter?"

The question surprised Cobb. "Yes, I did," he said. "Once, a long time ago."

"She was pretty?"

Cobb smiled as he remembered Elizabeth's face. He saw her running on a hillside in a white dress, one Sunday afternoon after church. She had been laughing and smiling, chasing butterflies as her parents walked blissfully behind her. "Yes," he said, quietly. "She was very pretty."

Silence filled the room, and Cobb feared that he might be alone again. "Rebecca?" He asked, after a moment.

"I was never pretty," said Rebecca, her voice a low whisper. "I wanted to be. I asked God to make me pretty, but He didn't."

There was such anguish in the phantom girl's voice that Cobb didn't know how to respond. Part of him was losing patience with what was clearly the spirit of someone who had long since died, but another part of him remembered how the pain of a child could cut right into a father's heart. He wanted to tell her that it was all right, that none of that mattered in the long run, but he knew it was pointless. The ghost had carried its pain for a very long time, and Cobb knew that after a while it was all they had left. The pain was what kept them from moving on, and sooner or later they would grow to love that pain because it was the only thing that reminded them of what it was like to be alive.

"I'm sorry, Rebecca," he said, eventually. "But there's nothing I can do about that."

"I know," the girl replied. "I know."

"Is there anything you can do to help me, Rebecca?" Cobb asked.

"I don't think so," the girl replied, a hint of fear in her voice. "I don't think the others would like that."

"Others?"

"They mostly leave me alone down here," said Rebecca quickly. "They stay together, but I like the dark. In the light they're mean to me."

Cobb thought about the eight ghosts he had met in the dining room, about the mother and the father and their strange little girl. "You mean the family?" He asked. "Who are they?"

"They're the Jeffries family," answered a deep, strangely echoed voice. "The first family to live in this house."

Cobb, surprised, looked around the room. No one else was visible, and Rebecca hadn't spoken. "Hello?" He asked. Was another ghost talking to him?

"Hello."

This time Cobb could tell where the voice was coming from. It was somewhere in front of him, but all he could see was the wooden table and its assorted occult junk.

"Who are you?" Cobb asked, his eyes moving over the things on the table.

"I'm a friend," said the voice, still from in front of him. "Whether or not I'm your friend is entirely up to you, though."

Cobb wasn't certain, but he thought that the voice was coming from underneath the black cloth on the table, from whatever it covered.

"What's your name?" He asked.

"I don't really have one," said the voice. "But you can call me 'Head.'"

Cobb snorted. That was a silly name. Something occurred to him and he tilted his head a bit towards his shoulder. "Rebecca? Are you still there?"

The girl didn't answer.

"She's probably gone," said Head from under his cloth. "The spirits of this house don't like talking to me and they don't like it when I'm awake either. It's enough to make me feel almost unappreciated."

"If you can get me out of here I'd be plenty appreciative," replied Cobb. "Why didn't you say anything earlier?"

"I wasn't awake earlier," Head told him. "I heard you talking to Phil, and then Rebecca after he left. I couldn't actually hear her, though, just you. Like I said, they don't like talking to me. It's only because you said her name that I even know who you were speaking to."

"Who is she?"

"She's Rebecca Ainsley," answered Head. "She was born in this house over a hundred years ago. The poor child came out deformed. She committed suicide after killing her mother and stepfather. Used her stepfather's sword. They never found it. They didn't even live here anymore, but her spirit came back. They always come back."

Cobb looked at the black cloth. "It wasn't her fault," explained Head. "This house did it to her. It did a lot of things to a lot of people."

"I can tell," said Cobb. "I met the...what did you call them? The Jeffries family?"

"Yes," said Head. "Ephraim built this house, but it didn't let any of them leave. Whole family just up and disappeared in 1799. Now they're here forever."

"How many more are there?"

"I'm not really sure. Phil has been after me to find out but that's not easy since they seem naturally repelled by me. The spirit of the house is very rude, to put it politely."

Cobb shook his head. He didn't know if he should trust this "Head," but he seemed to be more knowledgeable and stable than Rebecca. "What does Philip really want with me? How can I help him talk to the thing in this house?"

"You already have, just by coming here," Head explained. "As soon as you walked inside this building the house came alive, I'm sure you felt it. The spirits here have never been this active, at least not on any level that you should be able to perceive. Phil knew there was something unique about you, and the house likes that. That's why it likes children. There's nothing more explosively unique than a child's mind. You, though, you are something else, even more unique than a child. You're a wild card, an unknown that can be used for many different things. I did some asking around. There are a lot of nasty things that are afraid of you."

"Thanks," Cobb said sarcastically. "Is there anything you can do to get me out of here?"

"Not much," said Head. "Sorry."

Cobb swore and looked at the ground. His feet were chained at the ankles while the other ends of the chains were bolted to the wall. Both of his arms were pulled straight out to the sides, the ends around his wrists and ankles secured with padlocks. The tightness of the chains on his arms was probably putting a lot of strain on the metal, but he wasn't able to get enough leverage to exploit that. Besides, his arms were numb and his back was in agony.

He still had Head, though, so he decided to get some answers, if only to take his mind off of his situation. "Hey, Head," he called out, "you awake?"

"Yes."

"Tell me about the house. You said Ephraim Jeffries built it?"

"Back in 1797," replied Head, sounding almost happy. "There was a house here before that but it burned down. Ephraim built this one and moved in."

"But he disappeared?"

"Yes," said Head, dragging the word out dramatically. "The Ainsleys moved in next, but the husband died shortly after Rebecca was born. Tuberculosis, you see. The spirit of the house made contact with Rebecca. It twisted her body in the womb and worked on her mind afterwards. When she was growing up she spent hours at a time just sitting in the back yard, silently listening to it. Rebecca's mother married a second time to a military man in 1810."

"And they left, you said?"

Head let out a chuckle. "Not for long," it replied. Cobb's top lip curled back.

"And Farwell," he said. "What's his story?"

"I think he was born in Virginia," replied Head, slowly. "In 1895. He had an uncle who introduced him to the occult when he was ten years old. He eventually killed him and stole all of his books."

"How does he know so much about me?"

"From your own memories, like he said. He'd never seen you until the Kilroy incident, so he had Helena attack you in order to find out who and what you were. She read your mind that night. She saw a few things, including your name, and names are powerful."

Cobb cleared his throat. "So why is he using me?"

"He doesn't want to endanger that delicious wife of his," Head answered, his tone odd. "And Fletcher is too vulgar for the presence to care. Helena was able to act as a link, though, and that's how he got into your mind. I saw the whole thing—he did it right here in the basement."

Cobb nodded. He knew somewhere in the back of his mind that vampires usually had some sort of connection to the people they bit, but he had hoped he was immune to it. He was immune to a lot of other things.

"So, who are you?" He asked, deciding to change the subject. "What do you do for him?"

Head snorted. "I do as little as I can," he said. "That man is undeserving of my particular talents."

"And what are those?"

"I was built for conversation," Head explained. "I was supposed to delve into the mysteries of the cosmos and then talk about them, but Philip is only interested in little things, one at a time. I'm used to talking about the grand scheme, he only wants to see what he can steal or use right now."

"Well, anyone that would marry a vampire and make deals with people like Fletcher isn't thinking ahead," replied Cobb. He looked again at the bolts to his right.

"Well I can understand marrying Helena," said Head, that odd tone back in his voice, "but Fletcher is an animal. They let him nest outside, in the back. Did you see it?"

Cobb paused. "No," he said. "I didn't."

"Probably just as well. It's filled with bones from his most recent victims. He likes to go to the train station and grab people. I'm sure someone's noticed by now."

It wouldn't have been surprising if no one had, thought Cobb. People were very good at ignoring things. "What about Helena?" He asked. He gave the chains on his right a slow tug, testing their strength. "What's she all about?"

Head laughed quietly. "She's very, very old," he said. "Phil found her about five years ago, buried somewhere in Greece. That was before he found me. From what I understand she was some sort of queen in the old days, but they deposed her and she had to run. It's very sad, I suppose."

"Or not," said Cobb while he leaned to his left. He had wrapped his fingers around the chains and was pulling at the chain on his right, using the left for support. If he could pop the bolts out of the wall or find a weak link he could escape.

"She didn't look like that when he found her," Head continued. "She was much different, but she changed her shape for him. I guess he likes redheads. I know I do."

That comment got a glance from Cobb, but he quickly looked back at the chains. He tugged harder, trying to ignore the pain in the small of his back and the deadness of his arms. A low groan escaped him as his arms flexed.

"You'd better stop what you're doing," said Head. "I can hear you straining. Someone's coming down the steps."

Cobb stopped instantly, causing his body to jerk to his right before it resumed its normal position. As soon as it had done so, the door to the basement opened and Helena appeared. Cobb looked her over, remembered her wanton features from his dream. She was dressed in tan trousers and a white shirt, the sleeves rolled up past her elbows, her hair up. Laced calf-high boots covered her feet, trousers tucked in. She had the look of someone ready to move, and her gait only reinforced that impression.

"Hello," she said. "I was hoping I'd get a chance to speak with you."

"Yeah, me too," said Cobb, "only I was hoping that you'd be the one chained up."

"Naughty," Helena replied, her hands on her hips. "Don't let my husband hear you talking like that."

"If I had my way your husband wouldn't hear anything, and neither would you."

"Philip said you were in a foul mood," said Helena, a suggestive pout appearing on her face. "But I didn't think you'd be rude." She looked at the chains. "I wouldn't bother trying to break them," she said. "I tested them myself."

Cobb's eyes were hard. "What are you doing down here?" He asked. "If you and your idiot husband are going to kill me you should just get on with it."

"It's so rare that I get a chance to talk to someone like me," said the vampire as she walked over to stand next to Cobb. She leaned in close and smelled him. "Someone who doesn't age. Someone who understands the loneliness of immortality."

"Fuck off," growled Cobb. The scent of her perfume reminded him of his dream, which reminded him of Mary. There wasn't any trace of the grave smell this time, though. "I'm not lonely, there's plenty of people who want to talk to me."

"Yes, but none of them like you," said Helena as she smiled and ran her long fingers over Cobb's bare scalp. He tried to pull away from her cold skin, but the chains kept him from eluding her touch.

"Suits me fine."

"I knew men like you," said Helena. Her fingertips moved around to Cobb's neck. "Once, a long time ago. They were warriors, generals. They followed my every command. I had thousands of priests spreading my faith. Whole cities obeyed my whims. My armies offered up the blood of the conquered and I feasted from sundown to sunup."

"Yeah," came Cobb's quick reply, "but then they ran you out on a rail, didn't they?"

Helena's eyes narrowed. "How did you know that?" She asked. Cobb said nothing. Suddenly the woman's eyes focused on him intensely and Cobb felt her mind touch his. Cobb was ready for it this time and he resisted. He thought about Runs-in-Wind, he thought about the night he saw a shooting star when he was fifteen, he thought about anything except what she was looking for.

Eventually she gave up with a shake of her pretty head. "It doesn't matter," she said. "You're right, they turned against me. The followers of another god sowed discontent among my priests. They slaughtered my children just as you did. I barely escaped. That was many, many years ago. I had hoped to sleep just long enough to avoid slaughter, but something went wrong and I slept until Philip found me."

"Too bad," Cobb mocked. "Maybe you should just kill yourself."

Her lips twisted into an angry frown and Helena's fingernails lengthened into wicked claws, which she drove into the meat of Cobb's torso. She raked them downward and tore four long lines of red across his chest. He winced, but he didn't cry out.

"You will learn respect," the vampire snarled. "I will not be insulted by one such as you." She wiped her bloody fingertips on Cobb's shoulder, a disgusted look on her face.

"What, don't you like me anymore?" Cobb asked as faint trickles of blood ran from his wounds. "I thought we both understood the loneliness of immortality."

"You understand nothing. You only attack, only cause pain. I could have shown you more than that. I could have taught you to appreciate the beauty of power."

The vampire suddenly looked saddened. "You killed my children," she said quietly. "They weren't full-bloods, of course, but I didn't want any of those around yet, not until I knew enough of the world to be able to raise them properly. The half-breeds were good enough, but you killed them. Do you know how much trouble it was to make them? We had to strangle them just the right way to make sure they woke up. Could a parent work any harder?"

Cobb stared at the floor with a scornful look on his face. He didn't want to spend the rest of the night talking to this insane bitch. Finally, Helena stalked off.

His pig-headed refusal to answer was getting to her. After she had gone, Cobb looked back at Head with a smile.

"What the hell was that all about?" He asked.

"I think she likes you," said Head. "But I have to say, you're lucky she didn't take your head off."

"She's got a temper," agreed Cobb. "I think that's normal for vampires."

"Most of them, yes."

Cobb leaned left, resuming his plans for escape. "What are you doing?" Head asked at the sound of Cobb's straining.

Cobb answered between grunts. "I'm trying to get out of here," he said. Then he took in a deep breath and pulled. "Before Fletcher comes down and starts chewing on me."

The bolts in the wall shifted slightly; Cobb felt them move. He stopped, his face red, and smiled. "Almost out," he said. He took in a colossal breath and pulled again, his eyes on the bolts, and saw fragments of powdered stone fall from around them. He didn't know how long the bolts were, but they had to have a breaking point. He relaxed for a moment and then narrowed his eyes and gave a mighty heave, his mouth hanging open.

The chain snapped.

Cobb lurched and dropped onto one knee. For a moment he knelt there while the feeling returned to his arms and the pain in his back faded. Pushing himself onto his feet, he lifted his right arm to look at the length of chain and saw the broken, deformed link that still hung at the end.

He shook the link loose and turned his attention to the chain on his other arm. After grabbing the chain with both hands he began to pull, sinking and using his own weight to brace himself. There wasn't much slack in the chains around his ankles, but there was enough for proper leverage. With a minute of heavy pulling, the bolts gave, suddenly popping out of the wall. Cobb spun around and flopped onto his stomach, his face hitting the dirt hard as the chain whipped around and scraped the wall. He lay there for a short while, breathing heavily, and then he pushed himself up onto his knees and wiped dirt from his chest and face.

All that were left were the chains around his ankles, and those would pose no problem. He sat down on the ground and sidled up to the wall, planted his feet around the bolts securing the first chain and used the wall as a brace. With both hands on the chain, he yanked. The muscles in his shoulders and thighs bulged as he let out a long groan. Eventually the chain snapped, and he repeated the process on the second.

Finally free, Cobb got to his feet, the remnants of the chains still bound to his wrists and ankles. He had no way of getting the padlocks off; his fingers couldn't get enough purchase to snap them, so for now they'd have to stay.

With hurried steps Cobb walked over to the long table, chains rattling, and pulled off the black cover over Head. Head's eyes turned up to meet his, and the shaped and riveted brass plates that formed the object's surface surprised Cobb, who wasn't really sure what he had expected to see.

"So," he said, "you're Head."

"And you're Cobb," Head replied.

Cobb fought down the urge to put out his hand for Head to shake, and then looked at the other odds and ends on the table. None of them looked like a decent weapon.

"You'd better get out of here," said Head, casually. "I think they're going to come down here soon."

"What is this?" Cobb asked, and he looked down, saw the Glenbury parchment, and picked it up to show it to Head.

"That's something that Philip and Helena stole in England," sighed Head. "It's a formula for waking sleeping things up."

Cobb looked at it. "Will it work on their sleeping thing?"

"It might," said Head. "Philip thinks it will. He hasn't been paying much attention to it since he found out about you, though. I think it was written for something specific, but I'm not sure what."

With a shrug Cobb folded up the thick parchment and stuffed it into his pocket. Anything he could do to upset Philip's plans was worth it, he decided. He would need to get to his equipment and weapons back, though, if he wanted to finish this business once and for all.

Cobb turned to leave, but then paused and glanced down at Head. "What about you?" He asked. "You happy here?"

"What do you think? Phil keeps me under a sheet in this dank basement."

"Good enough," said Cobb, and he scooped up the brass head and tucked it under one arm. "You're coming with."

CHAPTER 24

▼

Cobb bolted towards the steps, forgetting for a moment about the chains that dangled from his limbs. When he hit the wooden staircase, however, those on his ankles knocked loudly against the steps. Cobb froze, waiting, hoping that no one heard them. Head's eyes darted back and forth, its mouth slightly open.

"Quiet," the brass head whispered. "Helena can hear very well, you know."

"Yes, she can."

Cobb turned and saw Helena at the top of the steps, a haughty smile on her face. Having no desire to wait for her to do anything, Cobb hurled Head up at her. The screaming, heavy brass object crashed into her chest and knocked her off her feet. She let out a small cry of surprise as Cobb bounded past, chains rattling and banging against the wood, no longer concerned with secrecy. The woman rolled Head off her and got back up, but he paid her no mind and made for the dining room. He ignored the fact that the table had been put back in place.

He didn't make it more than half of the way towards the kitchen and its back door before Helena was on him. She landed on his back with a snarl and reached over his shoulders, her claws deep in his chest.

With a surprised yelp Cobb reached up, grabbed one of her arms, and threw her over his shoulder. She landed hard on the table, the wood cracking under her back. In an instant she slithered away from him and hopped onto the floor, turning to look him in the eye. He avoided the contact, though, by keeping his eyes on the pit of her neck. She saw that she couldn't entrance him and lunged forward, only to take a blow to the face from the chain hanging from Cobb's right arm, swung like a whip as soon as she moved. She twisted to the side and dropped to one knee, her hands going to her face, and Cobb wasted no time in hitting her again. He knew that if given a chance to recover she would come at him. His fingers thrust into her hair and he drove her headfirst into the nearby wall, her skull punching a hole in the plaster. Not yet finished, Cobb smashed her face against the edge of the wooden table with a loud thump. The sounds of the battle were sharp and intrusive in the silence that had filled the house only a moment before.

Taking a moment to lift Helena's head, Cobb saw that her face and the table edge were streaked with blood. It wasn't nearly enough to finish any vampire, though, and Cobb knew it, so he shoved his hands under her armpits and threw her across the room into the wall. She bounced off and crashed to the floor in an inert heap. Satisfied that she was at least unconscious, Cobb headed for the entryway, but then remembered something, and went back to the top of the basement stairs where he found Head on its side, looking around frantically.

"I thought you'd forgotten me," said Head as Cobb picked him up. "Let's get out of here."

"Not yet," said Cobb. "I have a friend here, somewhere."

"The priest?" Head asked. "Forget him. It's too late."

Cobb's eyes widened and looked sharply at the brass head. "What do you mean, 'too late?' Did they kill him?"

"Not exactly—" Head started, but was promptly interrupted by a loud bang and a bullet bouncing off his temple with a loud, metallic clang. Head shouted in protest and Cobb ducked down while he looked towards the entryway. Philip was there, a smoking snub-nosed revolver in his hand.

"Damn you, Cobb," he shouted. "What have you done with my wife?"

Out of reflex Cobb looked over at Helena and saw that the vampire was stirring, already coming back to consciousness. Philip fired another shot and the bullet drilled a hole in the wall above Cobb.

"We have to get out of here," whispered Head, an inch-wide dent where the bullet had struck it. "Now."

The table was alongside Cobb; he looked at it once, and then came up with a very simple plan. He rolled Head under the table, past Philip's legs, the heavy brass head leaving gouges in the wooden floor while Philip dodged to one side. As he did so Cobb lifted the table from underneath and threw it at Philip, who saw it coming and crumpled down, protecting his head as the flat tabletop smacked into him. Taking his chance, Cobb leapt over the table, scooped up Head, and ran towards the stairs.

"The door! Go out the door!" Shouted Head. Cobb ignored him and leapt up the staircase instead, intent on finding McAllen. The second floor doors were all closed again, and Cobb threw open the door to the spare bedroom and was about to run by when he saw what was on the bed.

His possessions were there—all neatly piled up on the bed, the slouch hat on top. Cobb glanced over his shoulder and saw that no one had followed him, so he jumped into the bedroom, slammed the door behind him and locked it, though he knew that the light wooden door would do little to stop Helena if she really wanted to get inside. Time was a factor, so Cobb plopped Head on the mattress and popped the shackles from his wrists and ankles, using a Schofield to shoot the locks off. When he was finished the room was filled with smoke and the stench of burning powder.

Just as he finished and picked up his Stoeger the window behind him shattered, an explosion of powdered glass that sprayed across his back, but the bigger problem was the black shape that hurled itself through at him. Cobb took the full force of the impact and staggered forward before he crashed into the door. After turning his head he saw Helena come at him, her eyes crimson and her face terrible, black and blue marks around her nose and her fangs glinting. Cobb kicked her in the stomach, sent her flying backwards, and then fired the shotgun, hoping it was still loaded. Luckily it was. The blast struck her in the chest and sprayed blood out of her back onto the wall.

"Again," shouted Head, "shoot her again!"

Cobb complied and his second barrel emptied into the vampire's stomach. She fell backwards screaming, her tiny body pummeled by Cobb's weapon. He snatched at the shells on the bed to reload while trying to keep an eye on her, but he wasn't fast enough. Like an enraged beast she loped towards him and grabbed him by the shoulders to fling him into the wall. Stunned, he managed to duck down just in time to avoid her fist, which buried itself in the wall instead of his skull. With a spray of dust and plaster Helena wrenched her limb back before she drove her knee into Cobb's stomach while he tried to straighten, and followed up with a smashing forearm to his face.

He stumbled towards the open window, his vision blurry, and Helena clapped her hands on him, intent on throwing him out it. Cobb wasn't so disoriented that he would allow it, however, and he reversed the attack, hooked one arm around the vampire's waist and tossed her at the opening feet first. She screamed and struck her head against the top of the window frame before dropping out of sight towards the back yard.

"Damn," whispered Cobb, his breath coming in heavy gasps. He massaged his chest. Helena's blow to his stomach had cracked a few ribs, he could feel a sharp pain when he breathed in and his vision was still fuzzy.

It took a moment for him to get his bearings, but he did his best to dress quickly. In seconds he was put completely together, his weapons, ammunition, coat, hat, and boots back in their proper place. Cobb smiled while he loaded his shotgun and looked at the door, ready for whatever was beyond. He could see straight again, that was something.

He picked up Head and went back to the hall, still looking for McAllen. A quick check of the study found it empty. On the other side of the hall were the two doors he hadn't had time to look in earlier—he decided to try them. Across from the study was a bathroom, and a nice one, too, but no McAllen.

Cobb went to the second door, pushed it open slowly and reached in to turn on the light. It was a bedroom, with the same hardwood floors as the rest of the house, and a pair of matching dressers of dark brown wood set against the walls. Cobb looked at the canopied, black-sheeted bed and noticed that it hadn't been made in a while. A strange, stale odor hung in the air and the windows were covered in heavy black drapes that completely repelled the outside world. That was probably for Helena's sake, thought Cobb, the drapes kept out the sun during the daytime.

Cobb's eyes were drawn to the corner. There was a chair set there, and tied to it was a man in black, his head hung low and his white hair rumpled and messy.

"McAllen," whispered Cobb, and he rushed into the room and dropped Head onto the bed. He knelt by McAllen and put a gentle hand on the man's shoulder. "Wake up, priest."

The priest made a sound and Cobb smiled, glad that he was still alive.

"Come on," he whispered forcefully, "wake up. I'm getting you out of here."

McAllen lifted his head and looked at Cobb, his eyes red and a pair of long fangs in his mouth. He made a strange gurgling noise, only half-conscious. Cobb's heart sank.

"Damn them," he whispered. "Damn them to hell."

"Sebastian?" McAllen asked, weak, his eyes opening wider. "Sebastian, is that you?"

That's what Head meant by it being too late for the priest, Cobb realized, and for a moment he wondered why Head had said nothing else since then about it, but that answer was simple. Cobb simply wouldn't have accepted it until he saw it. Helena had transformed him into a vampire, and by the looks of him he was vampir, the higher species like her, instead of the savage upuir. He looked tired, though, the transformation probably taking a lot out of him. Cobb wasn't sure how long it took, or even what was involved other than drinking vampir blood, and he didn't care. They had done it to the priest, that's all he cared about. They would pay for that.

"I'm here, McAllen," said Cobb. "How are you feeling?"

"I'm thirsty," said the priest. "Very thirsty."

Nodding, Cobb patted McAllen on the shoulder. "I know," he said. "You stay here. I'll be right back."

Cobb straightened, his expression stern. McAllen was safe for now, being a vampire he wasn't as fragile as he had been, but Cobb didn't want him running around until he knew the specifics of his condition. Tied to a chair was probably the safest place for him. But Cobb's situation had changed. This wasn't about escape or rescue anymore. Now it was about revenge, as it always should have been.

Head looked at Cobb, sympathy in its eyes. "He'll be all right," said the brass thing, "he's just getting used to his new condition."

"It shouldn't have happened," said Cobb. "He's had his share of pain. He was a good person."

"He still is," Head explained. "He's just a vampire now. It doesn't make him evil by default, you know."

"But it means he's not human anymore, and that's not what he wanted," Cobb retorted. "He's got to drink human blood to stay alive, and he won't age. I doubt that's what he was after when he signed on for the priesthood."

"Isn't that what Communion is all about?" Asked Head. Cobb just stared, his eyes hard.

"You watch him," he said. "I'm going to put an end to this."

Head said something, but Cobb didn't hear him. Angry, he stalked out of the bedroom and into the hall. As soon as he made it, though, a pair of hands grabbed him from the side and yanked him towards the stairs. Cobb reached up and grasped his attacker's arms just in time for both of them to go tumbling down the stairs together, one over the other. The pair of huge men slapped onto the first floor, both spitting and snarling. Cobb's shotgun flew out of his hand and rolled away, out of reach.

"You're mine, Cobb," barked Fletcher. He twisted Cobb underneath him onto the floor and stared maniacally through his one good eye, the stench of his breath washing over Cobb's face. "It's over."

"Damn right it is," whispered Cobb, and he wedged his knee up and pushed his opponent away. Simultaneously they jumped to their feet and faced each other, their eyes locked. Neither of the titans moved, unspoken loathing twisting in the air between them.

"Now it's just us," said Fletcher, breaking the silence. "Will you fight me with your bare hands, or will you be a coward again and pull those pistols and shoot me down?"

For a second Cobb considered it. He could just go for his iron and punch holes through Fletcher's disgusting body, then move on to Helena and Philip. But he chose not to. Fletcher had not only blown him up and beaten him, but he had helped to capture McAllen and so was partly responsible for the priest's transformation. For all of that he deserved death at Cobb's hands. Cobb wanted to take his time killing this man.

A twist of Cobb's neck while he loosened up the muscles answered Fletcher, who smiled with obscene delight. Cobb's hat had been lost in the fall down the stairs, and the light of the entryway shined off his bald scalp. Fletcher lowered himself in preparation and Cobb did likewise, both men holding their arms out. Again they faced each other silently, both playing out the coming confrontation in their minds.

The moved as one, both giants colliding with the force of a pair of elephants. They locked their arms together, their faces twisted in cold abhorrence as each tried to wrestle the other down. The sounds of their panting filled the hall, and their faces went red with the strain.

Cobb felt his legs start to buckle, and he realized that this wasn't a fight he could win this way. Fletcher was stronger than him, the gifts of Yulgo Kharan more favorable in that aspect than whatever he had been given. So, he changed tactics. He let Fletcher twist him to the side and used the momentum to carry them both over to the wall. Fletcher cursed as Cobb tucked his head and let Fletcher's skull take the impact. The top of Fletcher's head cracked the plaster and the beast was stunned.

There was an instant before Cobb dealt Fletcher a vicious head butt to the snout, crushing it and spraying blood onto the faces of both men. They released each other and Cobb pressed his advantage. He began pummeling Fletcher's head with his huge fists, which came back red. Fletcher staggered, his face a bloody pulp, but he was still strong enough to send blows back to Cobb, who took them in the jaw and nose.

For several seconds they fought like this, each hammering the other with punches that would have shattered a rhino's skull. There was no beauty or art to the way they fought, no strategy or tactics involved. They just pounded each other. This was a contest of endurance, physical and mental, and it was to the man that had the most that victory would come.

In the end it was Cobb who won, his fortitude fueled by the white-hot rage that burned deep within him. Blood-spattered and battered, he brought both fists down on top of Fletcher's head and the porcine giant toppled like a house of cards, his jaw going slack. Quickly Cobb grabbed him by the shoulders and pulled him up to put his head through the nearby window. The glass shattered, leaving jagged edges that sliced Fletcher's flesh. Unfortunately it appeared that the pain from the cuts brought him back to consciousness and he howled. Cobb was immediately pushed back by Fletcher's beefy hand, and the last scion of Yulgo Kharan reared up, his face no longer recognizable as that of a man. Cobb had mashed it into a red and black monstrosity.

"No'gh meghr jamez," Fletcher dribbled, his words coming out as nonsense through his broken jaw. He lurched forward while Cobb took a moment to breathe. "Bi'll kill doo."

Fletcher bared his teeth and Cobb kicked him in the groin. The trick might not have worked on Yulgo Kharan but it worked just fine on its chosen favorite. It was a good kick, too. Cobb had used as much force as he could muster. The pig-worshipper squealed, his entire body trembled in a morbid spasm of shock and agony, and then he fell to his knees, clutching his crotch.

The battle was over, and now it was time to administer the final blow. Cobb picked up his shotgun and walked over to Fletcher, pointed the gun at his face. Fletcher, though, didn't know he'd been beaten. He reached up quickly and grabbed Cobb's forearm, twisted the weapon away.

Cobb had really had enough. He wrenched free from Fletcher's grasp and smashed the Stoeger into the side of the giant's head. Fletcher howled as his skull cracked, and Cobb hit him again. The barrels of the shotgun came away gleaming with blood. Fletcher fell back but Cobb held him up by the shirt collar and continued to batter him. Red splattered off the gun as he whipped it back and forth, but Cobb didn't stop, he beat him repeatedly with the steel muzzle, disgusted. He thought about the bomb that Baker had set, the victims that Yulgo Kharan had left behind, and the ones that Fletcher himself had undoubtedly claimed in the time since meeting the Pig. He thought about the priest upstairs, now a creature of darkness, and he thought about his own injuries caused by the giant. All of this went through his mind as he bashed his shotgun against Fletcher's skull. Any sympathy he might have felt the first time they met was gone, drowned out by the anger and hate that now filled him. All he wanted was to kill Fletcher, to make him dead, to bury him under the ground and never see him again.

By the time he finished he barely noticed that Fletcher wasn't moving. Cobb's hand opened and Fletcher crumpled to the floor, three hundred pounds of meat in need of a grinder. His lips pulled back over his teeth, Cobb reached down and pulled the giant's jaw down before stuffing his gun's muzzle into the open mouth.

"For your god," Cobb whispered, and then he fired both barrels. The blast exploded out of the top of Fletcher's head and spread the contents of his skull onto the floor, finished him for good. After he withdrew his gun Cobb wiped the blood off on the giant's shirt and reloaded.

He only had four more shells left, he realized, and two of them had just gone into the gun. That was all right, though—he still had the Schofields.

Cobb headed into the living room and wasn't really surprised to see the Jeffries family waiting for him. They stood in front of the door to the kitchen, all eight staring at him expectantly.

"Join us," said the family in unison, and Cobb realized that it wasn't really them talking. It was whatever force lived in the house, whatever it was that Philip Farwell had wanted to use him to contact. Cobb just ignored them and walked into the kitchen, passing through the bodies of Ephraim and his wife on the way. The ghosts screamed out a pitiful wail that almost split Cobb's ears. He kept his composure, though, and went through the open door to the back yard.

Outside Cobb looked around and saw that several poles had been set in a circle around the yard, by the trees. These poles were topped with torches, burning brightly, lending their light to the grassy clearing. He didn't know how long he'd been unconscious from his broken neck and he didn't care. It didn't matter if he'd been out for a few hours or a few days—he was going to end this.

Standing in the center of the clearing, his face lit by the ring of torches, Cobb turned to the back of the house. "Come and get me Farwells!" He shouted as he raised his shotgun over his head. "It's just the three of us now, let's finish this!"

Something flew out of the darkness and struck Cobb from the side. He reeled, waving his shotgun around, but could find no target. A woman's high-pitched laugh pierced the night.

"Bad idea," said Helena from the darkness above. "Fighting me in the open air is the worst thing you could do."

Cobb said nothing. He just searched the sky for the vampire, his shotgun ready. Licking his lips, he waited, the sound of his own breathing in his ears, the ground moist beneath his boots. She had to make some kind of sound, he thought, if he could just catch it before she attacked.

In the silence of the night, he caught it. Unfortunately he didn't have enough time to use it. The attack came from behind, Helena gliding down and kicking Cobb in the head just as he spun around. His shotgun fired into the empty air and Helena kicked him with her other leg. The blow sent him flying and he landed hard on his back. Cobb tried to recover, but the vampire landed alongside him and kicked the shotgun out of his hands as he reloaded.

"You've given us quite enough trouble for one night," she said, her shirt torn from Cobb's earlier shots but the pale flesh underneath showed no signs of damage. Cobb rolled away from her, onto his stomach, and tried pushing himself up but she drove her boot down onto the small of the back. He groaned, his face in the dirt.

"I wanted to be friends," she said, her foot holding him down, "but you had to be difficult. Now it's too late, and when Philip is through with you I'm going to suck every drop of blood out of your body. It's too bad Fletcher's dead. I would have liked to watch him tear you to shreds with his teeth."

"It's no real loss," said Philip as he came out of the shadows by the house, still holding his revolver. "Cobb just saved us the trouble of killing Fletcher ourselves."

Cobb looked at him with a defiant smile. "Come do it, Farwell," he barked, a patch of grass popping from under his jaw. "Come try your little magic trick."

"Don't you worry about that," Philip replied, entering the clearing. "I'm just about to begin."

CHAPTER 25

▼

"Did you see the preacher man?" Helena asked, grinding her boot down. Cobb snorted a reply. "I gave him my blood, did you like that? He's the first of my new children, and I'll make sure he's brought up right. He'll be feasting for the rest of eternity now. Doesn't that make you happy?"

"Bitch," whispered Cobb, another shove from the boot Helena's only retort. Philip smiled at her and pointed the revolver at Cobb's head.

"Get the formula," he said to his wife. "He's got to have it somewhere on him. I need it."

Cautiously, Helena complied while her husband covered Cobb, taking her foot off him and lifting his coat to go through his pants pockets. It took a moment, but she found it, folded into a square. Pleased with herself, the vampire handed it to her husband.

"Perfect," he said, holding it up. "Now watch him."

Helena put her foot on Cobb's shoulder, the inhuman strength of her tiny body pressing him down onto the dirt. He still had the pistols on his belt, but he was lying on his stomach and even if he could get them out the angle was impossible to aim from. Helena would tear him apart before he could get a good shot.

The parchment in his hands, Philip headed over to the center of the clearing. He examined the formula in the dim light, mumbling softly.

"The chant is complete," he said, almost to himself, "if a little archaic. I can adjust."

He looked at Cobb. "Do you know what this is? It's an incantation for rousing spirits of darkness. I can make it work for the presence under the house, now that

I've got the right kind of bait. It's already trying to wake itself. Your arrival started that. All it needs now is the right kind of help, and I'm going to give it."

He turned his face to the moonlit sky, the shadows from the torches dancing on his face, and cleared his throat. "Let this veil be torn asunder," he intoned, his voice loud and clear. "Let the sky be as a looking glass, let the earth tremble. I call thee, most ancient of forces, most potent of things, from the outer dark. Come unto me, and let this offering be thy guide," he pointed at Cobb. "Come unto me, powers of chaos, and lend me thy strength. I beg it, I command it, I desire it. Taste the soul of this one and be free!"

Something passed through the air, all three of them able to sense it. Cobb stiffened, felt a twitch deep inside his brain. Something was touching him, something he couldn't see or hear, but it was touching his mind. It was weak, but it was definitely there.

Philip smiled. "Come unto me!" He cried, laughing. "By my name and by my power, come!"

The contact with Cobb's mind strengthened, and suddenly Cobb was assaulted with images. Bits and pieces of old, forgotten things flashed through his mind—names, faces, feelings, and places. Everything he had done and everywhere he had been was swirling inside his brain like a hurricane. First the memories were blurry, indistinct, but then they gradually grew clearer and more vivid. The sounds got louder, the feelings more real. Something was reliving his life inside of his head, sifting through his memories like so many old papers.

"Yes!" Philip shouted, a charge in the air. "*Nuvos, Ghemnok, Hraadmon,*" he chanted, repeating words that were older than the Latin on the parchment. "By these names I conjure thee. *Jajjito, Laszop, Armog,* by their power I command thee!"

The ground began to tremble and Cobb felt himself growing more and more distant from what was taking place, as the chaos in his mind growing more and more lucid. He was remembering whole days, whole nights, huge spaces of time in an instant. He saw his human life, saw the day that his father taught him to hunt. The memory was perfect in every detail—the sights, the smells, the pounding in his heart as he lifted the musket, a deer just beyond. He remembered his first kiss with a girl he had met in the market place. They had giggled behind a barn, knowing that they were doing something forbidden but being excited all the same. He remembered the Revolutionary War. Remembered running across a battlefield, the sound of cannon in his ears, smoke in his nostrils, the gun in his hands. He remembered the fear of death, remembered watching his comrades fall in the face of the British guns. More than all of that played through his mind, his eyes wide as he saw nothing. A hundred and eighty years of memories tripped through his head, a cold sweat on his forehead as he struggled to stay conscious.

Things he had forgotten were there, things that had been buried by time, alcohol, or plain old forgetfulness. Most of these things jumped by so fast he barely noticed them, but something important came flashing in his mind's eye, something he saw once and tried desperately to hold onto. He saw Mary and Elizabeth tied to a stake; their necks cut, their bodies limp. He remembered the pain in his chest, the churning in his stomach as he neared them, unable to believe that they were dead. It seemed so terrible, so pointless. Who would do such a thing? Cobb knelt down and touched his wife's head, ran his hand through her hair. She had already gone cold. He felt the sting of tears in his eyes as he put his hands on the sides of her face, remembered how it looked like she had been sleeping. He wanted her to be sleeping instead of dead, wanted her and Elizabeth to open their eyes and see him. But he knew they wouldn't, knew they couldn't.

The memories began to fragment, but Cobb grabbed onto that picture of his family, refused to let them slip away again. He had to see what followed, had to know what had happened that night. A terrible stench assailed his nostrils, the telltale scent of sulfur and ash that he had grown accustomed to in the last fifteen decades, and in his mind he turned, saw the great and terrible thing that had been called by the black-robed men. They had called and it had answered, amused by this little man that had done away with its servants. Cobb remembered screaming in the face of what he thought had to be the Devil, his small mind unable to comprehend the full horror. Flames burned in its eye sockets, its jaws bristled with yellow fangs.

The thing had reached down and clutched him in its huge, clawed limb. His flesh burned where it touched him. In his mind he howled louder, trying to remember how to pray, but the words left him in the face of his blind agony.

A claw pierced him. Sebastian felt it rip through his torso, a scythe of black iron. His veins erupted in anguish, as if he were poisoned by the monster's touch. Then he went cold. On the ground outside of the Farwell home Cobb shivered as if he were covered in ice.

The memory broke apart, shattered like a sheet of fragile glass into a thousand pieces and gave way to a thousand other experiences. Cobb let himself be swept away, his mind crumbling as Philip's thing defiled it.

In the real world Philip was exultant. Had he been able to Cobb would have seen the vortex of invisible power around the sorcerer. He would have seen he change that had taken place in the air around them as the ground continued to shake. The separation between the planes was shifting, the thing beneath the house was coming to them.

As it was, though, Cobb was ignorant of all this. He had gone rigid on the ground, his eyes rolled back in his head. There was nothing he could do, the time was past for him to save himself.

"Yes," Philip went on. "Come to me, give me your power!"

A glowing ember of light appeared over him. Small at first, the faint pinpoint flared brighter, a glorious blue-white, and cast its light on Philip's face while he stared in ecstasy. It grew to the size of a baseball, a pulsing, bright mass of brilliance, a star that fell to earth. The light touched him and he was enveloped in blazing radiance.

"Hey, you bastards!"

Helena and Philip turned towards the unfamiliar voice. Standing on the side of the clearing, a pair of .44 revolvers in his hands and a burning cigar clamped in his mouth, was Detective LeGrasse, his hat perched firmly on his head and two bandoliers slung across his chest. "What the hell do you think you're doing out here?"

Not waiting for any sort of answer he shot Helena through the shoulder. The bullet twirled her around and Philip started after his wife, but then paused. He looked at the policeman, the light still over his head.

"You shouldn't have come here," he said, his voice distorted. "Die!"

The ground around LeGrasse trembled. The trees behind him began moving in a way that no wind could cause and the branches reached down towards LeGrasse, driven by the will of Philip and the power of what he had raised. The policeman ran forward, the slender limbs gouging at his flesh and trying to entwine his legs. He barely escaped them as he came the rest of the way into the clearing.

"Nice try," he called to Philip, pointing a pistol and firing. The bullet struck the ground next to Philip's foot and sent a burst of dirt into the air. Philip ducked to his left, away from the impact, left the brilliant globe of light floating where it was.

"Kill him, Helena," he shouted at his wife, who was still nursing her shoulder. "We're almost finished!"

Helena took to the air, disappearing into the darkness overhead. LeGrasse stumbled in a circle, looking upwards with wide eyes. In a moment she reappeared and hurtled down at him, her claws extended. He started firing, his bullets finding only empty air before she struck him. She dug a deep wound in his shoulder and knocked him onto the ground, cackling her delight.

LeGrasse ground his teeth together, laid out on his back, and Helena dropped back to the ground and started stalking towards him, her fangs glittering. He pointed a revolver and fired, a bullet crashing into her in the chest. She was rocked by the shot, but she didn't fall. LeGrasse fired again, missed, and then a third time, this time hitting her in the stomach. Still she came towards him, inexorable and malevolent. He pulled the trigger once more but the guns were empty.

"Come on, witch," he spat as he threw his pistols down. They landed on the grass with a heavy thud. "Come finish me."

She probably would have, if Cobb hadn't been there. After LeGrasse had shot her the first time Helena had taken her foot off him. He had been free but still completely catatonic. The memories had been cascading through his head, but then gunfire intruded on his senses. The smell of powder and screams dragged him back to the present, reminded him who and where he was. With a monumental effort he had forced himself back to the consciousness. His eyes cleared and he jumped to his feet just as LeGrasse dropped his guns.

Philip shouted to his wife, but it was too late. Cobb drew his Bowie knife and leapt onto Helena, drove the point between her ribs from behind. The vampire gave a startled cry as he twisted the weapon, separating the ribs and spilling out a huge spurt of blood. It would take more than that to finish the vampire, though, and she twisted around, forcing the knife out of Cobb's hand, and struck him in the chin. Helena roared, apparently tired of the constant desecration of her body, and lifted Cobb up before throwing him twenty feet through the air to crash onto the dirt. There was almost no sound as she ran at him, her feet barely touching the ground, and she kicked him across the jaw as he tried to stand up. He flopped onto his side and kicked at her as she moved in, his boot aimed at her stomach, but she caught it and twisted the leg. His whole body turned and he was face down on the ground again. There was a wet sound as she yanked the Bowie knife out of her side and she held it up, her eyes on the red-streaked blade.

"I'm going to take your head off with this," she said. "Then I'm going to feed your friend to the priest."

Cobb had run out of ideas when he felt something thrust into his right palm, just above his head. The muscles of his arm recognized the shape and his fingers wrapped around the long, narrow object before he turned, jumped up, and slashed blindly at Helena. The woman was completely surprised by the attack and had no chance to defend herself before the sword bit into her neck and hacked the head from her body. A mass of red hair flopped to the ground before it rolled away, and the vampire's form shook with violent spasms while her hands clawed at the empty air. A fountain of gore pumped out of the stump of her neck as her legs slowly kicked in a grotesque parody of conscious movement.

His broad chest heaved as Cobb looked at the decapitated corpse on the ground. He watched its movements gradually cease, and then he looked at the sword in his hand. Where had it come from? He wondered. It was a cavalry saber, with a long, curved blade and a brass hand guard, not unlike the kind he had grown proficient with during the Civil War. Blood covered the blade, more than should have come from the stroke that killed Helena.

Cobb looked to LeGrasse. The detective was still nursing his shoulder. LeGrasse raised a finger to his forehead in thankful salute and Cobb returned the gesture with a movement of his sword.

"No!"

Philip's cry was a desperate, horrified wail. Cobb faced him, the sword at his side. The magician stared white-faced at his wife's body, hands shaking.

"Damn you, Cobb," he barked. "Damn you!"

"It's over, Farwell," said Cobb. He took a step towards Philip. "You can't fight me."

A maniacal gleam appeared in Philip's eye. "Maybe not," he said, "but I know something that might able to finally kill you!"

With that he threw his hands up into the air and called out. "*Nuvos, Ghemnok, Hraadmon, Jajjito, Laszop, Armog, Baray, Ighctha*," he cried, "I command you to protect your servant! Come to me and smite my enemies! I bind thee to flesh by the names that created thee!"

Cobb jumped forward, intent on silencing the sorcerer, but it was too late. The ball of light, still where Philip had left it, flared once and the ground between them split, a wide black crevice in the grass appearing and widening until it was nearly twenty feet long and ten feet across.

Unfortunately for Philip, the hole opened right beneath him. He screamed, terrified, before he disappeared into the darkness, his body flailing madly. Silence filled the clearing, and Cobb took an uncertain step towards the crevice. Had the thing grown tired of Philip's commands? He wondered as he peered over the edge of the crevice, his eyes unable to pierce the black.

Cobb felt a surge of power push past him and he realized that the thing beneath the house was coming up, moving out from under the ground where it had slept for countless millennia. The ball of light changed from blue-white to yellow and then vanished. Cobb felt it coming, and he leapt back from the crevice just as it vomited up from the ground.

LeGrasse shrieked when he saw it, Cobb's face went white. Composed mostly of long, pulsing and undulating tentacles, the beast was literally a forest of limbs, all waving and swaying as they reached nearly fifty feet up into the air. Dark mottled green in color, several of the muscular tentacles ended in fanged, dripping mouths, lipless and wide, while others were tipped with barbs. Two of the shifting extremities ended in great, veined eyeballs, but as the mound was constantly moving and changing it was difficult for Cobb to see exactly how many eyes there were. A central sort of root mass protruded from the crevice, the tentacles emanated from its thickness and a giant central mouth gaped in the center while the rest of the body remained under the ground. Cobb stared, wide-eyed at the thing, wondering what kind of world could spawn such a creature. He knew intellectually that there were worlds out there where such things lived and thrived, but to actually see them always brought the question into his mind.

The eyes of the thing twisted towards him, the tentacles reaching down, and Cobb came on guard, the saber before him. Whatever this thing was it had made a mistake in coming up from the ground, a mistake that Cobb was determined to make it regret. He could still feel it boring into his mind, still trying to take some pleasure in his memories, but he didn't care.

"Join us," the thing said, using one of its lipless mouths, the voice recognizable as the young Jeffries girl. "Come with us and be forever."

"Join us," said another mouth, the voice that of Ephraim Jeffries.

Cobb sneered, his sword ready. A barbed tentacle wound towards him and Cobb chopped off the tip as it neared. The severed limb squirted black fluid as it thrashed in the air like an angry serpent.

"Come on," Cobb shouted. A lunatic's laugh escaped him. "Come get me!"

The thing obliged. Several tentacles lashed out and coiled around Cobb's legs and torso, held him while a fanged mouth approached. Cobb chopped the limbs apart, then stabbed into the mouth. It wasn't much of a plan but it was the best he could do.

The thing squealed strangely, black ichor spraying from the mouth as it pulled back, and the central mass of the creature lurched. Cobb realized that it was trying to pull itself completely out of the ground. After kicking the remnants of tentacles from his legs, he rushed forward fearlessly and drove the point of his sword into the beast's body, just beneath the giant mouth.

A mouthed limb shot down and clamped onto Cobb's shoulder, the needle-like fangs painfully piercing his body. Cobb let out a hoarse cry, pulled the sword free, and hacked the mouth off. The jaws went slack and he staggered back, pried the mouth off his shoulder with his blade. He winced as the teeth slid out of his flesh. The instant it dropped off, however, a barbed tentacle curved through the air and smashed him onto his back, a flash of pain pushing out from his spine. As he righted himself, gripping his sword tightly, he saw the great mouth of the beast flap open and closed in a peculiar fashion.

The mouth dropped open and a huge muscular column shot out, like a cylindrical tongue that was wide enough to almost fill it. It extended at Cobb, pink and fleshy, ribbed around most of its length like a great bony earthworm. Cobb was more interested in the end of it, however, as it shot towards him, wet and dripping.

From the end of the column grew the top half a human body, with a torso, head, and arms. Pale and naked, smeared with foul slime, the separation between torso and tongue formed at the waist. Cobb looked at the man-thing's face and recognized it immediately.

It was Philip. His eyes were malformed, the irises blotchy and indistinct, and his dark hair glistened with viscous sludge, but it was definitely Philip. The creature had taken him into itself, responding to his request for protection and power in the best way it could.

The Philip-thing pointed at Cobb, a psychotic grin on his face.

"Join us," he gurgled as he drooled greenish ichor. "Join us."

And then Philip grasped him by the shoulders with his powerful hands. Cobb reached up and seized Philip's neck, but the half-man just laughed back at him.

"I've seen into your soul, Cobb," Philip said as he leaned in close, oblivious to the fact that Cobb exerted enough pressure to crush a normal man's trachea. "I know what you are and what can kill you."

"Good for you," barked Cobb, angry. The smell of the sludge on Philip made him nauseous.

"Yes," said Philip. "Good for me. I'm going to roast you on a spit for the next thousand years, little monster. I'm going to set children on you to chew your balls off and I'll write music with your screams. You'll see your wife and your daughter every time you close your eyes, every time you beg for the mercy of death. You'll be bled dry to honor my wife and you'll be torn into a thousand pieces just to make me laugh!"

Cobb replied with a thrust of his sword up into Philip's armpit. The weapon slid in clear up to the hilt, the point shot out of the man-thing's opposite shoulder and into the air. Philip roared but he didn't release his opponent, instead he lifted him into the air while Cobb squirmed, twisted the hilt of his weapon and tore open the ragged wound he had made. Higher and higher into the air they rose, Philip's hands tight on Cobb's shoulders while the beast below let out a droning cry of pain.

As Philip ascended, Cobb slapped his free hand onto the man-thing's shoulder. Without saying a word, he started to feed on Philip, drawing out his essence. Philip howled and tried pulling away, but Cobb wouldn't let him break contact. He felt Philip's soul funneling into him and the elder thing's foul essence came with it.

Both Philip and tentacled monstrosity cried in anguish, and finally Philip managed to push Cobb off. He dropped like a stone, the transference ceasing as he let go of both Philip and his sword. There was a loud snap as Cobb landed on the grass, an explosion of pain pounding up from his left leg. This was nothing, however, compared to the disgust caused by the black essence he felt moving through him, strengthening his limbs. Just like he always did when he used his most hated weapon he felt some small part of his soul die.

The monster heaved again, and thrust out its tentacles into the surrounding trees, wrapped them around the thick trunks. The muscular limbs went taught as they pulled against the ancient trees and the thing hoisted itself up out of the crevice to reveal the rest of its giant body. This was an irregular oval shape, the collection of tentacles sprouting from the upper portion, while underneath it rested on something that looked like the foot of an enormous slug or snail. Once free of the hole, the tentacles released the trees and with rippling, rhythmic movements the massive slug-foot propelled the monster across the ground towards Cobb. He could see a pair of bent, almost vestigial legs hanging off the sides of the creature's body, just above the slug foot. They looked like the legs of an elephant, only thicker, with flat, blunt ends. These legs would periodically straighten to touch the ground as it moved, perhaps to balance it.

Cobb crawled backwards as the monster approached. He felt the bones of his broken leg grind together with every slow movement.

The Philip-thing was looking down on him, his supporting column pushed high into the air. "I wish you could see the world as I do, Cobb," he yelled. He seemed ignorant of the black-streaked blade jutting from his shoulder. "It's so small now, so insignificant and pointless. When we're finished with you it will suffer. Cities will be laid to waste, populations eradicated. Those that do not bow down in worship will be mutilated in ways you cannot dream of. The suffering will be extraordinary, the carnage legendary! Angels will weep tears of blood to hear it! Now that we are free, our power will only grow!"

"I'm sure," said Cobb, glancing around. He wasn't sure that he was going to win this fight, but he was going to try. "Come on," he taunted as he beckoned Philip with a hand. "Come get it like your wife did!"

His intention had been to bait Philip and it worked. With a terrifying growl the half-man shot forward and struck Cobb with the force of a charging bull. Hands balled into fists, Philip hammered at Cobb about the head and shoulders like a madman. A powerful blow bounced off of Cobb's skull and he felt his head swim.

Cobb wasted no time. He knew that if he lost consciousness the game was over. Focusing as best he could, he grabbed the sides of Philip's face and drove his thumbs into the sorcerer's eyes. Philip screamed as stinking black ichor oozed onto Cobb's hands. He tried pulling back, but Cobb held him fast, hate and rage written on his face. Like when he fought Fletcher he wanted nothing more than to drive his enemy into the dirt, wanted to hurt him as much as he could in the hopes of getting some kind of revenge. Philip had violated his mind, had mocked him with visions of his dead wife and he had tried to take his very soul. Only suffering would repay that insult. Agony was the only thing that Cobb wanted from Philip and he wanted it in massive quantities.

With one mighty effort Philip punched Cobb across the jaw. Rocked by the blow, Cobb let go, but as Philip pulled slowly away Cobb snatched back his sword and slashed sideways, clove through the Philip's temple and struck off the top of his head through the middle of the nose. Philip pulled up into the air, keening bizarrely as fluid spewed from the terrible wound, his eyes and most of his brain gone. The muscled, bony column retracted, sucked back down into the monster's central mouth.

Cobb got to his feet, grimacing in pain, and reached under his coat to pull out the three sticks of dynamite hanging from his belt. He lit the fuses on a nearby torch, and limped towards the creature, hacking away a barbed limb that tried to keep him back. With a grunt he threw the dynamite into the monster's gaping orifice, the explosives disappearing after the Philip-thing, just as another tentacle smashed him away. He flew to the edge of the clearing, crashed into the trunk of a tree, and then slid down onto the ground, unable to move.

The monster suddenly started to tremble, its tentacles waving about, and then it exploded. Cobb held up a protective hand while the monster erupted in a massive fireball, creating a maelstrom of gelatinous meat and black slime, the sound like thunder. A wave of thick, foul-smelling liquid slapped against Cobb's chest, and then everything went silent.

For a long, long time Cobb didn't move. He just sat against the tree, more tired than he had been in months. He stared at the remains of the thing, now a smoldering pile of black wreckage, long sections of tentacle or an eye visible here and there, all inanimate on the ground. Breathing heavily, Cobb allowed himself a small, satisfied smile. It was dead. At least as dead as such things could get. If he knew his work, the thing wouldn't be able to reform for quite some time, if at all. Philip's sorcery had given it a body and Cobb had obliterated it.

He turned his head and saw LeGrasse sitting at the edge of the clearing, the policeman examining the wound in his shoulder. Cobb was relieved that he had managed to pull himself to safety.

"Hey, cop," Cobb called. "You alive?"

"Yeah," LeGrasse called back. "How about you?"

"I think I'll make it," Cobb sighed.

CHAPTER 26

▼

Cobb and LeGrasse took a while in getting back into the house, both men moving with pained slowness, their limbs aching and weary. Cobb cleaned himself off in the Farwell's bathroom, noting as he went into the house that there seemed to be no spirits moving around nor any oppressive presence lingering about the place. It seemed rather peaceful, actually.

McAllen was still upstairs, tied to his chair, and the sight of the vampire priest blunted Cobb's feelings of triumph. McAllen had been the real victim here. The man would never be able go back to the life he knew. Awake and alert when Cobb came into the room, McAllen had listened carefully as both Cobb and Head explained what had been done to him. Tears welled up in the priest's eyes as the full weight of it came down on him, but Cobb tried to console him by telling him that he was still the person he had always been and could still keep his faith and live by its rules.

"You can still be the man you were," he said, a hand on the priest's shoulder, "you just have more time to be him."

It was small consolation, however, in light of the fact that he would never see the sun again and would have to live on blood.

The priest said he didn't blame Cobb, however, and that he knew the people responsible had been dealt with, which was something. Cobb told him to seek out other vampires if he needed help, but warned that many of them weren't as moral a people as they could have been. He told McAllen about the enmity between the different vampire masters, and about Matthias. If he ever needed help, Cobb explained, Matthias was the one to look for. McAllen nodded at all of this and said that he would try to find his own way as best he could.

After that Cobb spent about a half hour rifling through Philip's study, prying open drawers and ransacking bookcases. Among the things he kept were Philip's journal and his address book, scribbled with the names of several people that Cobb would have to keep an eye on. He also took a few handwritten books that looked very, very old. Locating a satchel in the study closet, Cobb packed these items away for later when he could leaf through them at his leisure.

LeGrasse let Cobb dress his wound, flinching as it was stitched up, using some mundane sewing supplies he found in the spare bedroom. Next he sewed up the tears in his coat, finishing just as the sun started to come up. While doing so, LeGrasse explained what had happened after Cobb was taken prisoner. Apparently LeGrasse had managed to escape the house, the last of the upuir giving chase, and had killed the creature out in the woods. There he had stayed, a few hours passing before Cobb came out and challenged the Farwells. Cobb was glad to hear that he had only been out for a little while, his broken neck healing in hours, not days.

"I nearly shit myself when I saw that thing," said LeGrasse, sitting on a chair in the living room while Cobb stitched his coat, McAllen safely upstairs in the Farwell's bedroom where the sun couldn't reach him. Cobb nodded, his bare scalp still streaked with dried ichor.

"Yeah it can be pretty terrifying the first few times," he said while he pulled his needle into the air, a long string behind it. He had a makeshift splint around his lower left leg and his bottom lip and right eye were puffy and purple. "I guess you get used to it."

LeGrasse chuckled softly and shook his head. "I don't want to get used to it," he said. "I'm finished with this business, thanks very much."

Cobb continued to sew. "I don't know, you handled yourself pretty well out there," he said. "Could make a career out of it if you want."

"Some career," said the policeman. "My wife would kill me."

"If you're lucky," said Cobb. He had finished closing up the holes in his coat and he held it up to check it over. "So what's next for you?" He asked.

"I don't know," LeGrasse replied. "New York's going to seem very dull compared to all of this, assuming I still have a job when I get back. Maybe I'll get a transfer, someplace like New Orleans, where things are a lot more sane."

Cobb chuckled. "I could tell you stories," he said, cryptically. LeGrasse raised a hand.

"Please. Don't," he said. "I'll hold onto my normal life, thanks."

There was a scraping sound as Cobb got to his feet and pulled on his heavy coat. "There isn't any such thing," he said.

"So what about you? Where are you going?"

Cobb thought before he answered. His Stoeger sat nearby and he picked it up and opened the breech, made sure it was safely unloaded. He had lots of options, now that this little mess with the Farwells was over. It hadn't been planned, that was for sure, and now he had to think of something.

Where would he go? Maybe to San Francisco, there was a psychic there that he would have liked to talk to. Also there was a monastery in China that he'd been hearing about, a place run by a monk that was supposed be almost a thousand years old and have great knowledge of the spirit world. Maybe they could do something to help him out, maybe find some answers to his condition.

If he didn't do any of that he could always go to a baseball game.

"I don't know, either," he said, looking through the empty barrels of the shotgun. "I think I might take a vacation, head to Boston. Maybe out west somewhere. I haven't been to California in over thirty years."

LeGrasse stood. "Well, take care of yourself," he said as Cobb closed his weapon and dropped it into the satchel with the books from Philip's study. He slung the bag over his shoulder and the policeman extended a hand. Cobb took it, the pair smiling at each other.

"You too, cop," said Cobb. "Try to stay clear of people like me, if you can."

"Can't imagine that'll be too hard," replied LeGrasse. "There can't be too many people like you around."

"I hope not," Cobb said. He frowned suddenly, looked up at the ceiling. "Can you take care of McAllen? I'm not going back through New York, I don't think."

"Don't worry about it," LeGrasse told him. "I'll make sure he gets back. Just keep the sunlight off him, right?"

"Right. Don't let him bite you."

LeGrasse's eyes widened. "I don't think it'll be a problem," said Cobb, quickly. "Find a cow or something if he complains. He'll figure out what to do."

With a shake of his head LeGrasse left the room and went upstairs. Cobb picked up his sword and put on his hat, and then he realized that the policeman's life had become more complicated in the past few days than he probably ever thought possible. He chuckled quietly at that thought and went to the back yard to clean up, pausing only to pick up a rake from a pile of tools set against the back of the house.

Cobb had intended to dispose of the charred remnants of the giant monster in the open crevice, but he saw that they had vanished. Only pools of greenish-black oil stained the grass where the fragments had once lain. He walked around the clearing, checked that nothing solid remained, and came across Helena's body, lying in the morning sun, the head still a few feet away. The fact that the body was still there was proof that she was completely dead, he realized, knowing that if any of the vampire's spirit still lingered in the flesh it would have burst into flames as soon as the sunlight touched it. He dropped the rake, and picked up the headless corpse. While he walked with it the stiffened limbs creaked softly. A smile on his face, Cobb tossed the body down the hole and watched it disappear with great pride. The head followed, thrown down almost as an afterthought before he left the yard.

Back inside, Cobb headed down into the basement, shotgun in one hand, the cavalry saber in the other, intent on making one more sweep of the room before bidding farewell to the house at 1128 Halfpenny Lane. He looked around at the odds and ends, saw that there wasn't really anything that anyone could do any damage with, and was about to leave when he felt an icy touch on his shoulder.

"You're all right now?" Asked Rebecca from behind. Cobb smiled.

"I'm all right," he said. "You're still here?"

"Only for a little while," the girl replied. "You can keep the sword if you want it."

Cobb looked at the weapon, at the silver-gray blade that he had cleaned of blood and ichor. "It's yours?" He asked.

"It was my stepfather's," said Rebecca. "I thought you might need it."

Cobb remembered the weapon's mysterious appearance while he had been at Helena's mercy. "Thank you," he said. "It saved me. You're sure you don't want it back?"

"I don't need it anymore," Rebecca answered. "I used it to keep the others away, but now they're gone."

"And you're leaving, too?"

"Soon. I'm tired, I just want to sleep."

"I understand," said Cobb. "I understand very well. Goodbye, Rebecca."

"Goodbye, Sebastian."

Cobb turned around and saw that the room was empty. Rebecca was gone and he knew that she wouldn't be coming back. Maybe it was the fact that the thing was gone and could no longer keep her in the house, or maybe it was the fact that she had finally let go of her pain. Cobb couldn't be sure. She was gone, though, and that was enough. He allowed himself a bit of satisfaction in that fact. Of all the ghosts he had met in that house she had seemed the most genuine—the Jeffries had been thralls of the thing, while she had simply been a frightened, sad little girl who had known that something was wrong in that place. Her torment was finally at an end.

There was only one corpse left. Once upstairs Cobb stared at Fletcher in the entryway, saw that the blood had dried and the giant's body was stiff on the floor. A triangular black blast mark on the shattered wood floorboards emanated from the top of his skull, spotted with chunks of bone and brain matter. Cobb gave the corpse a slight kick, assured himself that Fletcher was really dead, and then put down his sword and hefted the carcass up onto his shoulders. His skin crawled at the touch of Fletcher's waxen flesh, but he ignored this and carried the huge body out to the crevice. With the same amount of ceremony he would have given a sack of garbage Cobb dumped the servant of Yulgo Kharan into the pit, glad to see him go.

Finally there was Head. Cobb took it out of the upstairs bedroom, careful not to disturb McAllen, sleeping soundly on the bed while LeGrasse rested in a guest room and waited for nightfall. The brass head's eyes opened when Cobb touched him but Head obligingly waited until they were out of the room before he started talking.

"So what are you going to do with me?" Head asked as they both went down the stairs. Cobb shrugged.

"I was thinking of dropping you down the hole out back," he said, calmly. Head grunted.

"And why would you do that?" They went to the ground floor, Cobb stopping alongside the great pool of dried blood that marked Fletcher's place of death.

"I figure you're dangerous to just leave lying around," Cobb replied. "You gave Philip information about me, didn't you?"

"Just enough to get you here," said Head. "He never learned to ask the right questions, poor guy."

"It's because that you call him a 'poor guy' that I want to bury you," said Cobb. "Farwell got what he deserved."

"Call it human empathy," was Head's retort. "It's a lost art."

"So what do you want me to do with you?"

Head blinked. "Leave me on a hill somewhere, or under a tree. Someone will find me and maybe I'll get some decent conversation for once."

Cobb shook his head and started towards the back yard. "No," he said. "I can't take the risk that you'll start saying the wrong things to the wrong people."

"I promise I won't," Head replied quickly. "I never really cared about magic or incantations to move mountains anyway. Give me a chance and I'll prove I'm not like that."

"Maybe," said Cobb as he tucked Head under his arm. After a moment he decided to give Head a chance and went back to the front door. He picked up his sword and headed out onto the street. "I guess we'll see what happens."

His car was still parked on the side of the road, and Cobb went to it and opened the trunk. The early morning light exposed his luggage and he placed the sword alongside the case, and was about to put Head inside when he changed his mind. Instead he took it to the front, his guns safely stowed away, and planted Head on the passenger seat.

Cobb shut the door and looked back at the Farwell house. The owners were dead, McAllen was a vampire, LeGrasse's life would never be the same again, and he had a talking brass head waiting for him in the car. Had he changed? Perhaps he had and perhaps not. Fletcher had taught him to make sure his enemies were dead and he had a new sword, but other than that he wasn't sure. He did remember more about his transformation, at least a little more, but what good that would do him remained to be seen.

For a century and a half he'd been going through things like this, hurling himself against the unknown, and in all that time he'd tried learning to deal with it. He worried about getting revenge, worried about learning things that would help him understand his condition, worried about protecting the few people that tried to help him. Change was something he didn't spend much time worrying about.

He got in the driver's side and revved up the engine.

"Where to from here?" Head asked as Cobb rolled down his window and let out a long, heavy sigh. Cobb smiled and straightened his hat.

"West," he said. The car rolled forward and Cobb shifted in his seat, getting comfortable. "We go west."

"Sounds good to me."

Cobb glanced at Head as they sped up. "You ever eat?"

"Not usually," Head replied. "Can't swallow much, but I can taste. Why do you ask?"

"I'm hungry," said Cobb. "Could eat a horse."

0-595-32993-4